D0357635

THE SEA KING

JOLIE MATHIS

BERKLEY SENSATION, NEW YORK

THE BERKLEY PUBLISHING GROUP
Published by the Penguin Group
Penguin Group (USA) Inc.
375 Hudson Street, New York, New York 10014, USA
Penguin Group (Canada), 90 Eglinton Avenue East, Suite 700, Toronto, Ontario M4P 2Y3, Canada
(a division of Pearson Penguin Canada Inc.)
Penguin Books Ltd., 80 Strand, London WC2R 0RL, England
Penguin Group Ireland, 25 St. Stephen's Green, Dublin 2, Ireland (a division of Penguin Books Ltd.)
Penguin Group (Australia), 250 Camberwell Road, Camberwell, Victoria 3124, Australia
(a division of Pearson Australia Group Pty. Ltd.)
Penguin Books India Pvt. Ltd., 11 Community Centre, Panchsheel Park, New Delhi-110 017, India
Penguin Group (NZ), Cnr. Airborne and Rosedale Roads, Albany, Auckland 1310, New Zealand
(a division of Pearson New Zealand Ltd.)
Penguin Books (South Africa) (Pty.) Ltd., 24 Sturdee Avenue, Rosebank, Johannesburg 2196, South Africa

Penguin Books Ltd., Registered Offices: 80 Strand, London WC2R 0RL, England

This is a work of fiction. Names, characters, places, and incidents either are the product of the author's
imagination or are used fictitiously, and any resemblance to actual persons, living or dead, business es-
tablishments, events, or locales is entirely coincidental. The publisher does not have any control over
and does not assume any responsibility for author or third-party websites or their content.

THE SEA KING

A Berkley Sensation Book / published by arrangement with the author

PRINTING HISTORY
Berkley Sensation edition / June 2006

Copyright © 2006 by Kimberly Ungar.
Cover illustration by Franco Accornero.
Cover design by George Long.
Interior text design by Stacy Irwin.

ISBN: 0-425-21065-0

BERKLEY SENSATION®
Berkley Sensation Books are published by The Berkley Publishing Group,
a division of Penguin Group (USA) Inc.,
375 Hudson Street, New York, New York 10014.
BERKLEY SENSATION is a registered trademark belonging to Penguin Group (USA) Inc.
The "B" design is a trademark belonging to Penguin Group (USA) Inc.

PRINTED IN THE UNITED STATES OF AMERICA

10 9 8 7 6 5 4 3 2 1

For Eric
I fly because of you.

Acknowledgments

First and foremost, I would like to extend my thanks to my agent, Kim Lionetti, and my Berkley editor, Gina Bernal. They saw the magic in *The Sea King,* and without their expert guidance, the story would not have become a reality. Because of them, I will forever recall the publication of my first novel as a truly wonderful experience.

Heartfelt acknowledgment also goes to my parents, Lewis and Ella Dawn, who raised me to believe I was capable of achieving anything I put my mind to. And to my brother, Army Maj. Kelly Eiland, who is an amazing writer in his own right.

To my fantastic critique partners and writer pals who supported me from the start: Kim Starrett, Julia Templeton, Sydney Miles, Pam Litton, Amy Loos, and all the ladies at Romancing History.

Much appreciation to the experts at the Northvegr Foundation, the Icelandic Language Institute, and to the Ða Engliscan Gesiþas. It was very important for me to do justice to this early time and place, and I would not have been able to do so without the resources, education, and assistance offered by their staffs. Also, much gratitude goes to Stephen Pollington, whose wonderful books on pre-Conquest England rarely, if ever, left my desk during the writing of this novel.

And finally, to those masters of the quill who continue to inspire me: Laura Kinsale, Judith Ivory, Kathleen Woodiwiss, Anita Gordon, Katie MacAlister, Susan Squires, JoAnn Ross, and the late Christine Monson.

Chapter 1

I have always wondered what it would be like to touch a man."

Isabel stared into Merwyn's handsome face.

"A square jaw." Her fingers smoothed over the bristly hair on his chin. "Or a cheek."

Merwyn's eyes bulged back at her from either side of his narrow nose. He snorted.

"Forsooth, what a romantic swain thou art." She rubbed his nose and reached into her pocket for a handful of oats. "I suppose you've earned your treat. A captive audience, once again, to my dark confessions."

She supposed she would learn the answers to her questions soon enough. In the spring she would be married. Her betrothed was handsome and strong, and she liked him very much. They would make a good match, and perhaps he would allow her to have a horse as fine as this one for her very own.

Overhead the winter sky grew increasingly churlish. Gusts of wind tossed her woolen skirts. She tugged Merwyn's reins, urging him toward the river.

"After you drink, we should go. Berthilde will be quaking in her baggy woolens if she finds we've escaped again." When he had taken his fill, she swung into the saddle.

Isabel glanced at the sky. In the distance, thunder boomed. How she loathed returning to the keep, for it was rank with the scent of rancid tallow and unwashed bodies. Here, in the forest, the air carried the scent of rain and cleansed her senses. Merwyn whinnied and stamped.

"Aye, old man. One more jump won't hurt." As she brought the steed roundabout, the wind caught her hood and tore it from her hair. "The oak. Once more."

The fallen tree lay just a bow's arc away. At the urging of her heel, Merwyn trotted forward. The river rushed along beside them, undulating beyond the log, dull and gray as a molting serpent.

Faster.

They stormed forward. Clods of dirt flew out behind them, cast up by Merwyn's immense hooves.

Faster.

Isabel leaned forward, her thighs clenched. Her hair whipped about her face. How she relished the scant moment after Merwyn's hooves left the ground. Her breath caught in her throat.

They flew!

A flash blinded her. The sky crashed. Lightning!

Merwyn veered and balked. Leather burned across her palms. Isabel screamed. The river.

Pain. Enough to leave her stunned.

Darkness embraced her and with it a vague coldness. Which way was up, and why was there no air?

Panicked, she thrashed. An unseen hand held her, but no. 'Twas the spindly branches of a submerged tree, twisted in her tunic.

Water breached her lips and nose.

Ranulf would be so angry with her. How many times had he told her to listen? To behave?

Languor spread through her limbs. Could this really be happening? A shroud of unconsciousness descended over her, not altogether unpleasant.

Warmth. Strong arms. Sanctuary.

"Stúlka litla," he whispered against her hair.

Looking up, she saw the angel, the pure blue of his eyes. Rain fell from the sky, haloing his dark head like diamonds cast down from Heaven.

"Not my horse," she confessed.

"Shhhhh," he soothed.

So it was true what the sisters told her about Heaven. No sadness, no regrets.

Isabel awoke with a gasp, struggling against the cold darkness. A sky of dark crimson spread above her. Forsooth. *She had been sent to Hell.*

No, she quickly realized. 'Twas the rich curtain that adorned her own bed. A multitude of anxious female faces peered down at her. Saints above, somehow she had been returned to the bower.

"Thank Heavens the child will live," Berthilde sobbed. Tears beaded the corners of her brown eyes. "Eada, send word to our king at once." Eada scurried from the room, while other servants moved forward to ply Isabel with blankets and warmed wine.

Scratches scored her arms and legs, and burn marks reddened her palms. She ached to her very bones. And a knot the size of a goose egg throbbed upon her temple. Isabel struggled for explanation. She remembered riding Merwyn in the forest. Yes, there had been thunder. Lightning. She had been thrown into the river. She shivered, remembering how close she had come to death.

Her women scurried about her, speaking in hushed

tones. She snuggled deeper into the blankets, thankful to be alive. There could be only one answer. Someone must have seen her and rescued her before she drowned.

She'd been dressed as a peasant. Surely the person hadn't known they rescued the king's half sister. Perhaps Ranulf had provided her rescuer with a reward for her safe return. She imagined herself bestowing a garland of lovely flowers on a handsome, beaming hero.

What an adventure, she thought with a little smile.

She must learn the identity of the fortunate fellow.

"Berthilde, did someone—"

Berthilde shushed her. "Do not try to speak, child." Berthilde always called her "child" even though she was only twenty-eight winters to Isabel's seventeen. "You have naught else to fear. They've taken the blackheart to the pit and he's getting what he deserves."

Isabel frowned. "Who is getting what he deserves?"

Berthilde's cheeks pinked. "The pagan fiend who attacked you."

Isabel reviewed her available memories. "I was not attacked. Lightning struck nearby and Merwyn threw me into the river."

"Oh, my dearest. You've had a terrible shock. Perhaps 'tis best you do not remember."

Isabel propped herself on one elbow. Her hair, still damp, clung to her shoulders. "But I *do* remember. Merwyn threw me into the river, and 'twas my own fault. No one attacked me." If there had been a misunderstanding she must set things aright.

Berthilde bustled around the room, fretting aloud. "They were blessed with luck to find you. The rainstorm came on so suddenly. If that barbarian had killed you or worse, if he had—" Berthilde's face darkened red as rowanberries. "Oh, I do not know what I would have done." She wrung her plump hands together. "Filthy creature. He's getting his lashes as we speak."

"Lashes!"

As if to verify Berthilde's claims, the voice of a man, faint though it was, echoed out from the depths of the stronghold in combined fury and agony.

Isabel bolted up. A vague memory flashed. *Blue eyes. Her angel. He was real.*

"Nay," she shouted.

All eyes turned to her, stunned. She swung her legs over the side of the bed.

"Lie back," Berthilde ordered crossly, pressing her back into the bedclothes.

A stout young maid moved forward with a goblet of wine. "My lady, you must not allow yourself to become distressed. The Dane deserves no less than death for what he tried to do."

Isabel shoved the offer of wine aside. Garnet drops spattered the soft linen of her bed gown. "He did not harm me. There has been a mistake. This man, whoever he is, saved me from drowning. You must summon my brother and halt whatever—"

Berthilde interrupted. "That spawn of Satan—he came from the sea and grabbed the first woman he saw. My lady, that is your reward for sneaking out dressed no better than the cooper's daughter."

"Listen to me—"

Exasperated, Isabel again attempted to leave the bed. But Berthilde took the goblet from the maid and pressed it to Isabel's lips. "You must drink. The wine will calm you."

Isabel's temper flared. "I am sick unto death of being treated like a child." She grasped the collar of Berthilde's gunna and, through clenched teeth, demanded, "Bring Ranulf to me, anon." Wine spilled onto her chin, ran in small rivulets down her neck.

"Dearest, you are not yourself." With tight-pressed lips, Berthilde nodded at the burly maid who assisted her. Looking to Isabel, she intoned, "This is for your own good. Our king hath ordered it so."

Within the space of a breath, the maid had captured both of Isabel's arms. "King's orders," the young woman whispered, as if reassuring herself with the words. "King's orders. King's orders."

"Nay." Pinned beneath the bedclothes, Isabel squirmed. Berthilde's fingers pressed into her mouth and pried her teeth apart. Despite her efforts, the liquid slid into her mouth.

"No," she choked. The wine burned her throat. Soon her limbs grew too heavy to move.

Despite her slurred protests and demands to see her brother, no one listened. Escape! she willed her body, but the slothful bag of bones refused.

A prisoner of good intentions. No different than any other day of her life.

Isabel awoke to drawn bed curtains and a darkened room. Customarily her elder half sister, Rowena, shared the bed with her, but she must have slept below in the hall this night. Silence prevailed over her brother's timber palace.

Was her angel dead then? The effects of the wine slowly dissipated. She couldn't stop thinking about him, her blue-eyed savior. Imprisoned like a criminal for rescuing her. Was he a Dane as her maid had claimed? If so, then no amount of pleading would persuade her brother to release him. Ranulf hated the Danes for their past incursions onto English soil. As king of Norsex, a small kingdom coveted by the larger powers of the Mercians and the Northumbrians, he despised anyone who threatened his sovereignty.

But her instincts—her heart—told her the man who had pulled her from the river was no monster.

From her bed she crept. She winced at the soreness of her limbs, the throb of her head. She clasped the wood bedpost until the dizziness passed. Furtively she glanced toward Berthilde, who slept soundly on her pallet near the fire.

In silence she donned a kirtle and gunna. Over her head she draped a dark hood. Though rook black hair fell over her shoulders, her pale skin would draw notice like the moon on a cloudless night. On the trestle lay a trencher of bread and cheese. She shoved some into her pockets. Carefully she lifted the lid to Berthilde's trunk and retrieved a small pot of healing salve. She crossed the room, pulled aside a wall-hanging, and slipped into the narrow corridor.

Centuries before, Romans had built their mountainside fortification upon the subterranean labyrinth. Their ancient stone walls still surrounded parts of the burh and formed the almost impenetrable foundation of Ranulf's new keep. Her father, Aldrith's, older and smaller hall perched just above on an outcropping of stone, and had lately been divided into private chambers for the king's family.

From there, Isabel maneuvered through an ancient passageway few knew existed. She descended stairs cut of earth and stone, into the caves.

Her heart beating as fast as a bird's, she peered out from the hidden door. Two guards, posted at the entrance to the pit, occupied themselves with vulgar stories. From somewhere came the sound of perpetually trickling water. Isabel slipped from the hidden doorway, an anomaly of shadow and stone, into the naturally formed central corridor of her brother's prison. A torch burned from a bracket on the wall; she avoided its light and kept to the shadows. She took care not to be seen by the other prisoners, who might call out and reveal her presence.

She found him in the last, most remote cell, separated from the petty thieves and troublemakers. Although she remembered nothing but the blueness of his eyes, somehow she knew this was the man who had saved her.

Through a narrow slat in the door, she saw he knelt into the corner, his face pressed against the filthy stone wall.

Her heart constricted. Chains held his arms above his head. Coal black hair matted against his neck and shoulders. He could have sought rest by falling to the ground, but appeared to make some attempt, no matter how futile, at readiness. Though only the faintest light illuminated the cell, she *saw* the darkness, clearly contrasted against his shredded woolen tunic. The same darkness seeped downward to stain his braies. Blood.

Horrified, Isabel pressed a hand to her mouth. She did not understand. Her brother, though a young monarch, ruled fairly and had never been given to cruelty. Never before had she seen a prisoner so badly whipped.

The man was huge and finely formed. To see him so demeaned because of a misunderstanding over her foolish mishap brought tears to her eyes. He had saved her from death and this had been his reward.

There was no question of what she must do.

Amidst the shadows she returned to the mouth of the corridor. There, keys hung on the wall. She lifted them from the peg, wrapping her fingers around them to silence their rattle. Silent as a wraith she returned to the cell, slowly turned the key in the lock, and slipped inside.

Cautiously, she stepped toward the giant.

"Sir," she whispered. He made no response. Was he . . . dead? She touched the top of his shoulder, the only place where blood did not stain his shirt.

He whirled. The earth crunched beneath her knees. Captured within the steely vise of his legs, she bit her lip to silence a cry. The keys and salve fell from her hands to land with a soft thud on the earthen floor.

Unable to support her own weight she collapsed against his chest. The musky scent of him filled her nostrils. She raised her head to meet his gaze. She tasted blood, her own.

Warm and labored, his breath fell against her cheek. A single shaft of torchlight revealed two azure eyes. Fueled by anger and pain, they blazed at her from a bloodied, filthy face, his silent accusation of betrayal stabbing into her more trenchantly than any sword.

"I will help you," she whispered with great effort. Moisture seeped through her clothing, his sweat and blood. When his legs did not relax their hold she feared she would faint from lack of breath. "Please. You are crushing me."

"Litla min," he murmured and released her. She stumbled away, gasping for air. About her face she secured her hood, then bent to retrieve the keys and salve. *Little one.* His language was not so different from her own, that she could not understand.

Behind her the Dane struggled to stand, then fell against the stone wall.

"You cannot walk?" Her whisper echoed softly.

He tensed when she moved toward him. Holding the key in front of her she said, "I will release you. But you must try to walk."

Isabel saw the curl of his lip, the gleam of his eyes, and recognized blatant mistrust. But he faltered. One of his feet appeared to have been injured, perhaps intentionally to hinder any escape.

Knowing she risked her life by doing so, she unlocked the fetters. Instead of snatching for her throat as she feared, he steadied himself against the wall.

With a soft groan, he collapsed to his knees.

Isabel reached out and braced his fall. Her own muscles screamed in complaint. As he slumped, she knelt, struggling to guide his head into her lap. There she sat, rasping for breath.

Likely he'd been given a sleeping herb. How would they ever reach the forest? Even if she were not so weak from her own injuries, she could not carry such a giant. Perhaps after a few moments of rest he would be able to stand.

She worked the woolen tunic from his shoulders. Nothing prepared her for the sight of his wounds. Bile rose in her throat when she saw how the whip had cut through his back, tearing through skin and muscle. If he survived, he'd be scarred for life.

Forcing down her revulsion, she applied Berthilde's salve with the gentlest of care. As she continued her ministrations, his muscles relaxed.

Thinking him unconscious, she settled nervously into the darkness of the corner, his great head in her lap. Her ears remained keen to any sound that might bring about their discovery. Even in the darkness, she could see the powerful slant of his cheekbones and the square line of his jaw. His wife, if he had one, must think him very handsome. She had imagined all Norsemen were fair but this one was as dark as the devil Berthilde had proclaimed him to be.

She ran one finger along his cheek. Much nicer than Merwyn's bristly chin. She yearned to stroke his hair. Instead she contented herself with resting her hand upon his nape. Perhaps her presence might give him some comfort as he slept.

His large hand fumbled for her smaller one. Her breath caught in her throat as he clasped it with near-crushing strength. The last time a man had touched her in such a manner it had been her father as he died in the cold darkness of an early November morning.

"*Martröd,*" the Dane whispered.

"Yes, this is a dream. A very terrible dream." She squeezed his hand and gently laid her other hand upon the black crown of his head. Bending over him, she prayed in near-silent whispers. *Let him live.*

How much time had passed? She dared not allow him to sleep any longer. Darkness would not provide its cover indefinitely, and if he remained in the keep another day he would surely face death.

"Wake, Dane. Can you stand?"

His eyes opened, sharp and clear. Perhaps he had never been asleep at all, but merely gaining strength. Although his pain must have been overwhelming, he arose to his feet without her assistance. He seemed loathe to rely on her for support, preferring the wall.

She frowned. "You will have to put your weight on me, Norseman. The walls do not extend to the weald and I would not have you fall and reveal us both."

His eyes flashed but she saw understanding therein. He allowed her to pull his arm across her shoulder. With a low grunt, he took his first step without the support of the wall. Isabel almost collapsed beneath his weight. After a moment he relieved her of much of his bulk, despite his injured foot.

A cacophony of snores came from the guard post and the cells containing other prisoners. Though his injuries slowed them, Isabel was able to guide him out of the cell and toward the secret passageway, pausing only to return the keys to their peg.

With each passing moment she became more terrified. Although a member of the king's privileged household, she did not doubt Ranulf would imprison—or even execute her, if he discovered this treason.

"Anon, there's no time." She urged him down the pitch-dark passageway, into the nethermost regions of the Roman ruins.

They passed through a hundred years of dense and nearly impassible undergrowth. Roots and bramble snatched their clothing, and surely clawed the Dane's wounds, but he made no complaint.

Soon the scent of brine surrounded them, as did the sound of ocean waves crashing against Calldarington's rocky shores. She clasped the Dane's arm, and bade him be still. Her brother currently skirmished with the Northumbrian king over borderland territory and so defenses remained in place.

Hearing no movement of the sentries, Isabel guided the Norseman toward the forest beneath a blanket of ocean-borne fog. Once they crossed into the tree line he pulled away from her and leaned against an oak. He growled, low in his throat.

Remembering the bread and cheese she'd brought for him, she fumbled in her pocket. Had he come from a ship? Perhaps his companions waited for him in one of the many inlets to the south. She lifted her offering.

Before her eyes, he straightened, very slowly. For the first time, she comprehended his true size.

Without warning a hand clapped over her mouth and an arm seized her about the waist. The bread fell from her hand. She struggled—

Until she saw them. Five warriors surrounded her like ghosts in the mist. In the center stood her Norseman, flanked by his companions. Even bent in pain he stood taller, more proudly than the rest.

They would kill her now.

"*Hættu þessu.*" The command rumbled from the Dane's throat. Her hood fell to her shoulders as the sixth warrior set her free.

"Your name, little one?" he rasped.

Too startled to do otherwise, she issued a whispered truth. "Isabel."

The wind sang through the trees, silvery and hypnotic.

"God be with you, Isabel."

Though she dared not even blink, the warriors disappeared like apparitions into the night. Only the drying blood and sweat of the Dane remained on her peasant's tunic to assure her he'd ever really existed at all.

Chapter 2

Two winters hence

Kol Thorleksson stood at the apex of his army. Behind him, several hundred foot soldiers formed a massive wedge of human strength. Ocean spray rode upon the winter wind, dampening his hair and body with each gust, yet he felt no cold.

Vekell strode toward him, inspecting the line. Ice crystals glistened upon his golden beard. "My lord, we have given the Saxon sufficient time to rally. Must we tarry any longer?" Once he reached Kol's side he murmured, "We aught have burned his hall in the night. These Saxons are pitiably lax in the winter."

Kol assessed the steep incline they would ascend during the battle, and the great wooden keep, cut step-fashion into the earth and stone of the promontory crest.

"*Nei.* I shall have my vengeance here on the field of battle, before the eyes of my men and the Saxon people." He lifted a hand to his chest. The grooves of his crucifix were cool beneath his fingertips. "And before my God."

Vekell, pagan to the core, smiled. "But my lord, is not your God the god of forgiveness?"

With a sharp glance at his second-in-command, Kol caught the cross in his fist. "Some sins God can forgive." He concealed the amulet beneath his mail. "But I cannot."

Through narrowed eyes Kol watched Ranulf appear at the rear of the hastily gathered Norsexian forces. The king, splendidly armored and thickly guarded by a small cavalry, sat atop a black steed.

Kol nodded to Vekell.

"Aaaagh!" shouted the bearded warrior, his legs braced. He lunged forward and cast his spear over the entire gathered force of the enemy, a symbolic act to dedicate the Norsemen and their valor to their battle god. The shield carrying warriors roared in one unified voice. Beneath Kol's feet, the earth trembled.

A ripple of unrest shuddered through the ranks of the Saxons. Their animals whinnied and pranced, their fear scenting the air. A cluster of fyrd warriors broke free from their lines and ran for the forest.

For the first time in what seemed an age, Kol threw back his head and laughed.

He thrust his *vikingsword* into the air. Upon his signal, missile weapons, flung by his *hirdmen*, darkened the enemy's lines, wreaking destruction upon wood, metal, and flesh. Kol stepped forward and the battle rush began.

The next hours passed in a blur of movement and crimson.

Above the clash of battle and the cries of the dying, Vekell bellowed, "We've broken down the gate."

Kol wrenched his vikingsword from the body of his dead opponent. The war trance abated. He straightened to his full height and surveyed the field of battle. Already his standard flew upon the plateau just south of the keep.

But where was the Norsexian king?

During the melee Kol had lost sight of Ranulf. He knew

his foe had not fallen in battle. Kol's warriors had been instructed to leave Ranulf alive, for be it now or later, Kol
would be the one to finish him. Grimly disposing of another challenger, he crossed the field, the dewclaws of his
bearskin boots finding solid purchase in the frozen ground.
He joined his hirdmen, who stamped and paced, eager to
begin the sacking of the burh.

Svartkell gripped his two-handed ax and shouted toward the keep, "Saxon bastard. Why does he not show
himself?"

Ragi, an old berserker who fought without benefit of
any clothing, save for a swath of fur across his chest and
loins, licked the blood from his sword. With a leer he said,
"We have seen naught of him. No doubt the coward runs
to hide."

Vekell led Kol through the gate of the burh. "My *stallari*, I have been advised the king's women remain."

Kol spat on the ground but found his teeth intact. "'Tis
Ranulf I want."

"And Ranulf you shall have," Vekell grinned. "The
Saxon traitor tells us the women are the king's blood-kin.
His sisters."

Ragi broke into a yellow-toothed smile and rasped,
"Princesses."

Kol's lip curled. "What sort of man leaves his family
behind as recompense for his sins?" But he knew full well
the nature of the man he sought to destroy. "You are right,
old friend. If these women share blood with Ranulf I shall
take pleasure in making their lives hell as my hostages.
With them in hand, Ranulf will be drawn forth and I will
see him dead."

Warriors thronged about him, clamoring to continue the
siege. He lifted his sword. "A-viking, my hirdmen."

•   •   •

From the outer passage Isabel caught a glimpse of the women clustering in the courtyard to form a human fortress against the invaders.

Where was Ranulf? For as long as caution allowed, she had watched the battle from the high earthen rampart. She had not seen her brother fall. He had simply vanished.

"To the stairway, my lady." Berthilde slammed the door and turned with half-crazed eyes. "Follow the Princess Rowena to the old hall. Anon!"

Just as Isabel turned she heard screams. The massive door splintered. Isabel whirled, her instincts drawing her to protect the others, but Berthilde pushed her toward the stairs. The servant remained behind to offer her life in defense of her mistress.

"Berthilde," Isabel protested.

"Go, child. He waits for you in the forest."

The doorway collapsed inward with a groan. Isabel looked over her shoulder. A swarm of foreign warriors invaded the narrow hall. Berthilde's scream was cut short as a hulking Dane swatted her into the wall. Isabel rushed to defend her maid, dagger in hand.

At that moment, another Dane appeared. His immense frame filled the portal as he bent to enter. He wore a shirt of mail, not the common leather hauberk of the others. He straightened to a terrifying height. The wide iron nosepiece of his helmet prevented any humanizing view of his face. Blood, sticky and black, spattered his chest. He clenched a long, blood-darkened sword, the gold and silver weapon of a Scandinavian aristocrat. The hilt dangled with exotic decorations, trophies of past battles won. The Dane scanned the room.

"*Þarna!*" called the voice of a soldier. *There.* All eyes fixed upon her. Isabel's heart constricted in fear. She had to survive. *There was one who depended upon her to do so.* She snatched her head-rail close, as if the garment might make her disappear. She fled to the stairwell, slamming the oaken door behind her. She had not yet lowered its heavy bar when the door crashed open, narrowly missing her as she fell backward. Rolling to her belly, she scrambled up the stone cut stairs.

She heard him behind her, the tall, bloody Dane so distinguished from the others, his pursuit unhurried, as if he knew she could not escape.

Isabel fought panic, but stumbled over her gunna as she climbed. With luck, her half sister Rowena had already left the keep. *And her beloved. Let him be alive.* Reaching the top step, she dashed headlong into the room, her intention to turn and bar the door. She would vanish into one of the secret passages and escape the keep.

Two burly arms wrapped around her, nearly crushed her. She screamed. The scent of sweat, acrid and stale, invaded her nose. A Dane held her in an inescapable vise. He gripped her wrist and squeezed until her dagger fell to the ground. She clawed at him, but her nails met only the impenetrable barrier of a leather jerkin. With a laugh, he shoved her to the center of the room. At the same time, another warrior flung Rowena toward her.

Isabel's sister cleaved to her, her face a mask of terror.

With her eyes on the circling men, Isabel whispered to her elder half sister, "Are you hurt?"

Rowena stared at Isabel as if she no longer understood the spoken word. The scent of blood and sweat permeated the room. Men's triumphant exclamations, spoken in the Norse tongue, crowded Isabel's ears. The door of the secret passage hung open. Danes spilled forth from its darkened recesses. Confusion and fear swarmed her mind. How had they learned of its existence? Now she understood why the fortress had been penetrated with such ease.

The room fell silent.

Oh, God. How she *sensed* him. The hair on her neck stood on end and she turned to face the huge Norseman who stood in the doorway. Rowena clawed her arm. Isabel saw the deference given to the warrior by the others. It was he who would kill them, the sisters of a defeated Saxon king.

Isabel peered out from beneath her head-rail, awestruck as he approached. Trembling took hold of her body now that she faced her death. He *did* look like Death come to claim her. The blood of her people slid down the length of his sword to make a narrow trail upon the floor.

The Dane took another step toward her, skimming the tip of his blade along the floor. Its eerie, metallic death-song reverberated through the high-ceilinged room. Although stricken with terror, Isabel stood tall, determined to die with honor.

Who would tell the one she loved she had died bravely? Isabel raised her chin to meet her executioner's eye. Hateful blue eyes, like those of a banished angel, gleamed at her from behind the bloodied helm.

The Dane raised his sword. She flinched as its blade rasped through the air beside her cheek. Rather than severing her neck as she expected, he caught the point of his blade inside her veil and thrust so it fell to her shoulders.

The Dane stepped closer. Rousing shouts of victory arose from the horde, but their leader lifted his hand. Instantly the room fell silent.

Only Isabel heard his whispered curse, and then, "Is it you? Isabel?"

Her name arose in a murmur all around her, spoken at first by the men forming the inner perimeter and then the others. Before long, the room thundered with the unanimous acclaim of the Norsemen.

"Isabel!"

Isabel covered her ears against the damning sound. The room spun around her in a nightmarish vortex. *What had she done?*

As Rowena slumped to the floor, Isabel stared into the eyes of the man who still haunted her most secret dreams.

• • •

Upon the dais in Ranulf's great hall, Kol sat straight-backed in the king's *Yppe*, the ornately carved throne signifying its occupant's superiority upon the earth. Vekell stood beside him. Together they surveyed the fruits of their victory.

All around him, his soldiers celebrated. At his feet lay the bounty of the burh. Finely crafted weapons, jewelry and vessels. Gold and silver. Ruby and pearl. But nothing so fine as the amethyst eyes he'd stared into.

She had whispered simply, *"You."*

And then he had watched as her bravely veiled fear had transformed into hatred. The young peasant girl who had saved him from death two winters before was, in truth, Ranulf's sister. The Princess Isabel.

At this moment she stood motionless at the lower corner of the dais, cloaked in the mystery of her woman's clothing, glaring her hatred with her extraordinary eyes. The other, fair-haired princess crouched at her feet, and sobbed as his warriors presented each treasure.

Strange how he had forgotten her. But as soon as he had looked into her eyes he had remembered. Vividly.

Since that night two winters before, he had put her from his mind, she only the vague memory of a girl through the haze of his pain. Seasons had passed. He had thought of her rarely.

Usually only in dreams.

Beside him Vekell lowered into a crouch, his voice but a murmur amidst the boisterousness of the hall. "My lord, she leaves me speechless."

"Oh?" Kol shifted upon the throne. At his movement, his hounds, Hugin and Munin, leapt to their feet and settled again. "Of whom do you speak?"

Vekell stared him hard in the face.

The man knew him too well. A smile curved Kol's lips. "All this time I had assumed her a wicked little horse thief." His gaze settled upon her. God. How shockingly fine she was. Fine and sweet and lovely. And clearly *furious* with him. His smile grew. "I simply believed when she made her own escape she thought to take me with her."

Vekell purloined another look at the princess. "That night when I saw her there in the forest, by Thor, I believed—"

Kol interrupted with a low laugh. "Yes, how couldst I forget?" He smoothed the pad of his thumb over the swirl pattern carved into the chair's arm. "You claimed she was a swan maiden, sent by the goddess Freyja to spare me from an unworthy death."

Vekell frowned. "You scoff, but they exist."

"I was grateful to her then." Kol touched his goblet to his lips and sipped Ranulf's wine. Woodsy and sweet, it mellowed his mood. "Now, after learning her lineage, I question her motives."

Vekell shook his head, the set of his lips firm. "Whatever her intentions, she spared your life and I revere her for it. *Wyrd* did not intend for you to die without valor, chained and bleeding in a filthy cell."

No, indeed, thought Kol. *Wyrd, or Fate or God had other plans for him.* He tipped the goblet in mock gratitude to the spirit of the witch-mother who had cursed him so vengefully, when he was but a boy of twelve winters.

Vekell gave a dry chuckle. "I do not believe the princess would extend the courtesy again, if given the privilege."

Kol felt her eyes upon him. With a sideways glance he met her unwavering stare. A sudden fire blazed through his veins, and with it a primal urge to react. To pursue and claim. He exhaled through his teeth.

Fortunately he had grown skilled at controlling urges borne of impulse and heat. He splayed two fingers across his lips in an attempt to suppress his smile.

He could not deny it: *her fearlessness excited him.* He perceived not a bit of fright in her. She must truly despise him.

Whatever her reasons had been for setting him free from the pit, it pleased him beyond measure to learn she was sister to the very man who had chained and tortured him there. He wanted to crow her treason to the rafters.

Leaning forward in the chair, he mused aloud, "Dost thou believe Ranulf knew of her betrayal?"

Vekell twisted one end of his fork-braided beard. "Behold her rich clothing, the perfection of her skin. If he did know, she was not punished for it."

Kol did behold, and felt each muscle in his thighs, his abdomen, tighten. The face of Isabel, the woman, now obscured any memories of Isabel, the girl. A woman so beautiful it damned his very soul to look upon her. But, alas, he was already damned, despite the cross that hung from his neck.

For some men, redemption was not so easily earned.

The thought made him restless. Remembering what had brought him to this place, Kol turned his attention to matters of conquest. By the time night fell, he had disposed of mounds of treasure. More than generous with his own mercenary legion and those lesser chieftains who had lent their forces to his maneuver, he emptied Ranulf's coffers with astounding alacrity. As was his custom, he kept nothing for himself.

But for the first time, he felt tempted.

"Let the feasting begin," shouted Vekell.

Wood scraped upon stone as warriors dragged large trestle tables from the walls. Teary-eyed serving girls, selected from the scores of prisoners taken in the burh, brought forth steaming trenchers from the kitchens. In the center of the hall, a fire blazed upon a circular stone hearth.

Amidst the smoke and wavering light, Kol's finest warriors clustered around the princess, she a single nightbloom amongst a forest of trees if one did not acknowledge the other princess sniveling at her feet. A heavy curl escaped her veil to shine upon her shoulder. A perfect foil for her white skin and brilliant eyes.

The temptation grew too great.

Would her voice match the one swirling forth from his imagination, rich and smooth? He extended his hand and beckoned.

Betrayer, her sooty-lashed eyes accused. She did not obey his summons. The coil in his stomach grew tighter.

Ragi stepped forth from the soldiers who surrounded the women.

"Isabel," he exclaimed in so thick an accent, Kol wondered whether she recognized her own name. The gray-haired warrior extended his arm to her, offered his escort.

Did the princess see her name tattooed into the old man's chest? Did she realize she had become an object of devotion to legions for having saved his life? Kol doubted she saw past Ragi's naked skin, still painted with the blood and grime of battle.

The princess bestowed a scathing look upon the man and ascended the dais, her bearing as proud as any queen's. A flash of color drew Kol's attention downward. From beneath her hem appeared the tips of two red, pointed slippers. An unwitting flirtation.

Tejst litla. If they were lovers he would call her that, his red-footed blackbird.

A shriek shattered the moment. The sound came from the fair-haired princess who stumbled, white-faced, in her sister's wake. Staring horrified at Ragi, the young woman snatched at and hid amidst Isabel's skirts.

Isabel smoothed a hand over the crown of her sister's head, the only gesture of comfort she could manage, and took the final stair. No longer could she delay a confrontation with the monster whom she had gifted with life. From her brother's throne, he watched her, his eyes so startling in their clarity they seemed fueled by a supernatural light.

He spoke a single word in greeting: "Isabel."

God be with you, Isabel. The words—his voice—echoed up from the recesses of her memory. Two winters had passed. How steadfastly she had believed in his innocence only to find, too late, what a naive girl she had been.

Now, at last, she stood face to face with the man who had betrayed her. Waves of heat surged through her, and with it, a fury she'd kindled for what seemed an age.

When she spoke, her voice barely exceeded a whisper. Inside her flared sleeves, her nails dug into her palm. "What a fine gift thou dost bestow upon me, Norseman."

The warlord tilted his head, and peered at her all the more intently. "Gift, my lady?"

Though his words bore an accent, he spoke her language well.

"Aye." Her eyes slid down the length of him, and back up again. She could not prevent the curl of her lip. "My very own nightmare, come to life."

His face remained carved of the same stone as before.

She despised his silence. Did he have nothing to say to her? Two winters of night-spawned curses and maledictions crowded her throat, but she could take no chances with impassioned words.

She had a secret to protect, and protect it she would.

Remembering this, Isabel drew up her courage and spoke with the dignity expected of a Norsexian princess.

"You and your army must withdraw immediately from these shores."

He responded in a low voice. "You know I cannot."

Isabel stepped closer, her sister dragging behind.

In truth, the monster held her in complete and utter thrall; more so than on the night she had held his head in her lap and prayed for his life. A neat, close-clipped beard emphasized the angular strength of his face. And his eyes. *His eyes.* Two portals to the most dangerous of hearts. A perfect reflection of her wistful, girlhood dreams.

Impulsively she reached out and pressed her hand

against his cheek. His lips parted. The hall resounded with the hiss of drawn swords. The two wolfhounds circled, growling. The Norseman lifted a staying hand. His eyes did not waver from hers. Beneath her fingertips his skin felt warm and firm; the bone of his cheek, strong.

She whispered, "Satan, the sisters taught me, was physically beautiful. One of God's most brilliant angels, fallen from Heaven."

Abruptly Isabel withdrew her hand. "I am no longer a callow girl. I shall not confuse angel with devil again."

"Indeed?" His eyes darkened, or perhaps 'twas merely the smoke from the hearth.

She hated the intimacy of his gaze, for it claimed a connection they did not share.

"Indeed," she murmured, her heartbeat thunderous. Her caution, so recently imposed, fell away. "I would face my own death to kill you here and now."

She knelt between his knees, a false supplicant. "In this hall before your men." She opened one empty palm toward the rafters. "If only I held . . . a dagger . . . in my hand."

From all about came the low, astonished murmurs of his warriors.

His expression remained frozen. "We shall be enemies then?"

Isabel winced at his chosen words. Did he seek to take her back to another time and place? A time she had tried so desperately to forget?

"We should never have been anything else."

His nostrils flared in masculine displeasure. "Did you truly believe I would not return?" Still damp with the sweat of battle, his hair clung like polished onyx against his swarthy skin.

"I have prayed each and every day *you would not.*" The force of Isabel's words sent her swaying forward.

The Dane caught her arms. She gasped at the power of his touch, but could not stop her confession from spilling forth. "I have prayed *each and every day* to be blest with knowledge of your death."

The Dane's eyes flashed. Rowena sobbed a warning. Isabel tore her arms free from his grip and, with her hands, swept the remnants of treasure from the dais.

"You have what you came for," she hissed. A jeweled goblet thunked down the stairs. "So be gone from this place."

Yes, go, she prayed fervently. Ranulf must be alive. He must return to his throne in Calldarington and everything must return to the way it was, else all would be lost.

"Nei." The Dane's eyes scorched a path over her face to sear her lips. "Not yet."

The pitch of Rowena's sobs heightened.

Isabel thrust her hands into her skirts and stood. "Then allow a message to be sent to our uncle to the north, Ugbert of Wyfordon. He will pay whatever ransom you require."

"Will he?" the warlord murmured. One side of his mouth quirked upward.

Of course he would smile. 'Twas a shock he did not laugh outright in her face. Laugh at who she was, at the foolish thing she had done in setting him free.

She frowned. "Is that not what you desire? More riches? So much that your boats swell and sink beneath their weight?"

"That is not at all what I desire." From beneath dark lashes, his gaze narrowed. "I have come to this place to claim only one thing."

Isabel's heart ceased to beat.

Did he know her secret? The reason she had prayed so fervently he would never return?

"I desire Ranulf's death," he growled. "I will not depart until it is done."

Along the outer rim of her awareness Isabel heard Rowena's sobs escalate into outright wails.

The Dane's gaze shifted to Rowena. "If you do not quiet her, I will."

A retort sprang to Isabel's lips, but a scream interrupted from the far corner of the hall, from one of the Saxon women who had been forced to serve his warriors. The Dane did not even glance in the direction of unrest, but watched Isabel keenly.

Perhaps he expected her to cower and beg for their lives, their honor, but she was daughter of Aldrith and sister to Ranulf. She would do neither. She carried the pride of their Norsexian dynasty in her blood.

She challenged his stare. "My sister and I will go to our chambers now." Lifting her chin, she added, "And you will provide us with a suitable escort so we can safely make our way there."

A roar of bawdy laughter echoed off the timber walls. Earthenware shattered. Isabel's lip curled. "Unless you wish for us to remain and watch."

The smile disappeared. He caught the eye of a huge giant of a man, the one they called Vekell, and jerked his head in the direction of the unrest. At this, Vekell plowed through the men toward the source of the distressed cry.

In the next moment, the Danish warlord snapped an order to a nearby warrior. His eyes, when they returned to her, gave off flinty sparks. "You may take your leave." With raised hand he indicated she and Rowena should follow the soldier.

In the next breath he stood. Isabel froze, her limbs bound, as if by some wicked dream. He stopped just beside her and lowered his head, almost as if he intended a kiss. For a moment, they stood as close as lovers exchanging an endearment, she trapped merely by the intensity of his physical presence.

"'Twould be to your avail, Princess, to assist in drawing Ranulf forth." Though no part of him touched her, his tone ravished, and sent waves of heat down her spine. "We will discuss your choices further this eventide, you and I."

His gaze fell to her sister. His lip curved in disdain. "Alone."

He descended the dais and vanished into the wall of men.

You and I. Alone. Isabel summoned every bit of her hatred and used it to quell the rapid thrum of her heart, a reaction she could only attribute to fear.

This time things would be different. This time she was awake and aware and would not find herself—too late— a victim of the Dane's treacherous hand.

Perhaps his return was a gift from God. A chance to take her revenge. For her king and her people. For herself.

But first she must take care to hide her secret. Anxiety speared through her. Blessed Lord. Godric. He was still out there. Waiting for her.

Chapter 3

E verything was so perfect," railed Rowena. "So beautiful. And now 'tis all laid to waste."

Her sister lifted shredded garments, and, with glazed eyes, set various trunks aright. The women's rooms had been ransacked. Only a lantern's meager glow revealed the devastation.

Rowena lifted a jewel case and peeked inside. The box clattered, empty, to the floor, amidst the sound of her sobs. From the doorway their guard watched, unabashedly amused.

Isabel stood in the center of the room and touched nothing. The chamber held none of her belongings. She no longer resided in this sanctuary of chastity. The women's rooms were a place where a noble maiden's purity was protected. She had learned her lessons well.

No chastity—*no sanctuary*.

She wondered whether her own chambers had been plundered. Yet in truth she did not care. The air frosted with her shallow breath. Her hands hung at her sides, as heavy as loom weights. Blessed Lord, had fear turned her to stone?

No! Inside, her pulse thundered so loudly, even Rowena's wails grew faint to all but one thought. Isabel's gaze fixed upon the window.

Her beloved was out there. Just the thought of Godric waiting in the forest—

She crossed to the window. The Norseman's gaze narrowed, followed her. She drew aside the heavy pelt and pushed open the shutter. Winter chill struck her full in the face, leaving her without breath.

He would be so cold. Tears stung her eyes, painful and sharp in the frozen air. She blinked them away, and took a deep breath. She had to find him. If the Dane came for her tonight as he'd promised, she might not have another chance.

Isabel peered outward. Small fires dappled the narrow flatland surrounding the burh, evidence of their captors' presence. Beyond that, the forest encircled the western face of the keep, as dense and black as a sooted cauldron.

From the corridor a voice sounded. She gripped the windowsill as the guard opened the door. For a moment he leaned out and spoke, then he turned to indicate she and Rowena would remain under guard. He quit the room and closed the door. Footsteps faded, and there was silence. Rowena's gaze turned to her.

Beneath Isabel's palm, the edge of the window became numbingly cold. Her pulse raced. A sudden gust of wind, smelling of brine and kelp, tossed her veil across her lips and face.

She must go now. Their guard could return at any moment.

Rowena hissed, "I despise you with each breath I take."

But first she owed Rowena an explanation.

Tangled skeins of yarn fell from Rowena's hands as she

charged forward. Red blotches marred her skin and tears wet her cheeks.

"I defended you to everyone." Rowena said, jabbing a narrow finger toward Isabel. "All along what they said was true. You helped the Dane escape." Her blue eyes seared Isabel. "Prithee, tell me. Is what I say true? Is that not the same heathen beast whom our brother imprisoned for attacking you two winters ago?"

Never before had her elder half sister dared to ask the question, not when Ranulf had always been there to protect and interfere. He had commanded Isabel's silence, and though he'd never spoken the condition aloud, she had known her quiescent submission was the only way to guarantee her king's continued favor for the one she loved.

But how could Isabel lie to Rowena now? All along she had despised the cool distance that had cleaved between them as Ranulf's clear, but unsolicited favoritism had become more and more apparent. But their regent was absent now, perhaps dead. Isabel was left with only the counsel of her conscience.

"Aye, 'tis true."

Rowena's eyes widened. Her body trembled. Slowly she came to stand even closer to Isabel. She shrank not from the wind and cold.

'Twas almost a relief for Isabel to avow her crime. Perhaps it was not too late to allay the rivalry between them, the one she'd neither desired nor cultivated. "Sister, for so long I have wanted to confide in you." Isabel reached for Rowena.

Rowena snatched her hand away. In the next instant Isabel felt the sting of a palm against her cheek.

Her half sister bared her teeth. "Never call me sister. Never again."

Isabel stood stunned. Though her cheek blazed with the force of the blow, as well as the heat of humiliation, Isabel did not raise her hand to soothe away the burn. In this moment, she deserved whatever retribution Rowena saw fit to mete out.

"Forsooth," Isabel whispered with a nod of her head. "I understand your anger. Endlessly I have prayed for forgiveness for setting the Dane free."

Rowena lunged. Her hands clenched Isabel's neck.

Isabel grasped Rowena's fingers, desperate to pry them loose, but Rowena, larger and stronger, held her fast. She could not breathe. Tears wet the corners of her eyes. Her sister's face shone vividly pale in the half-lit room.

"Tell me, little sister, was your treachery intentional or spawned by stupidity? When you set him free were you aware of his sin? The terrible thing he had done?"

Unable to speak, Isabel shook her head.

Rowena's gleaming eyes suddenly went flat. "'Tis no matter. Stancliff is dead. Hermione saw him fall, and you are to blame." She thrust her thumbs into Isabel's throat.

No, Isabel thought, choking. Stancliff, Rowena's betrothed, and countless others lay dead upon the battlefield because of her. Murdered by the Norse monster she had unleashed upon the world. Perhaps even the blood of her half brother, the king, lay upon her hands, for in the midst of battle, where had he gone? Ranulf was among the most skilled of warriors, and no coward. She could not imagine him riding away to escape, no matter how fierce the foe.

Without air, Isabel's consciousness dimmed. How long would it take to die if she did not struggle?

From her psyche hurled forth a fragmented memory, of another time when she had felt the nearness of death. Water and darkness. An angel who carried her into the light.

No, no angel.

The Dane should have let her drown. If he had, he would have died in Ranulf's prison and none of this would have come to pass.

Godric.

Strength surged into her limbs. She tore Rowena's hands from her throat and shoved her away, hard. They both collapsed to the floor. Air flooded Isabel's lungs, painful and sweet.

"I hate you," Rowena wailed, her gunna bunched gracelessly at her hips. With one foot she kicked Isabel's thigh.

Isabel grasped the edge of a table and pulled herself up. The secret passageway. The same one she had taken those years before from this very chamber to descend into the pit. 'Twas her only hope. The tapestry hung heavy and thick in her hands. She lifted it and shoved the wood plank aside.

Light flickered up from the depths where there should only have been darkness. Amidst the voices of men, stone scraped upon stone.

"*Meira. Hérna.*" More, here.

The Norsemen sealed the passage.

Isabel's hope faded. She pulled the plank back and dropped the tapestry into place. How would she escape now? Think. *Think.* She turned.

Rowena lifted a weaving hook and stabbed.

Isabel shielded herself but fell beneath the force of the attack.

"Traitorous bitch!" Rowena's curses filled her ears.

The door crashed open. A male voice commanded, "*Nei. Hættu þessu!*"

Rowena thrashed as a soldier pulled her off. "You killed Stancliff! You killed them all." Isabel crawled away and stood.

"Shhh," the soldier soothed. He carried Rowena toward a stool. The chamber echoed with her screams. Aghast, Isabel retreated until the backs of her thighs touched the window.

The window.

Across the room the door hung open on its hinges.

Surely once they realized her absence they would assume she had escaped into the hallway.

Moments later Isabel clung to the face of the wall, her fingers and toes shallowly wedged in the crevices between its timbers. Ivy covered the wood, allowed to remain in place by Ranulf for the purpose of lessening the winter winds' penetration of private chambers of the upper hall. Even in the spring, the weak, spidery stems would never support the weight of a man. Yet, in the past, they had given support to an innocent girl brimming with mischief and curiosity for the world, one who sought to escape the women's rooms to visit animals in the stable or to deliver a basket of bread to the widow who lived at the far edge of the burh.

A desperate sound left Isabel's lips. That girl no longer resided within her. She was a woman full-grown, with a woman's weight and height. Her veil swirled off, claimed by the dark wind. Why had she believed herself capable of this?

She pressed her forehead against the brittle, winter-dead leaves and closed her eyes. From the haze, Godric's face appeared and with his image came courage. Cautiously she bent her legs and, with her foot, searched for the next gap in the timber. Vines snapped, and gave way. With a painful scoring of her nails against the wood, she caught herself upon a narrow ledge. Though nearly paralyzed by fear, she forced herself to continue her descent. After an eternity her feet found purchase in the thicker vines at the stone base.

She heard the voices of nearby soldiers, yet there were no cries of alarm. Nearly blinded by the night, she stumbled into the ditch that surrounded the burh. Brackish water permeated her slippers and skirts. So cold. She welcomed the discomfort, the numbness. How deeply she despised herself for having been inside the keep while Godric had suffered in the forest.

She had not thought the water would splash so loudly. Rigid and aware she stood, awaiting a horde of barbarians to descend upon her in a wave of death. But none came. Perhaps the moan of the wind and not-so-distant crash of the ocean had muted her haste. Warily she resumed her trek and ascended the opposite side of the ditch. Sodden earth crumbled and slid beneath her slippers, but she thrust her hands into the mud and climbed.

She halted, faced with the expanse of land that had been the day's battlefield. Having no other choice, she delved into the blackness. The scent of burned thatch and blood hung heavy in the air, along with a low-lying fog that teased her eyes with false images—surely false!—of the men slain there that day. All at once, a wall of trees rose up before her.

Into the thicket she darted. Godric must be safe and alive. She could not bear the loss of him. Panicked thoughts swarmed her mind. Had he been found? Captured? Killed? She approached the clearing.

"Godric," she called into the fathomless pitch. Her sodden skirts clung to her legs. " 'Tis I."

Frantic, she ran in circles. No response greeted her but the sound of the wind and the creaking of winter-bare trees.

"Godric!"

Just as a sob of grief arose in her throat, she saw a movement across the clearing. A flash of gray against the black. A person or the cursed fog? She could not be sure.

A familiar figure emerged. Her heart swelled with relief. She broke into a run. "Beloved."

From behind her came the sound of thunder. A winged figure swooped past her like a fiend from Hell, clods of frozen earth flying in its wake. Terror crashed through her.

Fool! How could she, in her sense-numbing fear, have allowed the Norse overlord to follow her to the hiding place of the treasure she held most dear? She watched in helpless terror as he swept low from his saddle, sword in hand, to capture Godric.

Her son.

A child. He held a very small child, no older than two winters, in his arms.

Kol had no time to consider the unexpected turn of events.

At her cry his head whipped around. 'Twas not a scream, but a challenge to do battle. Like a Valkyrie, the princess flew at him—her visage radiant with anger, her black hair evidenced only by its high sheen beneath the night sky.

So entranced was he by the sight, she was upon him before he could react. Her hands struck his thighs, clawed at his mantle as if she would dismount him from his horse. Holding the child close, he scabbarded his sword.

"Give him to me." Her face gleamed white with cold and whatever emotion that fueled her attack. Fear or hatred? Both, he surmised. He reined his mount to the side, so as not to trample her.

"Mama."

The child spoke softly but the word stung Kol's ears as if it had been shouted by an army of thousands. His gaze held hers as he allowed her to take the child. Of course. Beside him stood a noblewoman, full-grown. He should have known she would have a family. A child.

A husband.

So why did he feel as if he'd been dealt a blow by the flat side of a sword? A vision formed in Kol's mind, that of a shining, faceless hero. *Her husband.* Hatred and jealousy flared deep within, and with it a primal desire.

She backed away, her eyes narrowed. Against her breast she held the child tight and whispered against the small cheek. Kol jerked the reins and spurred his mount to follow her. Over the child's head she cast him a venomous glare, clearly intended to wound. The effect was opposite.

He wanted to touch her.

"Come here." He dismounted.

"Nay." The princess's eyes darkened, clearly sensing a new and different danger. "I will not."

Silence ruled the grove, save for the rush of the wind through the trees and the elusive patter of Heaven spilling its frozen, fragmented tears upon the earth.

Had he met her husband in battle? *He hoped so.* A succession of images flashed through his memory, one after the other. The men he had fought and defeated that day. Each and every death-moment.

He moved toward her. She retreated, turning the child's face against her neck.

A woman's cry and the sound of horses' hooves tore his attention from her. Vekell burst from the weald atop his mount. Before him scattered a dozen or so children and one very terrified woman. Soldiers quickly fenced them in.

"Hermione," the princess called. Kol's eyes descended over her wet garments, which molded against long, slender legs. "Children."

The woman sobbed and fell at Isabel's feet. "Forgive me, my lady. When the boy heard you he escaped my grasp, and I knew not where to take the others." Around her narrow shoulders she wore only a thin shawl. The children huddled together, their faces gaunt, their eyes wide and fixed on the giants who surrounded them. Most were not dressed to survive the elements. Some wore no shoes.

Realization struck Kol, and with it, an anger so intense, the fires of passion that had so consumed him moments before were summarily doused.

He leveled his gaze upon the princess. "You knew they were here."

Her face shone luminous, her lips black red. Droplets of ice glistened upon her hair like diamonds. Her silence confessed everything. His men waited upon their mounts, quiet and watchful. Behind him his steed snorted and pawed, as if sensing his fury. Wind surged through the trees.

Anger thickened his voice. "You would let them die of cold to spare them from me?" The princess did not look at him as a man, but as a monster.

The princess did not blink. She did not move. She merely stood holding her child like the statue of some long-dead martyr, challenging him with her violet eyes. Almost as if she had witnessed every sin he had ever committed.

He was damn sick of her eyes and the way they judged him. Striding forward he took hold of her arm.

The children cried out. Some of them screamed.

As if he were a bloody-fanged monster, come to eat them alive. He grew more furious. All around, the forest trees pitched and roiled, brandishing their branches as if they, too, protested his hold on her. He heard their whispers.

Unworthy. Unwanted. Soon to be forgotten.

He released her. To Vekell he ordered, "Take the children to the keep."

Kol caught the nearest boy and lifted him by the nape of his tunic into the saddle with Ragi. When he removed his hand he froze. A dark hand print—his own—stained the coarse wool of the boy's garment. He lifted his fingers to his nose. Instantly he recognized the scent. Blood.

He spun around, searching the darkness. The princess had been the only one he had touched. The blood must have come from her. She stood beneath an ash tree sparring with one of his men over possession of her son.

Her voice rang with authority. "You will not touch him." When the warrior stepped toward her she slapped him away.

Taking full advantage of her distraction, Kol approached from behind. Before she could react, he stole the boy from her arms and passed the warm little body to the man. The child, now fast asleep, did not waken. Though the princess tried to pursue, Kol blocked her path.

"Vermin!" Panic tainted her voice. Small-fisted blows jabbed into Kol's chest. He caught her hands.

"I hate you," she hissed, her face a mask of feminine rage.

"Really?" He bent so low, so close, their noses almost touched. "I had not noticed."

Her eyes flew wide in astonishment. For a moment they shared breath. How lovely she was, even pallid from cold and reeking of ditch water.

The sound of horses and men grew faint as the last of the soldiers departed with their small passengers.

Kol released her. She stumbled backward and fell onto her bottom.

"Your wound," he demanded. "Where is it?"

The princess snatched up a stick and hurled it at his head. Had his mood not been so foul, he would have laughed. He caught her weapon midair and cast it to the ground.

Pointing at her, he warned, "Cease your foolishness."

With the intention of helping her rise, he bent but she scooted away like a retreating crab. She sprang to her feet and fled toward the narrow path as if she too intended to gallop the entire distance to Calldarington.

He caught her; gently, given the injury he suspected.

"You bleed." Frowning, he ran his hands over her rigid shoulders. "Tell me where."

So dark was her gunna, he could not perceive any trace of blood or injury and her softly curved lips held their silence. Impatient for an answer, he smoothed his palms over her breasts. The princess jerked back.

"Stop!" The clearing echoed with her shrill command.

He grasped her arm.

"Ow," she yelped. For a moment her face lost its expression of hatred. But in the next breath, her fist almost contacted his jaw.

With her hand held in his, he growled, "I vow if you do that again I will smite you in kind." He wouldn't of course, but his threat achieved the desired effect. Defiance lit her eyes, but she yielded to his touch.

Be gentle, Kol reminded himself. Admittedly, he had little understanding of the female mind, having grown from child to man in the company of warriors.

With a deliberate lightness of hand, he inspected the princess's arm. He bit down a curse. The night was dark. He could not see. Abandoning his own caution, he grasped her woolen sleeve and ripped it, and the linen beneath, from cuff to shoulder.

She tried to shrug free, but he held her still. Beneath the moonlight her skin gleamed as exquisitely as Quanzhou silk.

At his touch, she gasped. Blood surged to his groin. The sound of the wind in the trees mingled with the rush of blood to his head. Thankfully, his jerkin fell to the tops of his thighs. Doubtless the princess's alarm would grow tenfold if she saw the robust tenting of his braies.

He commanded his attention to her arm and quickly found the source of the blood. A small, perfectly round puncture wound on her forearm, and another just above her elbow.

"Tell me how this occurred."

She glanced at her arm. Again, bewilderment softened her scowl. Had she even been aware of the wounds until this moment? But rather than answering him, she lifted her chin, her lips sealed more tightly than a regent's missive.

Could she not confide a simple fact to him? Irritated, he strode to his mount to retrieve linen to bind the wound.

Upon turning he found himself completely alone. He searched for something to kick, to curse, but there was only the condescending silence of the primeval forest around him.

He swung onto the horse and, with a jab of his heels, set off after her. She had run nearly to the tree line when he sighted her. Leaning low he claimed her by the waist and dragged her into his lap.

The princess sat between his thighs, an effigy of silent disdain. An occasional shiver broke her stillness. Encased in leather, Kol had little warmth to share, but still he pulled her against his chest, and banded his arm beneath her outthrust breasts. Her garments had hidden the extent of her slenderness. Her rib cage was as delicate as a bird's. Cold-hardened nipples jutted in defiance of her tunic.

Kol closed his eyes. Exhaled through his nose.

Each shift of her thighs along his, each press of her buttocks against him, enticed. Tempted. Deep within his chest, and even more so in his loins, his arousal grew rampant, but he would not allow this impulse to sway him from his course. The extermination of his final enemy could be his only goal.

Isabel shared his enemy's blood. The girl who had once saved his life—who had unknowingly, but valiantly challenged his demons—no longer existed. Perhaps that girl had never truly existed at all.

Ranulf lived. Kol sensed that much in the air about him. He would use the princess to draw the king forth. There could be no more escapes. No more defiance.

Already he held the key to her submission.

Chapter 4

Two winters before

I cannot have heard you correctly. For a moment I thought you said the princess . . . was with child."

The timber walls of the women's chambers absorbed each of Ranulf's words instantly, leaving the room so silent Isabel wondered—nay, prayed each of its occupants had been swept away to some faraway land. A land where they would lose all memory of what they had just heard.

On the bed she lay, with the furs pulled over her head. She clenched her hands into the bedclothes, and promised to whatever divine being granted wishes, that if she were, indeed, taken to another world she would never shed a tear over not being allowed to say goodbye.

Not to family or friends, not even Merwyn, whom she had not been allowed to visit, not even for a pat on the nose, since—

Since the afternoon the Dane had pulled her from the river.

Cursedly near-deaf, the medicus shouted as if he truly believed Ranulf had not heard his revelation the first time.

"Aye, the babe wilt be born before the first frosts settle upon the fields."

"Shhh!" Berthilde reprimanded sharply. Isabel covered her ears with her hands.

Surely countless other ears strained against the outside of the door. Curious servants hoping to be the first to carry news of the princess's mysterious ailment to the multitude. Isabel pressed her face into the linens. Already there were too many witnesses to her shame.

"Isabel?" Ranulf's hoarse utterance stabbed past the barrier of her flat-pressed hands. She knew he stood at the edge of the bed. For an eternity silence throbbed about her.

"Tell me these are lies!" His shout tore the breath from her.

The fur coverlet flew from her body. She cringed, exposed. Air and light razed her skin but Isabel remained just as she had since the medicus' humiliating examination, curled tight as a sheave. Berthilde's ragged sobs emanated from the corner of the room. Isabel embraced herself even tighter, as if the fragments of her heart could be held together by force alone.

"'Twas the Dane!" Ranulf raged.

"No," Isabel whispered into her pillow.

Her angel would not have done such a thing. In her mind she had pondered every moment of their togetherness. Despite the black moments, the missing memories, she was sure he had saved her life. That was all.

"You dare champion him?" her brother roared.

Forsooth, the Dane had been a stranger, but somehow she knew—

A sudden weight tilted the mattress. Berthilde cried out. Hands closed on her ankles. Linen bunched at her thighs as Ranulf dragged her from the bed and forced her to kneel before him.

Did he not understand? She wanted only to be still, to mend. Tears scalded her cheeks. Futilely her mind

*searched for an explanation for her missed courses, the
persistent sickness—but there were no answers.*

*Yea, the Norseman had come, and he had gone, and
now, inexplicably, she found herself with child, but she
remained steadfast in her belief he was blameless.*

*Ranulf's voice broke as he pronounced, "'Twas no im-
maculate conception."*

*Isabel stared upward, stricken by the amalgam of emo-
tion in his eyes. Fury, tenderness—and disappointment. "I
would never presume to say it was so."*

*Tears glazed his eyes, tears she had never before seen in
this warrior king who showed no weakness. "And you,
naive child. You set him free."*

*In a blink, Berthilde appeared along the watery edge of
Isabel's vision.*

*"Sire, please," she whispered in a supplicant's voice,
her hands pressed together as if in prayer to her king. "She
hath been punished enough."*

*Ranulf paled. He sank to his knees in front of Isabel.
Her half brother, the pride of their father, of their long and
valiant noble line. Sunlight, waned by the approaching
eve, stole through the window to shine off his golden hair.*

*"This is not what I had intended for you, sister. This is
not—" He lifted a hand to touch her cheek.*

*Isabel could not look at him. Instead she stood and
crawled to the center of the bed, where she turned from
him and lay down, her arms at her sides. The linens still
gave off the faintest bit of warmth.*

"Isabel." Against the mattress he grasped her hand.

*But another man's words, not Ranulf's, echoed through
her mind. "God be with you, Isabel."*

*With each moment, her memories of her blue-eyed sav-
ior grew more faint, more altered. Desperate to remember,
desperate to believe, she slid her other hand beneath the
pillow. There her fist curled around the relic.*

A bloodstained fragment of cloth, snatched from the fire when Berthilde had not been watching.

Her only remnant of him.

"I bid you, cease looking at me thusly." The Dane spoke quietly, over his shoulder. He placed another shard of kindling on the fire.

On the far corner of the bed Isabel remained conjoined with the bed pillar, where she had scrambled after he'd deposited her moments before. She watched his every move, his every breath, her muscles tensed for flight. Would he lunge at her and tear her clothing, or would he take pleasure in a slow assault?

He pivoted and sat back upon the low stone hearth, his elbows propped upon his knees.

"As if I were some sort of monster." With a tilt of his head he peered toward her. His voice rumbled up from his throat like an elusive, first thunder before a storm. "My name is Kol. Son of Thorlek."

At her continued silence he frowned. "I thought, mayhap, you would wish to know."

Kol. How long had she wondered?

But she did not wish to give him a name. Monsters did not have names.

Silence screamed between them. Shadows blackened the chamber, save for the fire's meager light.

Somehow the man who sat before her did not concur with the stark, shocking images of a slavering fiend her mind repeatedly produced. Forsooth, his long, dark lashes contradicted everything hard in him. Surely he had been carefully crafted by Satan to beguile unwary women into opening their hearts.

Just as she had done, once before.

From beneath those lashes, he glanced about the room.

Shadows darkened the skin beneath his eyes. He lifted a hand to rub the bridge of his nose.

"These are your chambers, are they not?" He flashed a smile. Isabel glimpsed his white, even teeth. "They smell like you. That is how I know."

Isabel did not so much as blink in response. Eventually his smile faded to bleak neutrality. Lips pursed, he lowered his gaze and found interest in some item near his feet. Her belongings. Unlike the bower belowstairs, her chamber had been left untouched.

Like a nervous bird, Isabel shifted on her roost, her eyes narrowed. He had no right to touch her things.

From a woven basket he lifted a styli. Between his long, blunt-tipped fingers he rolled the delicate instrument, the ivory snow-white against his dark skin. Again he peered into the basket, this time with clear expectancy. The faintest of smiles turned his lip as he retrieved her wax tablet.

Only yesterday she'd written a bit of verse. Not even a verse, just a silly batch of words she'd intended to share with Godric when he grew old enough to understand; to laugh and to see she wasn't the remote, too-old-for-her-days young woman the rest of Calldarington surely saw when they looked at Isabel, youngest daughter of Aldrith, princess of Norsex.

The Dane smoothed his fingertips over her words. Words intended only for her son.

"Put it down." Her voice arose no louder than a rustle of reeds. He looked up.

"As you wish." He returned the styli and tablet to the basket, and stood.

Isabel's heart nearly tore free from her breast. Surely she had angered him. Her gaze veered upward over an endless span of rough-hewn leather boots to thighs surely the thickness of Offa's dykes. Behind him, his shadow blackened the tapestries on the wall.

Slowly he lifted a hand and beckoned. "Come hither." With each word his neck corded powerfully. He moved toward her curtained haven, his boots making nary a sound. For one so large, he moved with unnerving grace. He bent to peer beneath the bed curtains. A strand of hair slid across his cheek. "I would see your wound in the light and tend to its dressing."

"I think not," Isabel whispered.

He lifted his knee, and half knelt upon the bed. The mattress tilted.

"I will not allow you to touch me. Never again," she warned. Her heart slammed against her ribs. She pressed so hard against the post she expected it to splinter against her spine.

Over time, she had found some small comfort in the lack of memories of the assault. Would she be able to retain her sanity if he were to attack her again, here and now, as she endured awake and fully aware?

He leaned toward her, eclipsing the fire's light. "If I intended to do you harm, I would have already done so." Surely his voice, his eyes, cast spells, for she almost believed.

She sprang off the bed. Her damp skirts tangled thickly between her legs. Frantic, her gaze swept the room. A weapon! Though her mother's jeweled dagger lay sheathed in Isabel's trunk, she would never be able to uncover it quickly enough. She saw nothing else. A low moan escaped her throat. From beside the hearth she snatched up a narrow log and whirled.

"Stand away!" She wielded the weapon, however paltry, between them as if it were a sword as worthy as his own. Her shredded sleeve dangled like ribbons from her shoulder. "You may stand larger and stronger than I, but this time I will fight. *This time* I will watch your every filthy sin with my eyes wide open."

He stood exactly where he had been when she'd leapt

from the bed. The hilt of his sword glimmered at his hip.
"I lose patience with you, little one. Put the stick down."

Her laugh rang harsh. "Is that what you believe? That
simply because you order me to surrender, I shall? Nay.
This time I have a voice. This time I protest."

Measured steps carried him forward. "My dispute is not
with you, but with Ranulf." He stopped, an arm's reach
from her.

"Nay, your dispute is with me." Fury cut through her
veins. *Mistakenly* she had assumed that once they were
alone, face-to-face, his assault of her person two winters
ago would be at the forefront of both their minds. Had she
been so inconsequential a victim? Isabel tightened her grip
on the branch and waggled it threateningly.

Apparently her display of force impressed him not, for
his expression remained the same. But oh, how she wanted
to intimidate him, just as he intimidated her.

Boldly, insanely, she tapped the branch at the center of
his breastplate. *Tap.*

Her teeth clenched as tight as a mollusk, she demanded,
"What of my dispute with you?" *Tap tap tap.*

If Isabel had expected surprise or shame from her attacker in the face of confrontation, Thorleksson gave her
neither.

Instead, the Danish warlord glared at the tip of her
scrawny weapon, his nostrils flared with annoyance. "I bid
you, what dispute have you with me, prior to this day?"

Isabel's mouth fell open. "Knave! Dare you pretend not
to know?"

He paced a half circle along the perimeter of her
weapon's reach. "I know I saved your life." Slowly, he unfastened his leather baldric.

"Only to destroy it," Isabel cried, her eyes fixed on his
hands as, carefully, he set the sword aside. Would he also
remove his jerkin? His tunic and braies? She swallowed,
nearly ill from the thought of a large, naked, and *hairy* man

pursuing her around the chamber. Despite her claims of bravery, she retreated from him until her backside jolted against a wooden cabinet.

He made no effort to remove any of his garments. For the time being, words continued to be his weapon of choice. "As I said, I saved your life. In return you spared mine."

He moved closer. Isabel clutched her makeshift cudgel, raised it between them. His eyes denounced her as strongly as his words. "There are no debts. I owe you naught."

"Nay. Methinks you owe me"—she churned the branch in his face—"you owe me that which can *never* be repaid!"

Anger darkened his features. "You cannot deny my valid claim to vengeance. You saw. I was imprisoned. Beaten unjustly."

"Unjustly," Isabel spat. "So I too once believed! But I was a stupid girl. You deserved each and every lash laid upon your back."

He leaned toward her, the gleam in his eye no longer merely dangerous, but murderous.

"Beast!" She swung. The branch swooshed through the air. Thorleksson stepped back. Her weapon missed his neck by a fingertip. He expelled air through his teeth.

He gritted, "Reveal to me, Princess, why your opinion of me hath changed so greatly since you saw fit to set me free from your brother's pit."

Did he think she did not know of his affront against her? *Must she say the words?* With a curl of her lip she hissed, "Perchance, do you think, it was the realization of your foul transgression against me?"

"Obstinate woman." He shook his head. His dark hair shone like polished jet. "You argue in regress. I intended you no harm. I did not know you were his sister. I did not expect to ever see you again. In truth, I believed you to be a peasant until this very day."

Isabel felt her face go hot and numb, in alternating waves. Rage pricked along her spine. No woman deserved rape, regardless of her status in life. "Would that have stopped you? If you had known who I was?"

"No," he exclaimed with a guttural shout. "You expect me to order my men back to the ships and sail away, simply because I have learned you are that wretch's sister? *Nei!* Nothing will stop me from achieving my due vengeance."

His vengeance? Was his attack on her as she lay senseless beside the river so meaningless he could not even recognize it as the foremost source of her bitterness? How like a man to think only of himself.

But . . . Isabel cautioned herself. If the memory of his attack upon her remained so distant from his mind, or so commonplace as to be unworthy of recall, perhaps Godric could somehow be protected. Perhaps the Dane would never even suspect the boy was his son and she could—

The moment of distraction nearly cost her everything. Thorleksson pounced. Isabel reacted, swung. Along the length of her arms she felt the snag. Contact!

The chamber quaked with—

"Fiskislor fyrir heila!" Fish guts for brains? Surely the most vile of Norse curses. Isabel shrank back against the cabinet, so hard it rocked on its corners. Against her breast she clutched her now highly esteemed, mightily worthy weapon.

A streak of blood surfaced upon his cheek. The Norseman lifted a hand, and touched the wound. He stared at his fingertips. His gaze shifted to her.

In a voice flinty with wrath he growled, "Are you so appalled to see me bleed?"

Isabel snapped her mouth shut.

Apparently unafraid of another injurious blow from her most exalted death-stick, he again advanced.

A cruel smile bent his lips. "Didst thou expect green

bile to spill from my veins? Or perchance vaporous poison?"

"Barbarian!"

"Barbarian?" His face grew tight. He jabbed one long, accusing finger between her breasts. A flush arose to her cheeks. "'Tis *you* who swing a club in *my* face as I attempt to converse with you with the utmost diplomacy."

She swung. His arm a blur of movement, he caught the stick in one hand. Their gazes met, as solid a bridge between them as the branch to which they both held fast.

"I am a man, Isabel. No monster."

One hard tug undermined her balance. Isabel fell forward against the hard wall of his body. His arm closed as tightly as a shield-rim at her waist. Unbidden heat raced up her legs, shot through her arms and blazed along her fingertips. With one hand beneath her chin he forced her gaze up. Eyes brim-full of savage emotion stared down at her.

"I am a man," he murmured. "Flesh and blood."

His head dipped. Isabel recoiled with a gasp.

He stared into her eyes, fiercely intent. She did not understand. Had never expected—

Panic hummed in her ears. She stared into his eyes, too transfixed to struggle, too breathless to scream.

Thorleksson's expression grew hard. His hand snaked up the back of her neck, into her hair. His mouth fell upon hers.

All around, the world imploded into darkness, Isabel aware only of the predatory insistence of his lips, the faint tang of salt as he bit her bottom lip. In the distance, waves crashed upon Calldarington's shores, then rolled softly into the sea. The sound merged with, became lost in the sound of their mingled breath, the crush of his leather against her gunna. She shoved against his shoulders, but he did not release her. His body, rigid against her, radiated all things masculine and powerful.

For one absurd moment, she yearned to wrap herself around him, to breathe his very strength into her lungs.

Innocent. He is innocent. Angel.

His tongue parted her lips, boldly intimate, boldly possessive.

He could not be innocent.

"Beast!" Isabel wrenched away. In that same moment she silenced the voice of the unsuspecting girl-Isabel whom she no longer granted audience.

Kol cursed, and pressed a hand to his mouth. Only when she saw the blood trickle from beneath did she realize she'd bitten him.

"Ply me not with the kisses of a swain." With the back of her hand she wiped her mouth, as if pestilence danced across her lips. "If you seek to attack, then do it like the beast you are."

His arm shot out. She attempted an escape, but he captured her by the nape. *"At . . . your . . . invitation."*

Slowly he lifted her, until her face hovered in front of his. Her toes dangled above the floor.

He scowled. "Wiggle wiggle, little bug."

"Oh!" Isabel gasped, her entire body gone numb with shock. The beast could read. 'Twas the verse she'd written upon the tablet for Godric. To hear him speak the words, so foolish, yet drawn straight and earnestly from her heart, was a trespass she could not abide.

He growled the next line. "How you seem to like the mud."

"Shut your mouth!" Like a cat held by its ruff, Isabel swung her claws. "The words—are not—for you to say."

The room spun about and all at once she felt the softness of the bed beneath her back. She felt his hands, his weight as he climbed atop to straddle her belly. To think, for even a moment, she had thought him innocent.

She thrashed. "How easy it was to draw forth your true nature."

"True nature?" Flushed, he glared down at her. "I have done nothing but defend myself against your vicious attacks and spoken affronts." He intercepted the vengeful talon of her hand. "I believe 'tis you, fair Princess, who hath proven to be the barbarian."

Isabel wrenched her arm free.

"Devil." She shoved her palm against his lips, but he wrenched his face aside. She snatched a handful of his hair and yanked. Reprisal came instantly. He wrapped a fist in her hair and, with steady tension, pulled upward until she lay taut beneath him.

A knock sounded at the door.

Rasping for breath, Isabel felt the rise and fall of his chest against her breast, as erratic as her own.

"Enter," he commanded, his teeth set in a white line. She tightened her grip on his hair and felt an immediate, retaliatory tug.

Vekell entered, carrying a bucket and a neatly folded bundle of cloth.

"As you requested, my lord. Warm water and linen—" The man halted midstep. His eyes grew large, seeing them thus entangled. "Ahem." In apparent reverence, he diverted his gaze.

Isabel looked upward and saw what the warrior must have seen: Kol's hair strewn in dark disarray. Blood streaked his cheek and lip.

Despite the danger of her position, a smile found its way to her lips. To have humiliated him so, and before one of his officers. Even if he killed her now, she would die tolerably content.

"Put it down, then go," Kol ordered with a sharp tilt of his head.

Above her he felt hot and heavy and excruciatingly vital. She could *feel* the blood course beneath his skin where she gripped his forearms.

"You are certain you require no assistance?" Vekell

queried. He slid a hand over his mouth to conceal what she felt sure was a smile.

"Leave us," the man above her growled.

The warrior did as his lord bid him to do. Without another word or glance, he departed, securing the door behind him. Wood snapped on the hearth. Shadows frolicked on the walls.

"Dare you smile!" In one rapid movement, he arced his arm upward and pried her grip from his hair.

"Get off!" Isabel bent her knees and kicked, however obliquely, at his leather-bound calves. Her torn sleeve twisted around her arm, damp and tight. He sank to a position between her thighs. Too easily he subdued her flailing limbs and drew her hands above her head until they met, pinned beneath one of his own. Stretched like a miscreant upon a torture-room rack, Isabel could only stare at the ceiling, her mind wildly searching for the means to escape. Against her thighs, her stomach, she felt his heat, the rigid flex of his muscles.

"Know that you have forced my hand," he muttered. A metallic hiss signaled the entrance of another contender into their melee.

"Nay!" Her heart did its best to tear its way from her breast. The Dane lifted a long knife. Isabel's throat constricted. The blade glinted in the light.

"Animal," she choked. "God will curse you for your sins."

For a moment he stilled. Then, rotating the knife, he brushed his knuckles over her cheek. "I'm afraid someone else already tended to that matter."

Deftly he inserted the blade into the neck of her tunic. Isabel turned her cheek against the bed as cool metal whispered against her naked skin. Despite her valiant promise to watch, to remember, she gave in to cowardice and closed her eyes. The sound of renting cloth cut the silence.

Like honey, warm air spread onto the still-damp skin of

her arm, her shoulder, and to her horror, one breast. Beneath him she writhed with renewed vigor, desperate to be free.

He grasped her arm.

"Ow," she yelled. She had forgotten her wounds.

"Be still." His utterance rang hoarse.

She did not know how, but in some way she seemed to have hurt him. Perhaps he had fallen on his own blade? She wriggled more fiercely.

"I command you to cease."

Something hard, but oddly pliant, pressed against the inside of her thigh—

"Oh." Realization made Isabel's entire body go hot, as if stricken by a sudden ague. Just as she mustered the strength to fight—

He pushed up and away. She lifted onto one elbow and watched him stalk toward the wall, one hand staved into his hair. Viciously he cursed. Her or the tapestry of The Great Flood, she was not certain.

Pivoting, he stormed past, toward a wooden chest, and threw open its lid. With stony intent, he peered inside. Almost at once, impatience shattered his features. From inside he grabbed an armful of clothing, and hurled the misshapen bundle at her. "Black Hell! Put something on."

She sat up, but made no move to touch the garments. She did not understand. If lust had ruled his actions a moment ago, why did he turn his eyes from her now? She smothered the little voice that had attempted to squeak out a claim of his innocence.

His blue eyes flashed. "Did it ever occur to you that two winters ago this—" He jabbed his finger at the center of his jerkin. "This *animal*, this barbarian as you call me, came to Calldarington as a guest? Because he was invited?"

"Invited," she scoffed. "Do you truly expect me to believe that?"

His eyes descended to where her hand covered her breast. Darkness hollowed the place beneath his cheekbones, and for a moment she believed what she saw was not lust, but yearning.

A wall, built deep inside her heart, threatened to give way. Impossible. A flush bloomed upward from her breasts, to heat her neck and face.

He stood, his legs braced wide. "Of course you would not believe." He swirled a hand in the air. "Barely a word spoken between us but already you know, verily, I speak only lies and treachery."

She forced an expression of scorn. "What sort of fool would have invited a Norse mercenary here, when there was no need?"

"What sort of fool?" the Dane repeated in a low voice.

"Yes, *fool.*" Her chin jutted out in defiance.

"Dare you call *me* a fool?" He clamped his mouth shut on the word. "The fool who bade me come to Norsex—"

"Yes?" she demanded.

His next words, though spoken softly, cut like a blade. "Why, Isabel, if you must know, 'twas the king himself."

With a sharp laugh she challenged his claim. "My brother despises outsiders, especially Northmen, and would never have invited you, let alone an army of raiders, into the kingdom."

His blue eyes darkened. Smoldered. "'Tis not your brother of whom I speak."

Not her brother?

Isabel's mouth snapped shut with a click.

Her father.

At this, the Dane grinned darkly and turned on his heel. As he crossed to the door, he hooked the heel of his boot against the edge of the water bucket and tipped it onto its side. Liquid spread like molten amber across the floor to dampen the tips of her once-scarlet slippers. From the table he lifted the linen Vekell had brought into the room and tossed it in a high arc. The bundle landed in her lap.

"Cleanse and bind your wound. No doubt the ditch surrounding this burh swarms with the vilest pestilence."

Isabel looked down at the sodden shreds of her clothing and sniffed. Heavens, she did smell foul. *But he had kissed her still.*

Shadows hid his eyes. She saw only his lips as they moved. "The salve you spread upon my back . . . use it if you have it still."

"Wait!" Isabel commanded, unease sharpening her tone. "My son. When will he be returned to me?"

Kol's long fingers clasped the edge of the door. Beyond him she saw the shoulder of a warrior who apparently had been posted to guard her door, but Kol moved to shield her from any outward view. "Until you wish to divulge Ranulf's whereabouts, you and I have no further cause to speak. Until that time, you may consider the boy . . . well, you may consider him to be mine."

As the door closed, the blood drained from Isabel's face.

Invited. He had been *invited*, damn her to Hell.

Angrily, Kol stripped to his braies and stood before the fire, allowing its heat to cauterize the rush of blood and emotion still raging, unchecked, through his body.

In the distance, waves crashed against Calldarington's shoreline. Even now, the wooden floor seemed to move beneath his feet, in cadence with the ocean.

Slowly his breathing returned to normal. So long ago, he had taken command of his anger, harnessed its energy to work for his benefit alone.

So what had just happened?

"Bolvaður sé hún," he muttered. He had simply wanted to tend her wound. To dress her in dry, warm clothing. In-

stead he had allowed himself to be provoked, and he had become exactly what she had called him.

A barbarian.

Remembering the insanely fierce surge of desire he'd experienced for the perplexing young woman from his past, he rubbed his palm against his forehead.

Alone. Alone. It was best he remain alone. He and his silent companions. Even now they danced on the wall, shades doing their very best to haunt him. Always there— in reality or as creations of his frozen conscience, he knew not—those remnants of souls he had sent into the afterlife. He had never attempted to make peace with them. Why trouble himself, when more would be added to their ranks? As was his custom, he ignored them. To acknowledge them in any way would make them real.

Instead he turned his attention to the mundane. He perused Ranulf's chambers. He had slept in better. He had slept in worse. The bed was large enough for his frame, and that was all that truly mattered. Sleep and seclusion were the only two luxuries he insisted upon for himself and his demons.

The day had been long. With steady hand he hung his hauberk and helm upon the wooden armor tree that had been Ranulf's. He folded the remainder of his clothing in an orderly bundle, and set his boots beside the fire to dry. Upon a stool he sat, the flames warming his back. With reverence, he oiled his sword and sheathed it in its scabbard. He commanded no servant to tend to his armor, to stoke his hearth.

He had always been alone and had somehow grown to prefer it so. Upon his birth he had been an unwanted child. His slave mother had cast him into the snow to die. Raised ever since by men of war, he was never without companions, without a brotherhood.

But somehow, always alone.

Finally he examined himself for injuries, running his

palms over his abdomen, shoulders, and thighs. 'Twould not be the first time he discovered an injury without first suffering so much as a slight irritation. His fingertips lingered upon the narrow gash upon his cheek, laid there by the princess in her fury. Each scar upon his body was a mark upon the path toward an inevitability he had long since given up trying to escape. This time he found no injury greater than a scratch.

Too easy. He was somewhat disappointed at how easy the taking of Calldarington had been. He had walked the rows of the Saxon dead, not once, but twice. The man he had come to challenge did not lie among them. *Coward,* to run and hide when the others died for him. For their families and their land.

Kol took up his knife and polished its blade. Tomorrow he would lead a force into the uplands in search of Norsex's craven king.

And once Ranulf had been eliminated—what then?

Although Kol's future held no happy ending, he could no longer ignore the wishes of his men. They could accompany him on his quest only so far. The rest he would travel alone. Perhaps soon he would truly be alone. In recent years his men had grown less satisfied with the mercenary way, despite the riches it brought. He smiled. He could not imagine Vekell as a simple farmer, married and with children.

Children. The smile faded from his lips. A memory of the princess, holding her child close, came forth from the dark place in his mind. Long ago he had renounced the pain and regret that came with the knowledge he would never sire a child of his own.

But something about this place challenged his inner peace.

'Twas *her.*

He moved toward the far side of the room to stare at the wall that separated them. She was there. Even with the thick barrier between them, he could feel her. He even imagined her scent transient upon the night air, sent aloft by the warmth of her beauty and hatred.

In the king's prison he had lain like a child with his head in her lap as she prayed over him. She had touched his face and hair with gentle hand. Her tears had dampened his skin. He did not understand. How could that benevolent girl have grown into the woman who now occupied the chambers next to his? The same one who glared at him, all the fire inside her dead except for the flame of hatred?

Kol frowned at the tapestry on the wall, a hunting scene. The huntsmen were narrow, weak-looking men, with no more collective prowess than a flock of pea fowl. Mentally he named each of the scrawny hunters "Ranulf".

Surely the princess had known he would return.

No warrior of substance could survive the bloody injustice he had and not return to seek vengeance. To do so in this age would mean only cowardice.

In his mind she had been preserved as a simple young creature, pure and chaste. The woman with whom he had reunited today was complex beyond his understanding.

"Who are you?" he said to the wall that separated them.

A huntsman moved. Kol was sure it had. Clearing his mind of all else, he stared at the tapestry. Again there was a wavering, slight but sure. Fisting his hand in the cloth, he ripped it from the wall. Her fragrance swirled about him, lavender and mint. He'd smelled such on her skin, and in her hair, when he'd held her close.

He passed his hand over the timber. Coldness came through, and yes, a faint glimmer of light. He bent for a closer look. The hole was small, almost imperceptible in the dark mortar between the stones. Perfectly round, it had most certainly been bored on purpose. He stared at the peephole, a portal to her sanctuary. He ran his finger around the edge, his mind circling the possible explanations.

Powerful men spied upon those whom they did not trust, that much he had experienced during his travels into the courts of the Franks and the Byzantines. Perhaps, in the past, visiting dignitaries had occupied the chamber, and the king had felt they required clandestine observation.

Or . . . could Ranulf have secretly observed his own sister? Nay, surely not. Just the thought made him uneasy. More likely the old king, Aldrith, had enjoyed spying upon his young queen, who, years before, had most certainly occupied the comfortable chambers next door.

Kol stared at the hole.

To look would be no weakness. After all, the hole could be used to spy upon *him*. Surely there had been a corresponding hole in the tapestry and if he were to lift the cloth and take the time to look, he would find it. Only a fool would decline to probe further.

Without further deliberation he bent and peered inside.

He saw light. A scant moment later his vision focused and he saw what lay beyond. The trestle and the hearth. But that knowledge registered only vaguely.

She stood beside the overturned bucket. Naked.

His mouth went dry. Low in his belly, it began. A slow, exquisite burn that spread to and filled his loins with molten flame.

Her skin shone flawless in the firelight's glow. She lifted a strip of linen to her arm. Shadows etched the delicate lines of her ribs, and shaded the undersides of two full, pink-tipped breasts.

The moment she turned away he suffered crushing disappointment, but was rewarded with the sight of her unbound hair. He remembered it. The slippery-clean feel of it against his cheek as they had struggled. Its scent, lavender and mint.

Darkly, the silken curtain fell over her back to tease his eye, just above her rounded—

Kol whispered a curse and stepped back from the peep-hole, his body raging with fire.

Her *deviant, damned half brother* had spied on her. What other purpose could the peephole have served?

He closed his eyes, but the memory of her nakedness remained scorched upon his mind. He should never have looked. He was *no better* than the one who had created the hole.

And, damn himself to Hell, all he could think of was how much he wanted to look again.

He stared at the opening.

Kinsman or saint, he was neither. In truth, he suffered a pitiably small conscience when it came to lust. Of the sins he had committed, this would be among his least.

With his fingers splayed against the stone, he bent and peered inside again. Isabel pulled a long, pale gown over her head. He snatched only the briefest view of her softly curving buttocks and long legs.

Isabel turned. She stared directly at the wall. At him. Surely she couldn't see him.

Tears streamed down her cheeks.

With a hiss, Kol closed his eyes.

Exercising more effort than he wished to admit, he stepped back. As far away from the hole as he could remove himself.

He fell back on Ranulf's bed and stared at the ceiling timbers, a crucifix above him.

Of course she would cry. Had he expected otherwise? She was a woman. Her home had been attacked, her loved ones defeated and killed. He had taken her child from her. And perhaps a beloved husband.

And he would change nothing if given the chance.

Closing his eyes, he immersed himself in the same self-taught meditation he had practiced since he was a child. He willed the blackness to consume his insides; his mind, heart, and soul, until he felt like nothing more than a shadow, transient upon the earth. Indifferent to the lot which awaited him in the coming days.

When he at last saw nothing, he slept.

And dreamt.

She came to his bed, her eyes brilliant as jewels against her white skin. There were no more tears. She gleamed with fearlessness. He smiled. She smiled in return.

He saw the glimmer near her breast.

'Twas no dream—

As quick as an asp, his hand shot up to halt the dagger's murderous plunge.

Chapter 5

How—?" Kol demanded, squeezing her wrist.

The tip of the blade quivered just above his bare chest. What of his guards? How had she breached the security of his chambers?

The princess peered down, her cheeks aflush, her eyes wide. Her upper lip twitched into half of a smile but behind, her teeth were clenched.

"I had an inkling you fancied knives, Thorleksson." With a tug she attempted to free her wrist. "So I brought you another."

Beside him, she crouched upon the bed, all curves and hazy softness. The glowing hearth, behind her, gave her a surreal glow. Two slender feet peeked out from the hem of her linen gown. How pretty she was.

God save his soul. He felt nothing but excitement with her bent above him, blade in hand.

"Who are you, Isabel?" Kol stared into her eyes. With one stiff shake of her wrist the blade clattered to the floor.

He arose to one elbow. "The suffering princess or the brave warrioress?"

Her smile grew by a hair. "Neither, Norseman."

"Then what?"

She bent low, so close he felt the quiver of her breath upon his lips. Silken tresses caressed his shoulder. Deep within his chest something staggered, and he recognized it as the beat of his heart. With gentle pressure, he pulled her hand to his chest. Cool, slender fingers splayed across his skin. Her pupils were huge. Fear shone in her eyes, but was he wrong to believe he also saw exhilaration?

He lifted his head, just a fraction, and brushed his lips across hers. She exhaled, then murmured, "Your executioner."

And in that instant her other hand swung up. Though he could not see the blade, *he knew*—

"Isabel!" he rasped, stunned by her ferocity.

Instinctively he deflected her attack, and at the same time scuttled back, up the mattress. His senses exploded in shock as *his own weapon* plunged between his legs, a hair's breadth from her original target.

His loins.

While he gaped, stunned, the princess tugged frantically at the blade, trying to get it free. Her knuckles brushed heavily against him. In one white-hot flash, blood surged into his member. A half-moan escaped his lips.

The princess ceased her struggle and stared at his groin. There, the hilt of the blade protruded rigid and phallic. Color suffused her cheeks.

The sight of her fingers, slender and white, around the shaft—

Jesu.

Kol felt heat flush his own cheeks. Dismayed, he clasped his hands over hers and, by proxy, took control of the weapon. Clenching her hands tight, he yanked the blade free and hurled it to the floor. God, how he wanted to put his hands on her. He pulled her forward, into his lap.

She shoved against him, all elbows and rigidity. "Godric is mine. I will kill you before you take him from me."

She attempted to scramble away, but he flipped her onto her back and with his own body pressed her into the bed.

"I do not want the boy."

Liquid-onyx hair fanned out around her shoulders, and rippled with each arch of her body. Beneath him, Isabel let out a low groan and set about shoving him off. Easily he held her, peering into wild, violet eyes. While she might want nothing more than to slay him, he could only imagine lifting her tunic to ease the erection presently wedged between their bodies like an iron pikestaff.

"Nei." He caught her clawing hands beside her head, weaving his fingers between hers. "I do not want the boy. Nor do I want Norsex."

Her eyes widened. "You lie. Every word you speak is a lie."

For a woman she displayed fair strength, but he aligned his thighs against hers.

"I want only Ranulf."

Her linen gown twisted about her body and gaped at the neck, revealing the round swell of her bosom. Desire, heavy and thick, mottled his thoughts. "Perhaps now I want more."

Some things were fated. He knew that truth too well. Why should he fight this? Isabel could be his, for as long as his destiny allowed.

As she lay trapped beneath him, he drew the backs of two fingers over her cheek. Emotion flashed in her eyes, but she did not turn away. Against his naked chest, he felt the beat of her heart, as rapid as his own.

"Your husband, does he live?" Though he spoke her language, for a moment she did not seem to understand. Dark lashes lowered, shutting him out.

"Aye."

Along the delicate line of her collarbone he brushed the same two fingers. She gave a shallow gasp.

"Then why is he not here, tearing down timber and stone to save you from me?"

Her pale skin blanched a shade more white. Through the fine gossamer of her gown, he felt her nipples against his chest and his mouth went dry.

His control weakened. "Do you honor him?"

The princess did not answer. His eyes roamed her face. How he wanted to be inside her, to drown himself in her crushed, tragic beauty. To consummate the hazy web of emotion between them, to experience the intensity of their unspoken connection as they made love. The dark fringe of her lashes fluttered, and her eyes closed. Beneath him, he felt her tremble. She tugged her hands free. What she did next sent his mind into a dizzying whirl.

Her hands bracketed his face. She lifted her head and brushed her lips over his in a kiss as soft as a butterfly's blush.

Oh, God. He closed his eyes, not believing. Pleasure surged through him. The world disappeared. He was left with nothing but the invitation of her body, warm and pliant, beneath his. Her sweet scent, all around him. Her mouth grew bolder in its foray.

Impatient to taste her completely, he thrust his tongue inside, vaguely aware of her uneven breath, her hands clenching his upper arms.

With a low groan, he fisted his hand in her hair and gently arched her neck back so that he might test her delicate skin with his lips, and his teeth. In the back of his mind, there rang satisfaction: He would have her in his enemy's bed. He smoothed a hand over the firm swell of her breast.

Isabel arched. "You will return the boy to me?"

Kol grew still. Slowly he drew back and looked into her

face, knowing, with a sudden and complete blackness of heart, what he would see. And indeed, he did see fear and hate, manifested in the tremble of her lip and the pallor of her skin.

She used her body as barter in an attempt to regain her child. Kol had never felt such self-disgust.

Fate? He nearly laughed out loud. Nay, 'twas merely blind lust on his part. Cursing, he lifted himself from her and backed away.

"But I am willing," she insisted in a low voice. "I will do as you wish if you will return my son to me."

He glared at the floor, where the two knives lay. "No trade." Bending, he retrieved them and placed them on the mantel.

He heard her intake of breath. Turning, he saw the horror clear on her face. His scars. She had seen them. His oath split the silence as he yanked a tunic over his head.

The princess sat up, the dark mantle of her hair falling over one shoulder. Upon her cheek there were small abrasions, where, in his passion, his beard had marred her skin. *Beast.* She thought him a beast.

He was a beast. Scarred, inside and out.

Though only his ears could hear them, the shades, cowering in their shadows, dared to laugh their disdain.

Unworthy. Unwanted. Soon to be forgotten.

Kol shut his eyes, not wanting to see the curve of her body, nor the bruised, vulnerable loveliness that had so destroyed his ability to reason. Even if she were willing, 'twould be senseless to give into such a temptation. Revenge and death could be his only mistresses.

In a low voice she asked, "Why would my father summon you?"

Kol stared at her. Would she believe the truth? Or did she already know why her father had sent his missive? Perhaps she merely feigned lack of knowledge to test his understanding of the intrigues of the Norsexian court.

He worded his response with caution. "At times, my army provides military services for pay."

"You are a mercenary." She made no move to leave his bed. By that, he assumed her invitation to barter for possession of her son remained in place, despite her knowledge of his deformity.

He tore his attention from her thin gown, and the alluring shadow of dusky peaks beneath. "Your father retained me thusly."

The princess's gaze dropped. A frown thinned her lips and she shook her head. Though her lips parted, he spoke before she could offer her denouncement.

"Do not think to accuse me of lies." Already, the old anger swelled his chest. The anger of being wrongfully accused.

Color darkened her cheeks. "But what you claim cannot be true. I would have known of any threat to my father's sovereignty, from within or without."

"'Tis only fair you hear my account."

Stone-faced, she sat. Kol waited until she nodded. Only then did he proceed.

"At your father's written invitation, my army sailed from Frankia, where we had spent most of the winter. But upon our arrival in Norsex, I found him already buried and Ranulf sitting upon his throne, waiting, with some expectation, to raze my existence from the face of this earth."

Confusion scored her brow. "None of what you say makes sense. If my father had extended an invitation to you and your men—which I altogether doubt—my brother would not rescind the summons, through violence, without provocation."

"Unless he was the source of the threat your father sought to quell through the retainment of my mercenary services."

She blurted, "That is ridiculous. My father adored Ranulf as a son, and honored him as his heir."

"Then who threatened Aldrith's throne?"

Isabel drew her knees up against her chest. "We have fended off the Northumbrians and Mercians for an age."

"Your father would not have felt so compelled to keep those foes a secret in his missives. The threat lay closer. Within his own ranks."

She refrained from meeting his gaze. "You offer no details which might render your accusations true."

"Why, Princess," he answered sharply. "You have given me little opportunity."

"I need hear no more." She shook her head. "Ranulf had every reason to seek your death and it had naught to do with my father or any *supposed* need for mercenary assistance."

Fists clenched against his temples, Kol turned toward the fire. Why had he even attempted to gain her understanding? He and the Saxon princess were nothing to one another, nothing but strangers, and foes. It mattered naught what she knew or believed about his intentions, or the truth behind them. This parlay of words had been a descent into stupidity on his part and he would end the fall now.

He would confine her to her chambers until Ranulf was dead, and then he would depart this place forever. There need not be any further discourse between them.

He turned toward the bed. Only rumpled bedclothes lay there.

He blinked, disbelieving. With a muttered oath, he walked the length of the room. He searched the shadows, even under the bed. No Isabel.

Fury arose inside him. Clearly Isabel *was not* ready for the truth, if, at the first glimpse of it she ran like a deer from the hunter. And curse her, the woman moved too easily for his liking. First in her escape from the bower and now from this chamber. Had his guards drunk too much of the sweet, Saxon mead? Were they, even now, asleep and senseless in the hallway outside his chamber? Furious, he strode to the door and yanked it open.

Two sentries straightened their stance, fully aware, their weapons lodged at their sides.

He slammed the door.

Of course. He had been so distracted by her appearance beside his bed he had not considered how she had come to be in his room in the first place.

A secret doorway or passage. They riddled the keep. His men had sealed all which led inward. Apparently one had gone undetected.

Because it joined two private rooms. The skin at the nape of his neck prickled in unease, in recollection of the peephole.

What of Isabel's husband in all of this?

Through narrowed eyes Kol surveyed the wall dividing their two chambers. Hands spread over the surface, he sought with touch what his eyes might not see, a portal large enough for a grown woman. Or a man.

He felt the aberration as soon as he entered the shadows along the far side of the room, where sun or firelight would rarely fall no matter the time of day. A slight crack in the mortar between the timber planks. His fingers ran over the almost imperceptible groove.

He could force his way inside, force her to hear the truth. But no, not while so many questions swarmed his mind. He glowered at the bed. He would find no rest this night, not in this fortress of breathing walls. He jerked his boots up his calves.

If he could not have sleep, he would at least have answers.

A short time later he strode into the great hall, tying the laces of his leather jerkin with impatient hands. All along the walls his warriors slept. Snores punctuated the silence. Near the fire lay the children from the forest. Several

Saxon women lay among them, those he supposed had been secured by his warriors to tend them.

He drew closer, searching for one child in particular. One with dark, shining curls and the face of an angel. He found the boy, nestled in the arms of a maiden. He drew closer, searching the boy's features. Long lashes lay against flushed, hearty cheeks. The boy would grow into a fine man.

Beneath his regard, the young woman who held the boy awoke, and seeing him, startled—then smiled the sort of smile he knew well. She misunderstood his interest.

Gently she moved the child from her arms, onto the fur beside her, and extended her arm in invitation to Kol. His eyes moved over her. She was comely, with large brown eyes, a small, pink mouth, and hair the color of honey. An ample bosom crowded the neckline of her tunic.

He smiled, but just a mite. There were always women among the defeated who sought out their conqueror. Sometimes he accepted what they offered. Most times he did not. He shook his head, and drew away.

Desire for another woman burned in his veins. A woman who likely hovered beside her hearth at this very moment, carving daggers from chicken bones or some such treachery, to further her next attempt on his life. Even so, a proxy would hold no true satisfaction. Kol left the woman and child.

From a shadowed corner Vekell arose. "My lord, is something amiss?"

Kol spoke quietly, so that none other could hear, in particular the women who lay nearby. "I wish to speak to the Saxon traitor. He has not yet departed?"

"*Nei*, he suffered wounds in the battle. Your physician has treated him and he will leave us before the sun rises."

A fire raged upon the huge stone hearth, but Kol did not need its ambient warmth. His blood remained kindled by his exchange with Isabel. Irritated, his hands fumbled with the broach at the shoulder of his cloak. The sharp prong of the emerald-eyed viper stabbed his palm and he cursed. Why was it things of beauty so often caused the most painful wounds?

His Celt mother, like Isabel, had been beautiful. But instead of bestowing a mother's love upon him, she had wished for his death from the moment of his birth. As a boy, he'd insisted upon seeing for himself the woman who despised him so much as to abandon him, a helpless babe, to a cruel death. He would never forget the moment Vekell finally agreed, and pointed to the madwoman who lived alone at the edge of their settlement. She'd remained there, completely removed from his life, until one night when he was a boy of twelve summers. After he'd led a tattered group of warriors and soundly avenged his father's murder, she had dragged him away from a feast to hiss a maelstrom of incantations above his head. He'd been accepted as a hero by his village, and yet she'd cursed him for being the son of a man who had, years before, forced his lusts upon her, a helpless slave. She had cursed Kol to die young, and without children to beget the jarl, Thorlek's, name.

At this very moment, he felt another woman's curses at work upon him. He glanced at the crossbeam ceiling. With a growl he pulled on his gloves, working the fitted leather over his fingers.

Vekell moved toward the entrance. "Come, my lord. I will take you to him."

Kol scabbarded his vikingsword into its leather baldric and, accompanied by his hounds, followed Vekell across the outer courtyard. The scent of the sea washed over him, cleansing him. He welcomed the utter darkness of the night and the shock of cold.

As he emerged from beneath the raised wooden gate, Svartkell appeared and fell behind to protect his flank as they walked across the shallow ditch toward a small hut on the outskirts of the burh. Outside stood several guards warming their hands above a fire, but with Kol's appearance they straightened and offered due greeting to their lord.

The animal-pelt door stretched cool and smooth beneath Kol's palm. "I wish to confer with him alone."

Kol opened the door and moved inside, leaving the men and his whining hounds behind. For a moment he perceived only peat-scented haze. Upon the earthen floor smoldered a fire, a small, burning pupil in the otherwise pitch-darkness of the room.

Something moved in the far corner. Kol rested his hand upon the pommel of his sword.

In Saxon, a man's voice demanded, "Who enters?"

"'Tis I," Kol responded with cool assurance. "Thorleksson."

With an oath, the man stood. "I had wondered if we would ever meet, or if I was worthy enough only for your seconds."

"Your wounds pain you. I bid you, please sit." Though his words were gracious, Kol did not bother to keep the edge from his voice. He took exception to the man's insolence.

Ranulf's traitor limped toward him. "Nay. I will stand in the presence of Kol, Son of Thorlek. The Banished One. King of the Sea."

The man wore his battle gear. Dim light quivered over a mail shirt still stained with blood. Sweat had dried his long hair into snakish strands.

Eye to eye they stood, staring at one another. Two wolves, each assessing the other's prowess.

Wolves hunted together. But sometimes turned on one another.

"Your injuries," Kol began, his gaze descending to a linen-wrapped thigh. "Are they grievous?"

"Nay, my Danish brethren." A slow smile curled the

spy's lips. "My wounds were salved by the satisfaction of our great victory today. That and the skill of your talented physician."

Kol trusted no traitor. However, the Saxon's hatred worked to his current benefit. He murmured, "I have been told you did not accept your reward."

The Saxon shook his head, his upper lip twitching into a sneer. "Gold is not the reward I seek."

This answer did not surprise Kol. Rarely did men turn traitor for greed's sake alone.

Still, a curious suspicion compelled him to ask, "Saxon, tell me then, what reward do you seek?"

The man turned from him, and retreated into the darkest shadows. "Ranulf's death will be reward enough." Kol heard the rattle of a scabbard being fastened, a sword finding its berth.

"Then go carefully. My captain will see you to the perimeter. In a fortnight we will meet at Leswick."

The man came forth. The stiffness of the wound must have eased, for now he barely limped. "Aye. I will be there, unless Death claims me first."

"Remember," Kol instructed evenly. "Ranulf is mine."

Kol watched the spy's lips tighten as he bent to remove the linen bindings from his legs. Beneath, dark stains marred the man's braies.

The Saxon straightened, and cast the linen onto the fire. "Though I crave the honor, I shall remember the oath I have made." The acrid scent of burned blood pressed into Kol's nostrils.

"I have one additional request."

Behind the man, white peat smoke arose from the fire, and streamed upward through the hut's smoke hole.

"What would please you, my lord?"

Reluctant to reveal the extent of his interest, Kol trained his gaze on the upward spiral of smoke. "Learn what you can of the Princess Isabel's husband."

"Her husband?" A low, dry laugh filled the hut.

Unaccustomed to being a source of mirth to anyone, Kol silently tucked the grudge away for later retribution.

"Yes." He met gleaming eyes. "Her husband. Confirm whether he fell this morn or whether he has joined Ranulf's surviving forces."

The man hesitated, as if savoring a flavorful tidbit. "I am afraid our princess is but a songless bird, caged in the splendor of the fortress on the hill."

"Caged? Caged by whom?"

"Ranulf. He hath disallowed her from having a husband." The words echoed like thunder inside Kol's head. Isabel had lied to him. Even as he vowed not to ask, he heard the question spring forth.

"Then who is the father of her child?"

"Christ's blood." The Norsexian traitor moved closer. Smoke danced in slender wisps around his face, obscuring his features. "You know naught?"

"Speak your knowledge," snapped Kol, impatient with the game.

The man tilted his head, his gaze as sharp as a sword.

"Why, my lord, you are."

Chapter 6

"B ut why would the princess tell such a outrageous lie?"
Vekell's gaze scorched outward to ensure no other
stood close enough to hear.

Morning's blush fell across the eastern side of the keep.
Beneath such rosy light the Saxons who lined the ground
at Kol's feet appeared almost alive. But each warrior remained just as dead as he had been the day before. Kol had
no doubt of this, for he had lifted the shroud from each
corpse, confirming once more, Ranulf did not lie among
the battle-fallen.

He nodded to a *degn* who stood nearby. "Allow the Saxons to claim their dead."

The soldier nodded, and with his spear, beckoned to
the multitude who hovered in a grim-faced mass along
the edge of the field. Heels sinking heavily into the
mud, Kol turned to depart. The crowd fragmented. Elbows jerked and arms shoved, as the conquered people
of Calldarington hastened to remove themselves from
his path.

Kol muttered to Vekell. "You tell me why a woman lies about the identity of her child's father."

His marshal shook his head. His breath, visible in the cold morning, puffed out to trail along behind them. "Fenrir's fangs! I would not have believed it of her."

"Believe it." Since hearing the traitor's revelation, Kol's anger had burgeoned tenfold.

Vekell mused, "She must have a reason to claim such a thing."

They walked into the shadow of the burh's high earthen battlement. Arrow shafts jutted forth from the wall, remnants of the previous day's battle. Kol reached out and wrenched one free.

"She hath accused me of rape. All of these people—" With the arrow he gestured at the small clusters of Saxons who skirted past. They hunkered into their dark, shapeless clothing, as if by doing so they could escape his notice. "By God, all of Norsex believes me to be the father of her child by force."

"It matters naught what they think." Only their footsteps sounded between them until Vekell murmured, "You and I both know what she claims is impossible."

The arrow snapped in Kol's fist. He dropped the pine shaft to the ground. Vekell paused to retrieve it.

Kol walked on. Why did it unseat him so severely to have one of his deepest desires so *twisted*? 'Twas true, there would be no sons or daughters for him. His mother's curses, contrived to end his father's line, had proven true. Only God knew how intensely he'd tested their power in his earlier years, fornicating his way across the earth with regretfully little consequence, none but a soul-deep emptiness no profusion of carnal pleasure could ever fill. In time he had accepted his fate. In more recent years he'd found contentment in spiritual exploration and an almost monastic way of life.

When the path narrowed, Kol stopped. From this elevated place, just outside the burh's gate, he surveyed Call-darington's harbor. The dragon bows of his ships coiled upward through the morning fog like newly sprouted vines seeking the light.

He had come to await his destiny with a certain amount of peace. But now that he had come to Norsex, the place where he'd fully anticipated his destiny to culminate, that hard-earned peace scattered. Beside him, Vekell twisted the arrow's head off the broken shaft.

"The princess hath no husband, you say?" From his waist he withdrew a small pouch. Opening it, he dropped the head inside.

"Aye, she is unwed. She hath always been unwed."

Vekell tied the pouch at his waist. "Then she protects someone. A lover. One who is already married or below her in eminence. An unworthy liaison for a princess."

Kol's feet, like his mind, moved forward. "I can think of no other explanation."

Vekell matched pace with his lord. "Mayhap 'tis why she set you free from the pit, for if you remained in Call-darington alive—"

"Aye." Kol's jaw tautened. He glanced at Isabel's window in the upper hall, visible just above the battlement. The shutters remained closed tight against the outside world. "She could not take the chance her lies would be revealed."

Vekell grasped Kol's shoulder. "If what we believe is true, you bore punishment for another man."

"Ranulf would have executed me regardless of Isabel's deception." Ranulf had been waiting for him. Ranulf had known he would come.

Vekell's lips twisted and he shook his head. "Still, something does not sit well with me in all this. May we not delay our judgment of the princess until we know for certain her motivation for telling such lies?"

"How quickly you fall under her spell," Kol teased, but

an underlying sharpness abided in his tone. "Her actions are betrayal enough."

Vekell's gaze skipped away. "She is not your mother. Do not assume she—"

Kol balked at any discussion of his past, especially when it had to do with women. "Our ships," he interjected. "Have they been duly unloaded?"

Vekell sighed, then nodded. "The furs have been laid out. The ivory and all the rest will be brought out in ample time."

"Good. Spread word amongst the citizenry of Calldar-ington, the harbor will open for commerce in a sennight."

"Aye, my lord."

Side by side he and Vekell walked beneath the wooden gate which led into the settlement. From all about came the greetings of men who worked to repair the damage of the previous day's conflict. Mostly Danes, but there were also Slavs, Arabs, and Franks among them, warriors of all lands who had, for whatever reasons of their own, joined his legions. Outside the stables, a contingent of his men prepared to ride, upon his orders, in search of Ranulf and any surviving North Saxon forces.

Kol suspected the king remained near in hopes the Danes would do as most Norse scavengers did, and simply leave once the burh had been divested of its riches.

Kol nodded toward the stables. "Be sure to choose a mount. Few of the Saxon animals remain, and our livestock will not arrive for another day, perhaps two. After noon you will ride with me to assess the available land. I do believe there is plenty for settling."

Vekell looked to him sharply. "I protest. You cannot mean—"

Kol lifted a hand. "I believe, with some care, the Saxons will become amenable to a foreign settlement."

Vekell glared at Kol's hand, and then at his lord. "And so, I suppose one morn we will awaken to find holes

gouged in the hulls of our ships and you gone, alone, under
cover of night so we may not follow?"

Kol smiled, despite the ache he felt in his chest. "I
would make no coward's farewell."

"You cannot simply leave us here. You are the only jarl
these men recognize. Every man here has sworn fealty to
you, and would stand by that vow until the end of his
days."

"Verily, my friend, I fear that would be a short time.
You know as well as I, my destiny draws near. The omens
appear more often in recent days. The men talk of dreams.
I hear the whispers. I see the way they look at me. As if I
am a dead man already."

"*Nei*, lord. You will be with us for countless days."

Kol wished that were true, but knew the truth of his
fate. 'Twas time to begin preparations. "'Tis not as if we
have a homeland to which we may return. We must make
a place for them here."

Vekell insisted, "I will hear no more talk of this."

Kol spread his hand on Vekell's shoulder. "You can accompany me only so far on this journey, my friend. The
rest I must confront alone. And so, until then, I must consider your future and the future of these men."

With a shake of his shaggy head, Vekell stopped, ankle-
deep in mud. Gray with gloom, his gaze scaled the high
front wall of Ranulf's keep.

After a moment of silence, he asked, "What do you intend to do with the princess?"

"Mama!"

As instructed by Kol's lone berserker, Ragi, Isabel did
not enter the great hall, but stood at the entrance, and
looked inward. Though she had not seen Kol this morn,
she felt his presence everywhere. In the foreign men
thronging about her. In the very air.

"Mama!" Godric wiggled like an unruly worm on Berthilde's lap. *Wiggle wiggle little bug.* Isabel flushed, remembering how the Danish lord's lips had formed those words the night before.

She could not help herself. She moved toward her son, over ancient mosaic tiles which proclaimed *Legio IX Severus*, the name of the Roman commander who had claimed the promontory now known as Calldarington, so very long ago. Already the strewing herbs, which lay amidst the floor rushes, grew brittle and stale. The room smelled of men.

Ragi also moved close. He shook his head. "No, no, no. My lord hath ordered it so. You do not touch the child."

"Have I touched him?" Isabel demanded in her most cutting voice.

His bushy eyebrows crept up like twin caterpillars. "*Nei*, lady princess."

She hissed, "Then stand off."

With jaw squared, the man stepped back, but remained close enough to observe any defiance of his lord's command.

Berthilde peered over the top of Godric's head. Bruises still purpled her cheek, but her hair and clothing appeared as tidy as ever. "My lady, I was told by young Wynflaed that our Godric passed the night well. She said the Dane's wolfhounds seemed to offer him distraction."

No hounds lazed at the hearth now. They must have accompanied their lord elsewhere. Isabel knelt beside her son and the maid, exerting every ounce of her will to keep her hands at her sides.

"My lady," warned Ragi, as she edged closer.

Isabel ignored the hoary old warrior. Godric smiled, golden-skinned and sweet.

Isabel lifted her hand to her maid's face. "Berthilde, your cheek. Doth it pain you greatly?"

Berthilde flushed. "Nay, one of the Danes—indeed, the

very warrior who caused me the injury, applied a dressing last eventide. 'Tis much improved."

'Twas difficult to imagine one of these warriors doing anything so benevolent. "Indeed?"

Berthilde nodded. Beneath the bruise, her blush deepened.

Isabel bit her lip. "What of Rowena? Have you seen my sister?" She both dreaded and craved her half sister's company, yet she had not seen her this morn, and feared for her well-being.

"Aye." Berthilde shrugged. When Godric reached for Isabel, the maid bounced him on her knee so that he clutched her leg and laughed. "She keeps to the bower with her women."

"Mama, see me ride horse." Godric giggled.

"Good boy." Isabel smiled, hoping he did not perceive her gloom. "But Rowena is well?"

"As well as *that one* can be, under our present circumstance." The maidservant rolled her gaze in the direction of the bower. "I hear her wails from time to time, but from what I have seen, the Danes have let her be." Berthilde sucked in her cheeks, as if she held back further comment.

Softly, Isabel chided. "Be kind."

Berthilde's brown eyes flashed. "She treats you with constant discourtesy."

Even now, the small wounds beneath Isabel's sleeve throbbed. "She hath been through much. Stancliff is dead."

"'Tis a tragedy." Berthilde shifted upon the stool, and drew Godric closer. "Still, you forgive too much."

"Berthilde, do not forget yourself."

"How can I, when always, you play my conscience?" Humor replaced the ire in her maid's eye, and from beneath the bruises, emerged the lively woman who, over time, had become Isabel's closest friend.

Isabel placed a hand upon Berthilde's knee. "Your smile always heartens me, and gives me hope."

Berthilde leaned toward her. "Hold that hope close, for all this will pass in due time."

"Mama, hold *me*." Godric strained toward Isabel. Her heart caved inward. She lifted her arms to him, only to have them forced down by Ragi's hands.

She pushed up from the floor, anguish fueling her fury. "How does separating me from my child serve your lord? I know not where my king hath gone, nor whether he lives."

The old man's lips parted, but he gave her no answer.

Through tears, Isabel comforted her son. "Beloved, I will hold you very soon. Until then, Berthilde will give you a thousand sweet kisses." She smiled, if only to assure the boy, then departed the hall, for she could not bear being so close to him without holding him in her arms.

Even if she did know where Ranulf had gone, did Thorleksson truly believe she would betray her king to satisfy her own maternal longings? She would not, for no matter how strong her instincts, no matter how much agony she felt at being torn from her child, Ranulf's survival and continued sovereignty had to be preserved.

Aside from the fond familial attachment she felt toward her brother, she could not forget that without him, there would be no protection for her son, no favor. Indeed, by Ranulf's mere absence, Godric's life might be in danger. Though a fatherless child, he bore the blood of kings in his veins, and that alone made him a threat to anyone who would seek to claim the rich kingdom of Norsex for their own. Children had been assassinated for less.

With those thoughts clouding her mind, she passed beneath the arched doorway, but a chest as broad as a ship hull barred her path. The giant called Vekell stood there.

The night before his eyes had glown with male interest and good nature, but his eyes held no warmth now. She gathered Kol must have informed the man of her attack on his life the night before. This warrior, like the others, seemed to look upon Thorleksson as some sort of god or king, and any offense against him would be construed as a strike against his legion as well.

Silently, he stepped back. With extended arm, he encouraged her to proceed. Though unnerved by his mute regard, she did so. She crossed into the outer passage, his footsteps sounding behind, heavy and long of pace. Along either wall, soldiers oiled swords and mended shields. Gazes lifted to consider her as she moved past.

She heard them speak her name, in heavily accented syllables.

Curse their pagan souls, how many mercenaries had Thorleksson brought with him to kill her brother? Not one made any move to engage her, but their stares were invasive. She hurried through the narrow passage. Their very presence reminded her all too clearly of the devastating change in her life, and the very real threat to her child's future.

Prior to the Danes' attack, her life had been no great pleasure, save for the love of her child. But her brother had guarded her interests. Godric's future had appeared promising with a king to foster and invest in him.

She pushed through the keep's wide oak doors. The unexpected glare of the sky caused her to lift a hand and squint. Winter air numbed her face and speared through her woolen gunna.

"Greetings, Calldarington," she murmured. A flutter of anxiety arose in her stomach, but she would not turn back now.

Truth be told, her descent from the window the night before had been her only departure from the keep in—

Forsooth, how long had it been? She supposed since before Godric's birth. How could that be?

If she were honest with herself, she could answer the question. Two winters before, Ranulf had quietly, but purposefully, brought her under the iron wing of his protection. He'd insisted the darkness that had inspired one man to violate her could reside in others as well. She knew not where that darkness hid, only that it existed.

But now, her haven had been overrun by that darkness. Peril hovered behind every curtain and wall of Ranulf's palatial keep. Indeed, the personification of everything she feared ensconced himself in the chamber beside hers.

The walls of the keep no longer provided her with any more sanctuary than the burh, or the lands beyond. She could not play the coward any longer.

Behind her, the door creaked, and she heard the Norse giant step out.

Before her, the dirt road thronged with foreign warriors and Saxons alike, thickly bundled in their cloaks. No such protection draped her own shoulders, but, loathe to retreat, she descended to the street.

Soldiers watched as she moved past, and conferred with one another in lowered tones. Her people did the same. She walked without direction. Vekell crunched along behind her.

Something struck her leg.

Isabel looked down. The remains of a rotten cabbage slid toward the hem of her gunna. Its foul stench rose up to taint the air.

"Norse whore!"

Her head snapped up. The words had been Saxon. A multitude of faces stared at her, but no one stepped forward to claim the affront.

Dread trickled over her. Of course. Now her punishment would begin. Two winters ago when Thorleksson had escaped Ranulf's prison the accusations had been whispered. She had never accepted blame, nor denied it. Surely after last night Rowena had let it be known the past suspicions were, indeed, truth.

A Norsexian princess had helped the Dane escape. Now Ranulf's protection was gone, there would be a reckoning.

Vekell moved to her side. Frowning, his gaze spanned outward. He bent, as if to brush the refuse from her garment.

"Do not." She moved out of his reach. "I do not require your assistance."

"As you wish." He straightened.

Just ahead she saw the high wall of the burh's church.

"I wish to pray," she announced to her unwanted companion. *Pray for wisdom. Pray for strength. Pray for the courage to take my revenge against your lord.*

Without waiting for the warrior to acquiesce, she trudged up the muddy incline toward the church, a place she had not visited in a very long time. Father Janus had seemed to understand her preference for the keep's small, enclosed chapel, and had served her spiritual needs there.

Three limestone steps led to the oaken doorway, steps where she, Rowena, and Ranulf had played together as children, waiting for their father to finish his Mass.

As soon as her hand touched the carved door, peace washed over her. But the moment she entered the church, that peace shattered.

Four warriors stood just inside the portal. They blocked her entry or any view of the altar. Fear stabbed through her, along with the remembrance of history lessons learned at Lindisfairne. Norsemen had come. Monks had been murdered, altars defiled. Had the barbarians from the north now desecrated Calldarington's Christian church? Did they intend to burn it to the ground? What of Father Janus who tended to the spiritual needs of the villagers and who had been so kind to her during such a difficult time in her life?

A dark figure hovered beside her.

"My lady," Vekell said, taking her elbow; pretending at civility when there was no need. "It appears he is almost finished."

As he led her aside, her imagination produced shocking, horrifying images. "Finished. Finished doing what?"

She pushed forward, bracing herself for the atrocities she would witness. Indeed, she *wanted* to witness them to make her hatred complete. Vekell stepped in front of her and took her forearms. Over his shoulder she saw what he sought to protect. His leader knelt in supplication before the altar. A goodly number of his warriors knelt alongside him.

"What is he doing?"

"Surely that is clear."

In amazement, Isabel watched Father Janus come forward, clothed in vestments, his eyes fixed upon the crown of the Danish invader's head. In a lowered voice he offered the sacrament.

"He is Christian?" A bitter laugh broke from her throat.

"Aye." He grimaced. "One of Rome's missionaries saw to that."

She jerked out of his hold. "And you?"

"I fear I remain just as steadfastly pagan as ever before." His smile did not ascend as far as his eyes.

Isabel returned her attention to the abomination in the chancel. "For what does he pray? The strength to destroy my people? For wisdom in stealing children from their mothers?"

Vekell's jaw tightened. "Do not speak of my lord so."

Reverence for the church kept her from shouting her demand. "Tell me for what such a man prays."

With a sudden fierceness, he tugged her close and whispered, "'Tis no secret. He prays for death."

"Death?" she repeated. "My brother's death? For my death? My people's?"

"*Nei*, my lady. For his own."

His words resonated inside her head. "What manner of man prays for his own death?"

"One who is *heljar-karl*."

"*Heljar-karl,*" she repeated.

His brow furrowed, as if he searched for the appropriate translation. "Accursed. Doomed to die."

Isabel stared at Kol's dark head lowered over the priest's hands. She had heard of such men. Warriors whom *Wyrd,* in her indifferent weaving of destinies, had marked for death.

She whispered, "A dangerous man, one who has nothing for which to live."

"Aye, and I would remember that if I were you."

Isabel was given no time to ponder whether his words should be considered a threat, for just then, Thorleksson arose and turned toward the nave. His eyes met hers as he lifted the crucifix from his chest. Solemnly he pressed his lips to the cross, and tucked it inside his jerkin.

Isabel gasped, for in that moment she caught a fleeting glimpse of the savior of her dreams, albeit a wounded one.

"No," she whispered, shaking her head. That savior did not exist. He *could* not exist, could not share existence with the beast who had stolen her innocence.

She backed through the doors and descended the stairs. An ocean-spawned wind whipped her hair across her face. Narrow alleys led between rows of peasants' huts. She hurried down the nearest. She did not dare look in his eyes again. Could not allow herself to doubt his guilt, nor fail to condemn him as completely as he deserved to be condemned.

The path led her into the darker heart of Calldarington. Faces peered through open doorways, but when she slowed, the doors slammed shut. Two women, upon seeing her, pressed back against the wall of a hovel and clutched their colorless cloaks at their throats. They considered her with dark, suspicious eyes.

No one called to her. No one offered sanctuary.

I am naught but a stranger in this place. Isabel's steps slowed. She turned around, her arms clasped at her waist.

As a girl she had known every nook and cranny of the burh. But now, she felt lost. Where did she go from here?

From behind, footsteps sounded, heavy upon the damp pathway. Her heart beat frantically in her chest. The Danes had followed her. *He had followed her.*

She turned to confront her pursuers. Three men stood there, bleak-faced Saxon men. Their sturdy bodies blocked the path down which she had come. The largest stepped forward, his meaty fists clenched into cudgels.

He taunted, "Why dost thou run, Princess?"

Isabel's blood ran cold.

Another sneered, his yellowed teeth gleaming like tallow in the mid-morning light. "Whore! Has your lover cast you out now that he has taken what he wants?"

The third man shouted, "Aye, our homes and our dead sons." His voice broke with emotion. "Traitoress."

The first man lunged. Isabel fell back, only to feel the hands of another man clench upon her waist. He pushed her to the ground so forcefully, breath forsook her lungs.

She tried to stand, but someone shoved her down again. Stones gouged her palms and her knees. In the periphery of her vision, a door opened. Light footsteps approached. Those of a woman? Surely a woman would offer her refuge.

"Bitch!" Something soft and wet struck the side of her face. The remains of a decaying onion fell to the ground. "My man is dead because of you."

Hands slapped her buttocks, yanked her hair. Toes and heels jabbed her sides. Laughter and curses flooded her ears. Isabel dug her fingers into the ground, and felt the jagged edges of crushed mollusk shells press into her skin. Amidst the clamor, someone sobbed, and she realized it was herself. She clamped her teeth shut, just as a stone struck her side. *She deserved this.* Mud splattered onto her back.

A shout pierced the haze of Isabel's misery. A woman

screamed. Footsteps retreated. Isabel lowered to crouch against the earth. Why could she not sink into it and disappear?

Two large hands touched her.

"No." She flinched. But the hands pushed her hair from her face, and moved over her back and sides. Men spoke the Norse tongue, in lowered voices.

He lifted her against his chest and for one astonishing moment she felt protected from all who threatened her. She did not need to look to know who held her.

His presence had become as familiar as her own.

Chapter 7

Kol kicked the oak plank shut in the faces of his guards, who clustered at the doorway to his chamber, doing their best to attain a glimpse of the princess. She curled like a sleeping child in his arms. He had held her once before like this.

As a girl, she had exuded innocence and light; whereas now, as a woman, her soul seemed cloaked in shadows.

How heartily he wished for her to cry, to curse him or even claw at his eyes. Instead she remained motionless, her face hidden against his chest.

He lay her on the bed. Though the chamber fire dwindled, her skin shone vivid against the furs. Tears glimmered on her lashes, but her eyes remained shut.

"Art thou injured?"

She made no response, save to lift her arms and cross them over her face. Kol diverted his gaze from the generous swell of breast, revealed by her damp, clinging gunna. At her knees, her skirts bunched haphazardly, and beneath, her stockings were torn. He pulled her hem down to cover her ankles, more for his comfort than hers.

"No scarlet slippers this day," he mused.

Instead she wore finely wrought leather boots, cut to display the delicate form of her ankle, the arch of her foot.

He much preferred the slippers. Perhaps because they offered a vision of Isabel he might never be allowed to see for himself. A vibrant young woman, with joy in her eyes, and laughter on her lips.

Had she been that woman before he'd loosed destruction upon her world? Having blazed so instantly and violently into her world, he knew not what assumptions to make. His gaze ascended the length of her body. Nothing bespoke an obvious injury. Betwixt her crossed arms, her mouth trembled.

Did she cry from emotional pain alone, or physical pain as well?

He made another attempt. "Art thou able to move your limbs?"

"Leave me," she ordered in a low, thick voice. She curled onto her side, away from him, and pressed her hands to her face. A sigh staggered from her lips.

"*Nei*, my lady. There are too many questions which require answers, and I would have those answers from you." He leaned forward to smooth the hair from her face. She jerked away, as he'd known she would.

He remained there, his hand motionless beside her cheek. How tempting it was to feel sympathy for her. To wish to comfort her. Did she inspire such a reaction in all men?

Was she the artful seductress he believed? A woman so wicked even her own people despised her? Something inside him did not find accord with that suspicion. At this moment she simply appeared to be a young woman whose heart had been shattered, but he recoiled from pitying someone who, like the enemies of his past, had chosen to betray him with lies.

"What sin did you commit that your own people would turn on you so completely?"

He did not expect an answer, only silence, and perhaps more tears. Instead she flung her arms from her face. A slight swelling affected her lower lip and a bruise formed on her temple. She lifted onto her elbows to glare at him with enough intensity to make his pulse trip, a rare occurrence, even in the most dire of battles.

"You wish to know my sin?" Heat sparked from deep within her eyes, and along with it, an obvious accusation of fault.

He frowned. "You look at me as if you hold me responsible for what they did."

"Oh, nay. I am entirely to blame." Acrimony tainted her voice. She pushed up to sit, wincing at some undisclosed discomfort. Tears swelled to her lashes. Beneath her stained gunna, her breasts rose and fell with ragged effort. "For if I had let you die in my brother's pit, none of this would have occurred."

He cautioned, "Perhaps it is best you return to your silence."

"You wish for me to be silent, when I have only just begun to speak?" She inhaled several times, as if breath eluded her. "Two winters ago I aided your escape for the simple reason I was a stupid girl who believed you had saved my life."

"And that I did."

Her scathing look told him she believed otherwise.

"That I did," he repeated harshly. "Do you believe the river spat you out of its own accord?"

She sat silently, but he saw the tremor which moved through her body. He knew she must be very cold. He withdrew to the hearth and added several logs, and kindling, to the ashen heap. All the while his mind worked.

Turning back, he demanded, "Of what do you accuse me, Isabel?"

" 'Tis no matter." She watched his every move with suspicion. "What matters is what they believe." She unfurled her arm toward the window, which, if opened, would overlook the burh.

"And what do they believe?"

Her face hardened, as if he forced her to confess a humiliation too shameful to bear. "They believe we were—"

She swallowed hard. Her face twisted, as if a bee had flown down her throat.

He found it difficult to contain his impatience. "Just say it."

"Lovers," she gritted.

Kol laughed, a sharp, mirthless sound. But in the next moment a stunning succession of images emerged from deep inside his mind. His body entwined with that of the princess. Sweat. Satiation and joy.

He rejected the visions.

He asked, "Why would they believe such a falsity? Have there been so many lovers in your past?"

The princess swept her hand over her cheeks, purging the tears which fell there. "Swine. You disgust me." She grabbed one of the embroidered cushions which lay like jewels atop the king's bed and flung it at him. He caught the cushion against his chest, a warning on his tongue— but Isabel went rigid atop the coverlet, and pressed her hand to her side. Short, shallow breaths came from her lips.

"Tröll hafi þig." He dropped the pillow and moved to her side. "You are injured. Twice in as many days. This self-endangerment must cease."

"I am not injured. I do not require your assistance." Pain weakened her voice, and undermined the legitimacy of her claims. Closing her eyes, she fell back onto the bed. "All I need is for you to leave, and to send my maidservant. She is called Berthilde and you will find her in the hall below."

"*Nei.*" Kol shook his head. Already his hands moved over her torso.

"Do not touch me." She gripped his hands. Hers were shockingly cold.

Their gazes clashed. For a moment, an odd sort of familiarity coursed between them, an intimacy borne, he supposed, of the previous night's kisses and bed-tussle.

"Your maid tends to the boy and will continue to do so."

Her dark lashes lowered, severing the connection. White teeth bit into her swollen lower lip. Clearly she had hoped he would allow her son to come with the maid. "If not her, then I beg you, please send for my sister."

"Speak you of the same sister who stabbed you last eventide?"

She shoved his hands away, her face white except for two vivid spots of color on her cheeks. "I would not have you tend to me in this manner."

Moving back, he shrugged his soiled jerkin to the floor, and rolled up his tunic sleeves. "I will entrust your care to no Saxon. Not after what I just witnessed."

Her gaze fell upon him, narrow and sharp.

"Do not misunderstand my concern. Two days henceforth we ride, and you must be well enough to travel at the pace of my men."

"Travel?" Alarm softened her tone. "Where?"

Gently, he took hold of her wrists. "Try to stand."

Frowning, she allowed him to raise her to her feet. Surely because she wished to get as far from the bed as possible.

She gripped his arm. "Answer me, please. Where do we ride?"

He guided her toward the hearth. "If I told you, then you'd have nothing to contemplate for the next two days."

Her furrowed brow and down-turned lips confirmed she

did not at all appreciate his humor. "What of my son? Will he travel with us?"

Kol pulled a chair into the circle of warmth.

She caught his arm. "Answer me. 'Tis not safe to leave him here alone and unprotected. Even now I fear—oh."

She bent toward him, her face pallid.

He lowered her onto the stool and knelt. "You must trust me now."

"Of course." No smile accompanied her laughter. "I shall do that without hesitation."

He pulled his knife from his belt. "We must determine your injury, and your garment fits too snugly to pull over your head without causing you more discomfort. Your inability to breathe fully and the pain in your side imply you have a broken or bruised rib."

Flat with dread, her eyes lowered to the blade. "This becomes an unwelcome habit."

"Cease placing yourself in danger's path, and I shall cease with the daily destruction of your garments." Though he sought to speak lightly, his words issued like a threat; he realized that in the instant stiffening of her frame. He attempted to ease her fears. "Please be assured I have much experience with regard to injuries."

"As one whose existence centers upon killing and maiming most certainly would."

Kol exhaled. He would not allow her to goad him into overreaction as she had the night before.

He caught her hem in his fist, careful not to take hold of the kirtle beneath. The princess did not struggle; she did not speak one word of protest. Indeed, she moved nary a muscle. Through the thick wool, his blade whispered upward until he severed the last bit between her breasts.

From her shoulders and arms he pushed the gown, until it fell over the sides of the chair, into a dark pool upon the floor.

For a long moment they stared at one another.

All at once she looked away, and shivered, her eyes fixed on the hearth. In a low, husky voice she asked, "I beg of you, might I have some water, with which to wash?"

Such was not an unreasonable request. The examination could wait until afterward. "Of course."

He stood and crossed to the hearth. From above the fire he unhooked a small cauldron. Inside, water sloshed against the rounded sides of the vessel. He returned and held it for her use. She cupped her hands, and lifted the crystalline fluid to her face.

The liquid glistened upon her skin, and trickled downward to dampen the linen over her breasts. The cloth took on the same delicate flush as her flesh beneath.

"Better?" His mouth had gone too dry to allow more complex speech.

"A little."

He watched, transfixed, as she drew her hair over one shoulder, and threaded her fingers through. "If you would allow me to do so, I would wash the stench from my hair." The dark fringe of her lashes concealed her eyes. "And from my skin."

'Twas a wonder the pot did not shatter, so tightly he did clench it. If she smelled foul from whatever the Saxon horde had pelted her with, he could not tell. Perhaps his eyes, trained so intently upon the shadowed channel between her breasts, weakened the abilities of his other senses.

"Please," she murmured. "I cannot bear the smell another moment more."

His blood expanded, thickened in his veins. At the same time there awakened a dark suspicion within him.

But her invitation enticed too sweetly to be declined. Lifting the pot, he tilted it and allowed the water to pour over her raised palms, and her upturned face. She smoothed her hands across her cheeks, and into her hair. The water cascaded over her shoulders. Her neck. Her breasts. The kirtle went sheer against her body, revealing tautened nipples, and lower, the dark shadow at the joining of her thighs.

How skilled she was with this false enticement. She sought to seduce him, he knew. Just as she had the night before. To gain the return of her son. To manipulate.

How foolish he had been, holding onto the hope she was an honorable wife and mother, when in truth she was as wicked and purposeful a seductress as Samson's Delilah.

The cauldron dripped, empty now. He lowered it to the ground and knelt before her. Water permeated the knees of his braies.

Droplets sparkled on her eyelashes. She did not avoid his heated stare.

"Tell me where you feel the pain most strongly."

She took his hand, and pressed it against her side. "Here."

Beneath the wet linen, her skin radiated with faint warmth. Her hair, longer now that it was wet, gleamed over her shoulders and breasts. Methodically he examined each rib, pressing his fingertips along her torso.

"Here?" Kol frowned, attempting to smooth a wrinkle in the cloth so that he might better discern any variation. 'Twas difficult to discern *anything* with the blood buzzing so heavily in his head.

"You may remove it."

Her words echoed amidst the thunder of his pulse. She grasped her kirtle at the knees. Slowly she drew the garment up. He heard the wet slide of it against her thighs. "Would you not see better without it?"

Every inch of Kol's body throbbed, as if he'd drunk too much wine. Desire swirled low, in his groin, like a warm tongue, well practiced and bold with its promise of pleasure.

Again, she took his hand, but this time she placed it at

his waist, over his knife. "Concern yourself not with my modesty. After all, you yourself said I must be prepared to ride, two days henceforth."

He pulled the knife free, and slit her kirtle up the center. Barely able to contain his anger, he stripped it from her limbs.

Her skin shone like amber in the firelight. Proudly she sat, her shoulders back, her breasts out-thrust. Legs covered only to the knee by her stockings, and slightly parted. He knew she watched him take his fill.

He slid close to the edge of the chasm. How easy it would be to accept what she offered, and to give her what she wanted in return. How pleasingly heavy her breasts would be in his hands.

His desire lengthened against his thigh. He drew his thumb along her naked skin, just beneath one breast.

He did not look at her face, for already he knew what he would see. He had seen it the night before. The sneer of her lips. The hatred in her eyes.

What a little fool she was to believe him so weak.

He splayed his hand over her naked skin. "You feel pain here?"

She nodded, turning her face aside, no doubt to hide her disgust.

In one sudden move he hooked his arm around her back. She gasped, and he knew he had hurt her.

"Is this what you want?" he demanded in a low whisper. He smoothed his hand over her breast.

"Aye," she breathed. "This is what I want." Did passion or hatred fuel the light in her eyes?

He lowered his mouth to hers, gently at first, but as his arousal grew, his anger also surged, and his kiss turned more aggressive in nature. With his mouth, he challenged her. Demanded she yield. And she did, parting her lips and accepting the thrust of his tongue deep within. He squeezed her breast, and lowered to take its tip in his mouth. She moaned, and he heard the scrape of her boot against the floor.

Almost as if her response was sincere.

He was no fool. He nipped her, and she cried out. Her head fell back in a perfect portrayal of passion. His arousal, tightly encased in his braies, cleaved between her outspread thighs.

He moved too close to the edge.

Beside her ear, he said, "Is this how you always get what you desire?"

She stiffened against him.

"The boy. You want him returned to you."

"You know I do." She sounded choked.

"And you would give anything to have him."

"Aye." Her hands fisted into his tunic. "Anything."

He drew away, holding her firmly in place by her shoulders. Naked and vulnerable, she trembled, but held his stare with her own.

"Return him to me." She tried to wrap her arms around his waist, but he stood and left her with arms outstretched. Confusion lay plain upon her face. Had she never failed in her attempts to seduce?

Now. Throw her lies in her face.

"Explain to me, Isabel, why would I need to barter for possession of something that in truth already belongs to me?"

"What?" she gasped, her expression, not unlike a battlefield opponent who had received a spear to the stomach.

"The boy." His breathing slowed. She floundered, and he enjoyed seeing it. She deserved this for her lies. "Did you think I would not learn the truth?"

Speak the truth, Isabel. Speak it, and I may forgive.

The princess, however, did not choose to confess her lies. Instead she stood from the chair, a bit unsteadily, and left her garments behind. Naked, except for her stockings and boots, she walked away.

He wanted to grab her. To force her to reveal the name of her lover, the father of her child. The man whose punishment striped his back in deep furrows.

From the bed she lifted a fur and pulled it over her shoulders.

"I insist you rest," he commanded cooly. "You suffer a bruised rib. Not a serious injury, but one which should not be worsened."

"I wish to leave." She turned to search the wall. He knew she searched for the hidden portal. Simple as that, the seduction had failed and so now she sought to leave his company.

"You may wish for anything you like, but you will remain here." He wanted to be cruel, to inflict the same torment she inflicted upon him

"Do not bother with the doorway. After your visit last night, and your display of pretty knives, I had it sealed."

She whirled, her eyes flat with hatred. "I want away from you."

His eyes slid over her. "'Tis clear you cannot be trusted, and must be watched. So the answer is no, you may not leave. You will remain here, in these chambers, until I decide otherwise. Your rooms will be given to my marshal for his use."

"I must remain in these chambers?" Horror whitened her features. "With you?"

"Princess," he chided. "From your actions just moments ago, I truly believed you cared for me."

The princess screamed and reached for an empty trencher.

Kol slammed the door behind him, just in time to hear the vessel crash against the other side.

The laughter which welled up from his chest felt good. Very good indeed.

• • •

Later that night, in the keep's great hall, his warriors ceased their storytelling and put their games away. Long after his final companion had settled down onto a bench, Kol sat beside the fire. All around him slept his warriors, and a few scattered Saxons. Although weariness had long ago settled into his bones, he knew he would not be able to sleep.

He could not stop thinking about Isabel. He both resented and wanted her. What sort of logic was that? Because of the animosity which coursed between them, he despised each moment they spent together. And yet here he sat, sleepless for a second night, trying to contrive a reason to return to her chamber.

A tug at his sleeve startled him. From over the arm of the chair, two large, dark eyes peered up at him.

'Twas Isabel's boy.

"Seepy?"

Kol did not answer. Instead he turned and searched the darkness of the room. The child's maid, the woman called Berthilde, snored upon her pallet. Vekell slept on a bench near her feet. He looked back to the child.

"Seepy?" the youngling asked again.

Kol delighted in children . . . in an uneasy sort of way. He'd simply never had the opportunity to interact with one, not without the mother or father hovering about, fearful he would consider their offspring a nuisance and . . . and what? Squash them?

He supposed the child was entitled to an answer. "*Nei*, I am not sleepy. Why do you ask?"

The boy shrugged. He spoke softly, a sound that reminded Kol of a chirping bird. "Me not seepy. Want play?" From beneath the cuff of his tunic he produced two small wooden warriors. He held them to the light. One had clearly been fashioned to resemble Ranulf.

"Only if I get that one." Kol pointed to the other, a warrior with dark hair and a red tunic.

Godric extended the toy, and Kol took it. When the child gripped his thumb, he allowed himself to be led from the chair, toward the boy's pallet. Kol's wolfhounds stood and whined, then padded along behind.

Godric plopped down and glanced over his shoulder at Berthilde. He lifted a finger to his lips. "Shhh."

Kol nodded, finding unexpected pleasure in this moment of conspiracy. They both lay down on their sides, facing one another. The dogs sidled in betwixt those who slept on either side, and stretched out, Hugin on one side, and Munin on the other. The boy's eyes met Kol's. Silently they moved their warriors into battle positions.

'Twas not long before Godric's eyelids drooped. Soon he dozed, his dimpled fingers clasping the wooden image of his uncle. When he was sure the boy slept, Kol tugged the toy free and eased the dark-haired warrior into its place. He sat upright and twisted toward the hearth. He threw the toy. The tiny missile flew in an arc over the bodies of three slumbering men, and produced a shower of sparks as it struck the logs.

Kol returned to the pallet. Beside him Godric slept, his skin smooth and ruddy in the firelight. His small chest lifted and fell with each breath. Kol stared at him for a long time, wishing he could forget the things he and Isabel had said to one another. The things they had done to hurt one another.

He wished he knew who the boy's father was, and why Isabel had chosen to lie about the circumstance of his birth.

He wished with his entire being, he was a different man.

Chapter 8

Boy-warrior,
Fostered by men.
By sword and by cunning,
Avenged his father-jarl's death

Leader of men! No child, he.
Let the skalds forever proclaim.
Kol the Shining!
Remember him,
In rune, in song.

Isabel stood just outside the entrance to the great hall. Her hand rested upon the carved archway, which had been fashioned by her brother's craftsman to depict entwined vines, a flock of sparrows, and one carefully placed serpent.

Kol had commanded her presence at the evening feast, and she had complied in hopes of reuniting with her son. But as she approached the threshold she'd heard the voice

of the Danish skald, imbued with such earnestness she
could not bring herself to interrupt.

> *Witch, honorless mother.*
> *Love never swelled*
> *Within her breast.*
> *Her vengeance she swore*
> *On an blameless son*
> *For his father's deeds.*
>
> *Her curses sprang.*
> *Death to our bravest lord!*
> *Death, whilst life's valor*
> *still seeks to be spent.*
>
> *Men still followed him,*
> *the Accursed One,* heljar-karl.
> *Voices shout: Leader of warriors!*
> *Leader of men!*
>
> *In the darker mists, the shadows,*
> *Half brother coveted,*
> *His ruler-chair not enough.*
> *Our Fairest warrior condemned.*
> *Unjustly banished.*

Isabel leaned against the wall. Why did her heart ache
at hearing this dark history? A witch-mother who had
cursed him when he was but a boy? And a half brother who
had banished him? Wrongfully, if the account were true.

> *We follow this King of the Sea.*
> *Mother, dost thou not protect thine son?*
> *Nei. He meets his Death alone,*
> *Sword raised. Eyes open.*

Oh, ye bards, remember.
He shall live forever,
In the hearts of warriors.
Forever in rune,
Forever in memory.

The hall exuded silence. Perhaps the feast had not begun, and the skald sat alone in preparation for his evening performance. She stepped forward to see for herself, but a hand gripped her arm and turned her until she felt the wall against her back.

She stared into his eyes. The Sea King. The man whom these mercenaries looked to as their ruler upon the earth. The same man she'd vowed to hate, and avenge herself upon.

But, as much as it shamed her, in this moment she felt no enmity or revulsion, only fascination. Had his wicked touch last eventide bespelled her in some way?

"Come," he said. If any emotion dwelled within him, his expression revealed none of it.

He escorted her beneath the archway, his hand beneath her elbow. To her astonishment, warriors lined the walls, and the rows between the trestles. All stood, she realized, in expectation of their lord. Neither Godric nor Rowena was anywhere to be seen. Nay, no Saxons stood among them.

Through the weald of men he guided her. Isabel could not keep her eyes from him. Not from his rigid jaw, nor the shadowed hollow beneath his cheek. How cold and distant he appeared. Was he furious with her for the seduction she had attempted the night before? In truth, she was furious with herself for the same reason, but she had been so desperate to regain possession of her son. Had Thorleksson summoned her to the hall to punish her before the gathered ranks of his men?

Vekell stood on the dais, his back to the shield-wall. She

did not miss the look of displeasure Kol leveled on the man. Perhaps his anger was not directed toward her, after all. Kol assisted her up the steps, but remained behind to speak to one of the ðegns who lined the edges of the platform.

Vekell pulled the bench from the table and helped her to her seat. She leaned toward him. "He is angry?"

He echoed her low pitch. "He disapproves of the song." For one moment, 'twas as if she and the Dane were co-conspirators. She rejected him instantly, drawing back to end the alliance. In the far corner of the hall, the skald stood, with arms crossed at his chest and his eyes tightly shut, clearly anguished by his lord's disapproval.

Kol seated himself beside her but his attention remained elsewhere, as if her presence remained below his notice or care. He smelled of wood-smoke and spice, scents which addled Isabel's mind. Tonight he wore a tunic of the darkest blue. Two bold stripes, accented by gold-threaded embroidery, ascended the garment from hem to neck, and slashed over his shoulders to descend his back. The exotic decoration only emphasized his powerful build. A well-traveled merchant had once presented Ranulf with a similar choice, but her brother had rejected the Byzantine style. She had found such garments fascinating. They offered a glimpse of faraway worlds, worlds she had yearned to see with her own eyes—before her life had changed.

Since then she had seen nothing but the inside of the keep, and whatever else she could experience from her window.

Serving maids brought forth trenchers heaped with bread and boiled meat. Pitchers of wine and mead were set upon the tables. The gathered multitude spoke amongst themselves in lowered tones.

Isabel did not at all mind Kol's lack of interest. Indeed, she worried if he turned to her, he would see the havoc written upon her face. After their encounter the night before, she had dressed in one of his tunics, for that was all she could find to cover her nakedness. She had returned to sit before the hearth to await his return. How she had feared his return! But truth be told, anticipation had consorted with that fear.

Last eventide he had desired her. She had sensed that clearly. But he had scorned her attempt at seduction. If he were the feral beast of her shadowed past, why did he not act upon his desire and feast rampant upon that which she had offered? Why did her motives disturb him, when a defiler of women would react instantly on whatever dark impulse resided within?

She had been given plenty of time to ponder those questions, for Kol had never returned. She had been left alone, though under guard, the entire day until his summons had come, along with a large trunk of her clothing.

Now, as she sat here beside him, her confusion over his nature grew tenfold. With no small amount of dismay, she had come to realize the dreams of a girl still resided within her heart. Dreams of a hero. Of a savior.

She had believed in him so steadfastly, once before.

But if he were not Godric's father, who was? At this question, a dark infinity opened up inside her mind.

Someone she trusted.

At the same time, she could not imagine anyone within her brother's *werod* daring to commit such a crime against her.

Even if Kol was not the attacker who left her with child two winters ago, his conflict with Ranulf had gone too far to be resolved peacefully.

Or had it?

Before such a judgment could be made, she had to learn the truth. Had her father summoned the Danish mercenary to Norsex, and if so, why?

Kol had claimed Ranulf waited for his arrival. Waited to

kill him. Could this be true? She would not know until she spoke to Ranulf.

"You are well?" Kol's voice cut into her thoughts.

A maid leaned forward to fill his claw beaker with wine. Beneath the table, his thigh brushed hers.

"Aye." Awareness heated her blood. Unsettled by his intense regard, she lifted her hand to her bruised temple. How difficult it was to forget, for even a moment, how intimately he had touched her the night before. She remembered, too clearly, the friction of his warm, weapon-calloused hands against her skin. She swallowed hard, for her memories went much further than that, to his mouth on her breast, and his arousal, hard against her body. Despite the child she'd birthed, she had only the experience of a virgin to call upon, so each kiss, each touch, remained emblazoned in her memory.

"The pain in your side has lessened?"

"Aye, almost completely." Her tongue felt as if it were spun of wool.

"Good." He nodded. Though his expression remained cool, he reached for the trencher and, using an ivory-handled knife, apportioned her a goodly share of meat. "You must eat."

Isabel considered her plate. 'Twas true. She had not eaten since the day of the battle. Food had been brought to her this morn, but she had been too anxious over all that had passed to eat.

After swallowing the first bite, she asked the question which lay foremost in her mind. "Should I be prepared to ride in the morning?"

For a moment, he kept silent. "*Nei.* I have reconsidered. You shall remain here, with Vekell to guard your safety."

She had little time to react to his announcement, for at that moment Berthilde approached the dais with Godric in her arms.

Isabel stood. At Kol's nod, Berthilde placed the boy

upon the platform. His small face crinkled with a smile. "Mama!"

But he did not run into her arms. Instead he reached for Kol. "Em-eer. Hold me."

"Greetings, little one." Kol swung the boy onto his lap.

Isabel frowned. "What did he call you?"

"Ymir." For the first time that evening, a smile twitched to his lips. "Aye, Godric? Ymir, the frost giant, borne of melting ice and hot steam."

He bit his lower lip and, in playfulness, bore Godric's small head beneath his arm. "From his armpit sprang both man and maid. Which are you, little one?"

Godric squealed and giggled. Isabel's displeasure burgeoned.

"You have spent time with him." She dropped into her seat.

Kol shrugged, his shoulders so broad they eclipsed any view of her child. From the trencher, he lifted a small wooden bowl. Inside glistened a chunk of bread, drizzled with honey. Godric's favorite.

"Um!" Her son dragged the bowl close.

Kol leaned so close to Isabel, his breath touched her ear. "A father should take an interest in his child, should he not?"

Isabel's chest tightened.

Did he claim the boy in truth? Was this an admission of his sin? Or had he heard the rumor of the child's paternity elsewhere, and now taunted her in his anger at being wrongfully accused?

She could not bring herself to demand the truth of her violation now; not before this roomful of strangers. "You are cruel. 'Tis not right a child be taken from his mother when her care is all he has ever known."

From beneath the dark shadow of his lashes, Kol's eyes gleamed. "What of your husband?" Anger tautened his jaw. "Hath he declined to accept my son as his own?"

The lies soured upon Kol's lips. *Your husband. My son.*

Against his chest the child nestled, a small bundle of warmth. Kol tried not to look. Not at the glossy curls peeking from beneath the woolen cap, nor the boy's curving cheek.

How badly he wanted a child. Just like this one, if he could so choose. Why had God granted Isabel, a woman who spun deceit all around the boy, with such a blessing, when there were those such as himself who would give anything for such a divine gift? What father would deny a son so fine?

"Dog!" Godric laughed. Beneath the table, Hugin and Munin nuzzled for scraps.

Kol stared into the upturned face of the woman who continued to intrigue and attract him despite all the evidence against her. Hurting her had not proven as fulfilling as he'd expected. Perhaps honesty on his part was the only way to elicit the truth.

"'Tis not I who have been cruel, but you."

Confusion clouded her gaze. "I do not understand your accusation."

Though the room thronged with movement, in that moment it seemed the world held only the two of them.

He spanned one hand over Godric's ear. "I didst not sire this child. Why have you allowed it to be so believed?"

Tears sprang to her eyes, but she did not look away. "Do not seek to lie to me when there can be no other truth."

"I am not his father." He read no deceit upon her face, which led him to a previously unconsidered possibility. Beneath the table, he grasped her wrist. "Do you have no memory of the event in which the boy was conceived?"

She did not pull away. "'Tis a blessing, for I do not believe I could survive such a cruel remembrance."

"I did not attack you. Nothing of that sort occurred between us that day."

Emotion thickened her voice. "Then tell me how I came

to be with child, when I have been alone with no other man."

Perplexed by her claim, Kol looked down at the crown of the boy's head.

"Dog?" Godric called. "Dog, come here."

"Ach!" Kol struck the bowl of bread from the boy's hand. With a loud rap, it bounced off the table, to the floor in front of the dais. Countless warriors sprang to their feet. Godric bellowed.

Isabel gripped his arm. "Why did you do that?"

Kol did not answer. There was no time. He pressed Godric into the crook of his arm, and gripped the boy's jaw.

"Open your mouth." He squeezed until the child cried out.

"My lord, what is amiss?" Vekell's shadow fell over them.

"Move back, I cannot see."

Isabel pulled his sleeve in an attempt to claim her child. "You are hurting him. Give my son to me!"

"The hounds," Kol hissed through bared teeth. "The hounds ate the bread."

Isabel bent to peer beneath the table. In the next breath, he heard her fear-strangled gasp, "Godric!"

In his mind, the image of the wolfhounds superimposed over the face of the boy. White froth upon their mouths. Their eyes glazed in pain.

In death.

Godric sobbed against Kol's shoulder. "Hungry puppies. Feed puppies."

"Touch not your fare," shouted Vekell to the occupants of the great hall. "For all may be tainted."

Isabel heard the murmur go up from the multitude.

"Poison."

"Treachery!"

Warriors rushed forward to examine the hounds. Others

charged out the portal which led to the keep's kitchen, surely to question those who had prepared the meal.

Isabel cried out, and reached for her son. Finally satisfied the boy had eaten none of the bread, Kol relinquished him.

Godric clung to his mother. Tears spiked his dark lashes. "Mean man. Hurt my mouth."

Kol cursed himself. Though he realized the threat to the boy and had already arranged for his protection, he had not anticipated such an attack might occur, here, in the keep, as the boy sat in his very arms.

Isabel looked up, her expression that of a cornered elk, wild and afraid. With the child in her arms, she pushed up from the table.

"Last eventide I warned you he was not safe. Do you not understand? There are those who await the day when Ranulf has been dethroned, so they may lay claim to Norsex. Godric's existence challenges any claim, for through me, he bears the blood of the Norsexian dynasty."

"I will protect the boy." Kol stood. "While I continue to seek the truth of this place."

"You cannot protect him while at the same time, you seek Ranulf's death." She quaked with anger.

"There is no reason you and I must be enemies."

"You are but one enemy, among many." She hurried to descend the dais.

"Princess." Kol sought to allay the scene unfolding in full view of his legion. "Return to the bench, so that we may confer on these matters further." He indicated the seat beside him.

Isabel shook her head. "To sit with you is to forgive your presence in this kingdom. 'Twas a mistake for me to have sat beside you for even a moment." Her breasts rose and fell with vehemence. "I hold you to blame for my child's endangerment. Before you came, he was safe."

Warriors stood as she rushed past, their eyes riveted to

her. Kol could not blame them. Emotion heightened her beauty. At the doorway she turned and, across the large and assembled room, met his eyes. "Dare you try to take him from me again, and I will tear your throat out with my hands."

She whirled away, her scarlet gunna leaving a fiery trail in his mind.

Isabel awakened to the darkness of drawn bed curtains, and the sound of horses and men below her window. She shifted, easing the ache in her bruised side.

The night before, she'd resumed residence in her own chamber, in defiance of Kol's edict. She had expected him to pursue her from the great hall, but he had not. On the contrary, she and Godric had been allowed to pass the night in peace. How thankful she was, for she had not slept in two nights and had felt nearly overwhelmed by exhaustion. She had held Godric until he slept, and she remembered no more.

Now Kol prepared to depart Calldarington without her.

She burrowed more deeply into the furs and told herself not to care. Not to remember the dark and brooding expression he'd worn as she'd left the hall last eventide. Godric had been returned to her and naught else but his continued well-being mattered. In the darkness, she reached for her son.

She found nothing. No warm little boy. No warm bedclothes.

With one hand she parted the bed curtain. Pale blue light speared across the pillows.

"Godric, where are you?" The sound of her fear rang sharp in the empty room. She clambered from the bed to kneel upon frigid timbers to peer underneath the frame, but saw clear to the other side.

She stood. *"Godric!"*

A horse whinnied without. A chill that had naught to do with a winter's morn, slid down Isabel's spine.

"No." She hurried to the window and shoved back its covering. She cast open the shutter.

In the distance, an army of foot soldiers moved up the mountain road. Even from this distance she heard their collective step upon the earth. Below her window, more warriors prepared to depart the burh. These men sat atop horses; large animals like none she had ever seen. Dawn shimmered off the mail shirt of their leader. He sat atop the largest and blackest beast. To her astonishment, Rowena also sat among the gathered contingent, heavily cloaked as if for a journey.

Kol bent, as if to speak to a shaggy bundle on his lap. Even from this distance, Isabel recognized the upturned face of her son.

"No!" She ran from the window and threw open the door. Two guards stood against the wall as she flew past, apparently too stunned by her sudden appearance to react, but their steps thundered behind as she raced barefoot down the stairs. She shoved through the lower passage. Figures bumped against her, their faces blurred. She pushed through the high oaken doors.

Already the line of mounted soldiers rode toward the gate. She delved into the wall of horseflesh, her feet slapping into the mud. The animals shied and complained as she veered in and out of their midst.

Like a shadow upon the earth, the great black horse and its rider rose up before her.

"Thorleksson!" she shouted.

When Kol turned in his saddle, Godric peeked around his side. Rowena also turned.

"Get thee into the keep," Kol ordered. His animal never dropped pace.

"You cannot take him from me." She ran alongside him. Her breath clouded the air in sharp bursts. She caught hold of his braies, and hooked her fingers into his leather greaves.

He braced the boy with his arm. "I ensure his protection."

Godric pushed out of his dense wrapping. "Mama, look. I ride big horse."

"Wherever he goes, so shall I." Desperately, she grabbed hold of the stirrup. The cold silver stung her hands.

"Release me." He yanked his foot and the stirrup free. With his heel, he prodded the horse forward. Isabel stumbled, but at the last moment, reached out and grabbed the steed's tail.

She would not let him take her son.

Jerked from her feet, she fell into the mud. Dampness permeated to her skin.

Godric cried, "No, no, no. My mama."

Despair gripped her, but she held onto the animal's tail. The movement reawakened her injury and pain seared her side. Abruptly, the violent travel ceased.

She lay in the mud, her hands tangled in the horse's tail.

"Curse you, get up."

"My lord," someone chastened in a low voice, and splashed to the ground beside her. Vekell raised her to her feet.

Still saddled, Kol glared his rage down on her. "You wish to come? Then come. Remember, 'twas your choice."

Though Vekell still held her arm, Isabel reached up toward Kol's saddle, her intention to mount behind him.

With a jerk of the reins, he cantered the animal aside. "Get your own damn horse. Anon. Already our time grows short."

Chapter 9

He should not have allowed her to come. But when the child had begun to cry, his mortared heart had weakened.

Kol guided Morke between the dull, flat stones of the old Roman road. Alongside him, his outriders wove in and out of the trees, searching for any enemy presence. Before and aft rode his warrior escorts. Although he did not fear a confrontation with his Saxon foe, he would tread carefully in this foreign land.

'Twas not far to the abbey.

In the courtyard he had behaved badly. How he wished he could despise Isabel, just as much as she despised him. Late into the night he had contemplated his weakness for her. She sensed it, he knew, and could not allow her to use that weakness against him.

With that caution in mind, did he dare believe her claim? Did she truly believe him to be the father of her child, or did she seek to play upon his sympathy with an outlandish story of missing memories?

When her attempts to seduce him had not succeeded, perhaps she sought an alternative method of manipulation. Perhaps this fierce connection he felt between them was not at all genuine, but forged by the princess to further her motives.

He felt her gaze bore into the base of his neck. He still held the memory of Isabel climbing atop a hastily saddled mare, one of the smaller Saxon stocks he and his men had quickly discarded when their heartier Arab breeds had arrived on the livestock ships. Her mud-stained kirtle had peeked from beneath the gunna she'd donned in the presence of his men. She had been shielded only by her maid-servant, who had held a cloak high, in an meager attempt to offer her lady privacy.

Afterward he'd given over possession of the boy to Isabel, avoiding her eyes, which were so desirous of reassurances he would not be cruel, that he would not bring harm to her or her child. But he resolved not to give her that comfort. He could not allow her to thwart his vengeance against Ranulf when he suspected that very ambition motivated her every word and action.

Kol looked up into the sky. There, a wintering raven flew with wings outspread. He must remove himself from the emotion of the situation, and make his conclusions based upon truth, not the absurd yearnings of his heart. Now his mind was clear, and free of the weariness of the night before.

The *truth* was: she had attempted to seduce him, skillfully, and on more than one occasion. By her own admission, she would do anything to get what she wanted, be that the return of her son, or the return of her brother, the king, to his throne.

How close he had come to believing her claims the night before. From where had this callow nature of his arisen? Most likely the princess continued to ply her deceptions to her advantage. She sought to win his sympathy, and by doing so, bring down his defenses.

He found himself eager to test the last remaining false-hood between them. Any continued deception on her part would confirm his suspicions.

With a tug of his reins, he slowed his mount and fell into place alongside Isabel, who sheltered her sleeping child beneath her cloak. Behind them, the Princess Rowena rode out of hearing distance. She had not endeavored to ride beside her sister.

To his surprise, Isabel spoke before he did.

"Have you determined who wrought the attempt against my son last eventide?"

Nearby the raven alighted upon a branch. Its fathomless black eyes observed their passage. Kol heard the murmurs of his men, and knew they too had taken notice of the omen.

He looked away from the unlucky carrion-bird and answered the woman beside him. "Our search resulted in naught but a kitchen full of hysterical women who provided no useful details. In the future, any food will be prepared and tasted by the women themselves in the presence of my marshal."

"Do you truly believe 'twas the kitchen women who undertook to end my son's life?" Isabel snapped, and bore her child closer.

"Perhaps at the direction of another."

Isabel looked away, her expression pained.

After a moment, Kol said, "'Tis lovely here."

She answered him not.

"Did you and your husband ride these paths together often?"

Her gaze fell to her son. "Aye," she answered unsteadily. "That we did."

She continued to lie. What more evidence of her duplicity did he require? *Let her think you believe.* The truth would be revealed soon enough, along with his judgment.

He nudged his mount into a quicker pace. Inside he grew so black, he no longer perceived the sway and creak of the forest trees lining the path. He closed his eyes, and allowed the beast to carry him forward through the pitch of his own mind.

Why did it torture him so, to be lied to? To be wrongly accused? 'Twas not as if it were the first time in his life he were punished for a crime he did not commit. If given the chance, to whom would he proclaim his innocence? To Ranulf? The idea was laughable. Even if Ranulf had tortured him believing he'd stolen his sister's innocence, Kol could not forget there was more to this intrigue.

In his mind, the pieces of the puzzle converged, but did not fit. Some were missing.

That day the king's hounds had torn into his flesh. Manacles had been fastened around his wrists. Faced with death, he'd identified himself and had revealed Aldrith's summons for his mercenary legion.

Even now, he remembered the moment with perfect clarity.

Ranulf's face had gone as white as the clays which lined these northern fenlands. He had gripped the wooden handle of the whip, and had said, "I knew you would come."

In the distance the walls of the abbey arose from a wreath of evergreens. Relief flooded Kol. He lived his life solely in the present for good reason. 'Twas because he despised almost every single remembrance of his past. Why had he believed, even for the passing of a breath, Isabel would accord him a different sort of memories, when like the others, she too betrayed him, with her lies and her intentions.

The gate of the abbey swung open. Out walked the abbess and several sisters, their eyes wary upon his war-

riors. He had sent a messenger to announce his arrival and
to assure the sisters they were in no danger from his forces.
But surely assurances from a Norse barbarian meant very
little to them.

And although he felt like a monster for what he intended to do, he would not be swayed, not by a child's
tears or a mother's demands.

He dismounted and looked to the princess. She rode
forward, her mud-spattered kirtle hanging down on either
side of the saddle. He saw her relief. For the first time
since he had thundered into her life, she almost smiled.

In a breathless voice, she said, "You wish for Godric
and I to remain here, at the abbey?"

"*Nei*, Isabel. Not you."

The hope faded from her countenance. Good. She understood.

Only Godric would remain.

"May I not stay with him?" She looked at her son, her
lip trembling. Beautiful, violet eyes blinked away tears.

"You may not." Kol took her mare's harness in hand,
and led her toward the abbess. "The boy will be safe here."
*And you will not be able to use him to manipulate my
weaknesses further.*

Tears plumped on her lashes. "I beg you, please."

"Give him to the abbess, Isabel."

"Why does my sister stay?" Isabel's watery gaze fell
upon Rowena, who was already disappearing within the
high walls.

"Because she displeases me." Kol looked to the trees,
wanting to see anything but her face. "She cries all the
time."

"Do I not displease you as well?" She pressed her face
against the child's neck.

"Aye, but in a different way."

"I'll only try to kill you again."

"Take the child to the abbess, Isabel."

She exhaled jaggedly. "You are right. 'Tis better this way." She dismounted. Her eyes did not waver from his. "Because he will be away from you. Still, I should be allowed to stay with him." A single tear fell to her cheek. She kissed the slumbering child's forehead, wiped her tears from where they had fallen onto his skin, and strode forward to place him in the abbess's arms.

Despite Kol's resolve, an almost unbearable weight clamped onto his heart.

As the princess strode past to return to her mount, she raked him with her hate-filled gaze. "I will not forgive this. Not ever."

Kol watched her flounce past. His eyes descended to the swirl of her skirts, against her slender legs. God help him. They were in the midst of what should be an excruciatingly heartrending moment and he had sprouted an erection the size of his Frankish sword.

What, he demanded of his traitorous body, happened to forgetting his desire for her? To despising her with the same intensity with which he despised her brother? The memory of what lay beneath her shapeless, mud-stained garments caused him the greatest agony.

Thankfully, distraction came quickly. The thud of hooves announced an approaching rider. With the hiss of drawn swords, Kol's men positioned themselves to protect the narrow path upon which they had come. The rider, duly identified, passed through their ranks.

Svartkell thundered into view. His long, copper-colored locks flew back over his shoulders.

"My lord!" he called, as he jumped to the earth and came to stand before Kol. A smile broke over his face. "You will be exceedingly pleased. The Northumbrian has agreed to your terms. We shall observe his acceptance on the morrow."

Moments later, Kol pulled his cloak from his shoulders and traversed to the far side of the clearing. There, Isabel sat upon her mount, her eyes fixed upon the abbess, who stood with Godric between the open gates.

"Put this on." Upon two hooked fingers he lifted the garment.

With a haughty lift of her chin, she refused. "I want nothing from you."

"Your mantle, while lovely, lacks warmth."

"My hatred for you keeps me warm enough." She gripped the pommel of the saddle. He saw the underside of her wrist, the pale translucence of her skin. A chill shook her lithe frame.

He knew she was cold. With one hand he covered hers on the pommel. Her eyes flew open in astonishment as he climbed into the saddle, his larger, more muscular legs bracing hers astride. Beneath his palms her hands were frozen.

"Get off," she demanded. Beneath them, the beast canted sideways, protesting his weight. Between his thighs Isabel twisted. Her elbow jabbed his chest. He slipped an arm about her waist.

Just below the circular broach which held her mantle, he saw a flash of her skin. A delightful flush crept up her neck from the place where her breasts swelled beneath her tunic. If he pressed his lips there, against her throat, her skin would be warm and fragrant.

From across the clearing, Kol felt Vekell's disapproval bear down upon him. Why that caused him such annoyance, he did not know.

"You must learn to follow the edicts of your master, Isabel," he murmured close to her ear.

"You are not my master," she hissed, turning to glare.

Still holding her waist, he pulled his cloak about her rigid shoulders and fastened its viper broach at her throat. He felt the tension in her, the rebellion. He resisted the impulse to bury his hands in her hair and draw the silken mass from beneath his garment.

"You will be grateful for the warmth." He held his cool demeanor. "For we do not return to the burh."

Dread burdened her voice. "Where do we go?"

Beneath the cloak, his hand spread across her belly. Against his palm he felt the nervous clench of her muscles.

"Perhaps curiosity will bind you to me?"

Why did he feel compelled to touch her so possessively, here, with his warriors milling about? And in full view of the abbess? Because suddenly the urge to test her proved overwhelming. He was certain, now; he had been a fool before. Isabel was no innocent bride, but rather a woman experienced in illicit love. How much would she allow?

Nothing, he quickly learned. She clasped his hand, and pried it from her. Agitation bloomed on her cheeks.

"Nay, my lord." She did not turn to meet his eyes. "My curiosity has been duly satisfied. Prithee, allow me to return to the burh. I have duties, and they have been neglected due to your interruption into our lives."

He relented, easing his hold. Her punishment would come when the time was right. Not here, in full view of his men and the abbey walls. Between his teeth, he expelled the aggression built up within.

"Your duties will keep." Around either side of her waist he tugged the reins, setting her mare into motion. "This morning you insisted on coming, and so you will complete the journey." Moreover, he could not spare the armed escort. He steered her mount alongside his.

He thrust his boot into the silver stirrup and crossed over to his steed. Cold air eradicated the warmth their bodies had created against his thighs and chest. He took one last look into her furious, amethyst eyes, and urged his horse away.

Why did he crave her, despite his knowledge of her duplicitous nature? Each husky utterance from her lips sent a thrill down his spine. The slightest brush of her body sent waves of awareness blazing through him.

Did she please her lover, or lovers, well? Jealousy reared up within Kol.

As if to defy him, the princess cantered past, taking a place at the forefront of the party. His eyes followed the straight line of her back into the saddle. His cloak concealed her buttocks, but he'd felt her, pressed against the center of his thighs just moments ago. Warm, soft and feminine.

Shamed, he bit down a curse. He tugged one rein, whirling his horse about, and set off toward the abbess. She shrank away, but only a step. Bundled in furs, Godric lay in her arms. What would he do when he awoke to find his mother gone?

Kol removed the crucifix from where it hung at his neck, and laid it upon the tiny form. "'Tis costly. Consider it my bestowal, in the name of the princess's child. In addition, I leave a contingent behind to defend the abbey."

"To defend the abbey?" Confusion mottled her expression. "From whom?"

Kol did not answer. "Keep the boy close to you, always."

He urged his mount to join the others. His act of contrition had done nothing to empty his mind of that which tortured him. Who about him would suspect that behind his emotionless mask, an amalgam of past encounters pulsed in shocking flashes of black and red. But the flushed female faces, the writhing, sweat-slick bodies were replaced by images of another. A woman he had not yet experienced.

Into his hair he thrust his fingers, raking a path for the cold along his scalp. Lord knew he no longer needed his damn cloak—or the crucifix. He felt eaten up inside.

As they rode north, into the forest, he caught a glimpse of his ghosts, dancing in the shadows of the trees. They laughed and taunted, pointing their long, skeletal fingers at the princess.

Not yours, they snickered. *Never yours.*

Not good enough for a mother's love, not good enough for a woman's.

Chapter 10

I t was late afternoon when Isabel saw Kol signal to Vekell to stop and water the horses. She urged her mount alongside Kol's marshal. "There is a river, just past that copse of trees."

Vekell's brows raised in question, but she rode on without offering explanation. Aye, she knew this land well enough, though it had been some time since she had visited. It belonged to Aiken of Leswick, the young warrior-*eorl* who acted as cupbearer to her brother and king. Aiken had also been her betrothed.

Once they came to the river, Isabel nudged her mare forward to drink. Several of the Danes, after allowing their mounts to take their fill, rode into the forest.

"Where do they go?" Isabel asked Vekell, who remained close to her, as always.

"To hunt." He knelt to the ground and lifted his mount's foreleg. From his belt he took his blade, and pried the packed dirt from the animal's hoof. "If you require a moment alone, my lady, now would be the time."

Without further contemplation she rode in the opposite direction of the soldiers, into the darker shadows of the forest. Finding a sheltered spot, she dismounted. She fisted her hands in her skirts, and almost lifted them, but her eyes perceived a slight movement in the nearby trees.

A scream arose within her throat.

There, just a stone's throw away, stood a man, his back pressed against the trunk of a tree. Mud covered his entire body. Through the filth, the whites of his eyes shone shockingly bright.

"Isabel," he gasped.

"Aiken." Aiken, the man who had withdrawn his suit after it had become known she carried another man's child.

For a moment he did not move. He only stared, his expression aggrieved. With one white-knuckled hand, he gripped his sword. With a groan, he slid down the tree to sit at its base. Isabel rushed forward and fell to her knees beside him.

He groaned. "Tell me . . . tell me you have not been harmed." One bloodstained hand gripped her sleeve. He still wore his battle garb. Embedded in his mail shirt were bits of leaves and grass. Mud matted his long, golden hair.

And there was blood, on his braies and splattered upon the leather of his boots. Frantically, Isabel skimmed her hand over his knee, and up his thigh, but she found no injury. When she reached the area of his groin he caught her hand.

"No." His voice was hoarse, but firm. He clutched her hand so tightly it hurt. "I do not want you to see."

Though she trembled, she forced a stern expression. "Aiken, you are injured. You must allow me tend to you." She could at least stanch the flow of blood with mud or leaves, and hide him where he would not be found by the Danes.

He touched her cheek, but his hand fell to his side, as if

the gesture had required too much energy. Green eyes burned with physical and emotional pain.

"There is naught you can do."

The resignation Isabel heard in his voice terrified her. While they had not exchanged more than a greeting since Godric's birth, she still cared for this man. Presented to her father's court when she was but fourteen summers, he'd quickly engendered her admiration. And despite the pain his disavowal of their betrothal had inflicted upon her, she had understood his reasons for walking away.

She pulled his arm across her shoulder and urged him to rise. "Anon, Aiken. You must hasten to the border, as fast as you can. There someone will help you."

Hewn of a warrior's muscle and bone, he weighed three times as much as she. He refused to budge.

"Nay," he gritted between clenched teeth. Carefully he withdrew his arm. For the briefest moment, his hand touched her hair. Naked longing gleamed in his eyes.

This she did not understand.

"Take her," Isabel insisted, pointing at the mare. Her heart beat erratically with urgency and fear. "Now. You must go *now*. Soon, they will come looking for me."

Slowly he stood, bracing himself against the trunk of the tree. With great effort, together they lifted and sheathed his sword. His breath came in sharp bursts, as if his lungs did not allow him to take in enough air.

"Only if you come with me."

"No." Isabel shook her head. "The Dane holds Godric and Rowena captive and I will not leave without them."

Aiken's injuries slowed their progress across the distance to where Isabel's mare stood, her ears alert and twitching.

"Can you mount? I will divert them somehow, until you have escaped."

"No, you will not," he hissed, his palm pressed hard

against his wound. He avowed, "I would rather die than leave you to them."

Isabel experienced an almost overwhelming urge to cling to Aiken, to beg him to save her, to find some way to save her son. But she knew to run away would only prolong the inevitable confrontation between herself and the Dane.

Kol would never let her go. Somehow he considered her a prize. And as she had been the one to unleash him upon the world, she intended to be the one to end his rampage of conquest and terror. Even if she sacrificed her life to the quest, she owed that much to her family and to her people, even if it never brought about their forgiveness.

With a steady heart, she met Aiken's gaze. "Do not be foolish. Your gallantry is wasted on me."

It took all her strength to pry his hands from her shoulders. Firmly, she took his chin in hand. In a softer voice, she pled, "Look at me and listen."

The hand he raised to cover hers trembled, but his voice did not. "You cannot force me to leave you here. What man of honor would abandon you to them? To him? It is him, is it not, Isabel? The beast who—"

"You must," she insisted. "The survival of Norsex outweighs your concern for my safety. You must reach Ranulf. Tell him the Danes entrench themselves for the long term."

Aiken pulled away, and turned toward the mare. He gripped the pommel, but did not mount. Instead he rested his forehead against the saddle. Exhaustion manifested itself in the sag of his great shoulders, the raggedness of his every breath.

Suddenly he turned, his eyes ablaze.

"Has he touched you, Isabel?" A grimace contorted his face, as if the words were the foulest bile. "Have *any* of those barbarians touched you?"

Isabel swallowed hard. In a brilliant flash, she remem-

bered Kol's face above her, the hard planes of his cheekbones reflected by firelight, his eyes burning with need.

"No," Isabel lied.

Beneath the intensity of Aiken's silent stare, Isabel
flushed. The smooth skin of his brow furrowed, and his
nostrils flared.

"If I had pressed my suit to Ranulf sooner, we could
have been married and perhaps you would never have suffered the Dane's—"

"No." Fervently, Isabel shook her head. "There is
naught you could have done."

His bottom lip out-thrust, he retorted. "You would not
have been out riding that day alone if you had been my
bride."

Isabel laughed, despite her fear that they would be discovered at any moment. "What makes you so certain?"

"Wildling." Sadness dimmed his smile.

Aiken had always conducted himself with the utmost
formality, both before and after their betrothal. She had
never suspected he had such an intensity of feelings for
her, and certainly not as strong as the ones written plainly
on his face.

Feelings she had once told herself she felt for him.

Abruptly he said, "I have delayed in finding a bride because 'twas you I wanted."

Isabel frowned. "You ended our betrothal."

"Nay. My king commanded me to sever that which
bound us together."

This revelation stunned Isabel. Why would Ranulf have
done such a thing? Nearby a tree creaked loudly in the
wind, startling them both.

"We have no time for this." Isabel tightened the straps
of the saddle. "Now, go. You will be of no help to our king
nor our people if you lie dead in the forest."

Forlorn, he swung, with visible pain and effort, into the
saddle. Isabel slapped the mare's rump, hard. The horse

cantered away. But Aiken whirled the animal about and
drew up beside her. He leaned low. His hand caught the
back of her head and he pulled her close.

"I should have fought for you."

His mouth brushed hers, and then he was gone. Isabel
stared after him, her fingertips pressed to her lips.

"Aye," she murmured. "You should have fought for me.
But you did not." She watched until she could see him no
more. Then she turned.

And gasped.

Kol stood an arm's length away. In that instant, she
could not breathe. Her heartbeat drummed over the nearby
rush and gurgle of the river. His eyes revealed nothing, no
anger, no condemnation. No suspicion. Would he not display all of those things if he had seen Aiken? His sword
still berthed in its scabbard.

She lied to fill the silence. "My horse. She wandered
away. I have been searching for her here and there."

"Wicked animal," he responded quietly.

"Yes. Wicked. Wicked, indeed." Isabel licked her lips,
feigning an expression of concern. "She has been contrary
all day. I am not at all surprised she has ignored my calls
to return."

"Oh, yes?" He affixed his blue gaze on her. Inwardly
her composure faltered. *Had he seen?* She felt rather as if
he were a wolf, watching her. Making his decision.

"Yes," she confirmed softly, her voice nearly stolen by
fear.

"Do you ride often?" He took one step closer.

"Ride?" She blinked, stepping back. With his advance,
her mind scattered. What had he asked her?

"Yes, ride. That day, two winters ago, I saw you riding.
Clearly you found joy in it. At least up until that moment
your horse tossed you into the river."

Beneath her heavy garments, Isabel grew cold. The
Dane's words tugged her memory dangerously close to the

gaping hole of nothingness, a time she did not remember, but which terrified her still. Had he watched her from the forest, like a predator waiting for the most fortuitous time to attack?

"I am not allowed to ride. Not any longer, not after you—" She looked down, at nothing in particular. Anything but him. Layer upon layer of moldering leaves covered the forest floor. Their earthy aroma rose up to scent the air about them. "Not after what happened. Ranulf does not allow it."

His voice took on an unmistakable edginess. "You told me earlier you rode often with your husband. Was that not true?" He stepped close. "Did I misunderstand?"

She grew flustered. "What I meant was that I am no longer allowed to ride without the company of my husband, or without a ridiculous escort, so why do it? The freedom is gone."

With an unsteady hand she pushed aside a branch and looked very hard into the dense forest, as if searching for the missing animal. Anything not to look at him.

"I did not take your freedom, Isabel."

"Yes you did." She whirled to meet his gaze.

"I did nothing but save your life that day."

A black chasm spread all around her, threatened to swallow her whole.

"I don't want to talk about this."

What was wrong with her? She had wanted nothing more than to confront him about what he had done, to scream her accusations at the top of her voice. But now the opportunity was here, staring into her face with such blue-eyed intensity, she did nothing but shrink from it.

He did not so much as blink. "All right. We'll talk about something else."

She stood, fixated by his gaze. As if through a tunnel, she saw his lips move.

"Was that your husband?"

The question echoed inside her head with such force she nearly stumbled. Requiring support, she pressed her hand against the trunk of a tree.

"What?"

He stepped nearer, and nearer still. "Sitting atop your wicked horse." She stared at his lips. "The man who kissed you. Was that your husband?"

Her breath came in quick, shallow gasps. His hand cupped her chin, and disallowed her from looking away. The set of his mouth had gone cruel.

"'Tis not a difficult question to answer."

Slowly, with one hand he pulled the mantle from her hair. His eyes fixed upon her mouth. Oh, God. She felt the burn of his stare, the heat radiate from his body.

"Yes," she blurted, pressing against the tree. "He is my husband."

Perhaps if he believed she held the status of wife, he would not touch her again, would not awaken the deplorable weakness in her.

"You would not lie to me?"

Blood pounded in her head. She barely heard herself whisper, "No."

He withdrew his hand. Something in his features cooled. "Then I can understand, of course, why you would help him escape."

He stepped back. "Come. Let us return to the others."

Isabel hesitated. Was that all? Relief trickled through her veins in tiny, near-strangled streams. There would be no punishment? Of course, the man she despised still held her prisoner, but Aiken would have ridden far by now.

Silent and brooding, the Dane followed her down the narrow trail. How she craved even the company of his hated Danish warriors.

They entered the clearing where the others waited. Immediately she sensed a sharp edge of excitement in the air. Some officers were mounted. Their steeds danced and cir-

cled about some common quarry. Others were on foot. But
they blocked her view. They swarmed like wolves on a
hunt.

Her mare wandered nearby, riderless.

"No. Aiken." In one horrifying glimpse she saw he was
there in the center of the Danes. On his knees, beaten and
bloodied, a leather noose about his neck. She ran forward,
only to be captured from behind. Kol took hold of her forearm and pulled her toward the melee.

Aiken looked up through the curtain of his hair. Hatred
exploded in his eyes.

"You," he shouted at Kol, springing to his feet. "Do not
touch her."

Isabel cried out, and tried to rush forward, but Kol held
her. Isabel watched, sickened, as the men subdued Aiken
with a kick to his groin and a tug of the noose. He fell to
all fours, groaned, and collapsed facedown in the mud.

"No," she sobbed.

Kol pulled her forward, through the gathered circle of
warriors. There, he pushed her down, and forced her to
kneel beside the fallen Saxon. Cruelly, he did not allow her
to touch him.

Kol crouched between them. He grasped a fistful of hair
and lifted Aiken's head. The man moaned, insensible.

"Look at him," Kol commanded quietly.

Isabel did look. Beneath the filth, Aiken's skin cast a
deathly pallor. She had to do something. She would continue the lie if it would save him.

"You cannot kill him," she cried. "*Please.* He is my husband."

Kol looked at Aiken as if he were a chicken being considered for the pot. Without passion, he murmured, "He
will most likely die of his wounds."

"Then help him. You must have physicians."

He stared at her, his eyes devoid of sympathy.

Isabel's anger exceeded her fear. "You said you understood."

"And that I do." His voice was gentle, but deceitfully so, considering he still held Aiken's head by the hair, one step away from its becoming a trophy. "I understand you have lied to me. That this man is not your husband."

Isabel's head snapped up and she stared at him. It was as if a thunderous clap of lightning resounded in her head. *He knew the truth.* All along, he had known she had no husband and had simply been toying with her.

He leaned close. She found herself unable to look away from his eyes. "And I understand, Isabel, that this man, whatever he means to you, kissed you, and rode away, leaving you to me. For that alone, does he not deserve to die?"

The world seemed formed of silence. He released Aiken's hair. The Saxon's head thudded to the ground.

Moments later two warriors hoisted Aiken across the back of a horse and led him in the direction from whence they had come, toward Calldarington. About her, men secured whatever fowl or game had been culled in the hunt. Isabel arose, numb to her soul. She walked toward her mare and waited there silent and apart from the others, until the party resumed the journey inland.

Soon, Leswick appeared, atop a large, extended knoll. Though the hall and outbuildings still stood, no smoke arose from the roofs. No one called out a warning of the Danes' arrival. Leswick appeared deserted.

Vekell circled his mount to ride beside her. "We will pass the night here."

Isabel gathered her cloak tightly about her, for the harsh cold of a winter night had begun to spread across the earth.

How could she ever find comfort here, knowing the man to whom it belonged might already be dead?

Chapter 11

W here have they gone?" Isabel stepped into the hall.
While a large structure, Aiken's familial dwelling
did not boast the private chambers of Ranulf's great keep.

Her gaze swept the dim interior. He had been trying to
come here. Perhaps to die.

She walked to the center of the room and held her palms
over the hearth. Though ashen, the logs still gave off faint
heat.

"Of whom do you inquire?" Vekell walked the perimeter of the room. His eyes consumed every detail.

Upon the walls hung an array of rich tapestries, but in
betwixt the exquisitely rendered pieces emerged a reminder
of the violence of the day: the outlines of absent shields and
swords, etched by hearth smoke upon the whitewashed timber. The male members of the household would have
snatched the weapons from their berths as soon as they'd
learned of the Danish threat. Like all loyal thegns, Aiken
had hastened to his king's defense, and dutifully offered
every man in his *folc* in the defense of the kingdom.

Isabel traced the outline of a short sword with her finger. "A family resided here, and many others along with them. I wish to know if they are well."

Aiken's widowed mother and his young sister would have waited here for his return, along with the wives and children of their numerous vassals.

Vekell shrugged. "We did not force them away. Whoever was here before our arrival, left of their own accord."

Isabel nodded, relieved. Though this man remained her enemy, she trusted he spoke the truth. He had no reason to lie to her. 'Twas her most fervent hope the people of Leswick had crossed the Northumbrian border and found sanctuary with kinsfolk.

Footsteps sounded at the threshold. Though Isabel's pulse quickened, Kol did not appear. Instead several warriors entered, their arms laden with wood. Soon the dormant hearth blazed anew. Above the flames they hung a boar upon a spit, one of the beasts hunted and captured by the Danes.

Just as the lord of this hall had been hunted and captured.

Isabel avoided looking at the animal's lifeless eyes, but she could not silence the sound of its lifeblood as it fell and hissed into the flames.

The warriors left. Beside the fire, Vekell rubbed his hands together and smiled. "Odin's tree! It seems an age since I have tasted boar. I have eaten so much fish in recent days, I expect to grow gills."

She felt his eyes upon her, expectant of some response. Beneath Kol's cloak she rubbed her arms and looked away.

"Hmph." He strode toward several wooden chests which lined the wall. After a moment of rummaging, he pulled out two pelts, and turned to walk a straight line toward the hearth. He dropped the furs, one beside the other. With the tip of his boot he spread them flat.

"Sit. 'Tis warm here beside the fire."

With the tip of *her* boot, Isabel dragged one of the furs a goodly distance away from the other. Holding the two cloaks about her, she sat.

Vekell sat on the other, as stout and sturdy as an ancient yew. "My company displeases you."

"Yes, it does." She met his eyes. "But why should that matter to you?"

He shrugged. "I suppose because I hold you in such high esteem."

"We are enemies."

"Not so long ago, you spared my lord's life." He looked down at his hands, large-knuckled and scarred. "We should not have to be enemies."

"As long as your lord seeks to murder my brother, and whilst your foreign army continues to occupy this kingdom, we can be nothing but."

Flames painted dancing shadows on the wall. For a long moment, he remained silent. "Do you *truly* believe my lord to be Godric's sire?"

With indignation on her face, Isabel answered, "You have no right to be so bold."

He looked about the room, then hunkered forward. "No one is about, and the truth must be spoken."

Curiously, Isabel felt no threat from the giant seated before her. So why not speak plainly? Surely he, of all people, knew the darker side of his lord and she would be able to read the truth upon his face.

"Thorleksson is the father of my son." Her eyes glazed at the humiliation of voicing the accusation aloud to a stranger. She blinked the tears away. "Of that I have no doubt."

She didn't doubt that. Not anymore. At least that's what she told herself when the alternative of another attacker, a Saxon, seemed so unreal.

Vekell straightened, as if surprised by the frankness of her charge—or perhaps unseated by her tears. Although they remained alone in the vast room, he lowered his voice. "Surely then, you do not remember the event in which the child was conceived?"

Why should she bare her heart to this stranger? She stiffened. "I am sure he hath told you my account."

His eyes became bright pools of candor. "My lord is a private man. He hath said nothing of this to me."

Isabel wrung the edge of Kol's cloak.

Ah-ha! shouted his expression. "If you do not remember, how can you be so certain of my lord's guilt?"

She waved an impatient hand. "You have only to look to see their likenesses."

Vekell's words grew thick, his accent more pronounced. "The boy's features are yours exactly. My lord's dark coloring may only be coincidence."

"I do not go about falling into states of senselessness where any man can—" She closed her eyes, feeling the heat climb to her cheeks. "What I mean to say, is there hath been only one opportunity for a man to—" She swallowed hard. The discussion grew far too intimate for her comfort.

In contemplation, Vekell chewed the corner of his thumbnail. "There has to be some other explanation."

"Why, when this one is so clearly the truth? Aye, he rescued me from death. And believing him a hero, I helped him escape." Against her knees, she fisted her hands. "But he was no hero."

"A hero he was. I was with him from the moment he pulled you from the river, and watched as he carried you toward the burh. He risked his life for you, and still bears the scar of the Saxon arrow he took as he held you, protecting you with his own body." With one fist, Vekell pounded his shoulder.

Isabel pulled her veil closer to her face. "I cannot believe you. 'Tis near impossible a Saxon of my brother's ranks would have dared assault me."

"'Near impossible' is not 'impossible.'"

"No," Isabel whispered. "Even if such an atrocity had occurred, when would such an attack have taken place, that I would not recall it?"

Though she had expected him to become angry, his tone gentled. "Do not hide from this truth, little one. What reason have I to tell you lies? My lord commanded I remain in the forest, but I watched from there. Did he drop you to the ground as the arrow pierced flesh and bone?"

Isabel pressed her palms to her ears, but she heard the words still.

"*Nei.* He held you." He unfolded his legs, as if he prepared to crawl toward her. "Held you until they pried you from his arms and dragged him inside the walls of your brother's fort. Surely that alone testifies to his respect for a maiden's protection."

"Stop, please. I do not wish to hear."

But his words, and their proclamation of Kol's honor, echoed inside her head. Vekell simply sat, staring at her. Slowly, she lowered her hands. From outside the hall, the voices of men drew near.

Vekell implored her. "He is not guilty of what you accuse. 'Tis impossible, for reasons I have no right to impart." Firelight glimmered upon his braids. For the first time, she saw the threads of gray, and the creases of age across his skin. He pressed a fist against his chest. "I vow, he is blameless."

Kol crossed the threshold. With him entered several *degns*. His eyes lowered to Vekell and Isabel, who remained upon their furs. When he spoke his voice was as light as she'd ever heard it.

"What? Thou hast not prepared a feast for us?"

Vekell clasped his hands atop one knee and grimaced as he arose. "Apologies, my lord. These battered bones, once settled, are reluctant to stir again." He chuckled and moved to turn the boar upon its pike.

"A lamentable excuse if I ever heard one." Kol's smile

appeared forced, as a smile would be when its wearer did not often put it to use.

Isabel paid little attention to their banter, for her mind buzzed full of questions, namely, whether Vekell spoke the truth.

She watched from beneath her veil as Kol nodded to a young soldier. "Thrand, I require your assistance."

Together they walked to the far end of the hall and pulled out several tall wooden screens. These they dragged close to the fire, and draped with linen. Once they had finished, Kol returned to her side.

"I apologize for the lack of privacy, but I do believe you will be comfortable and warm this night."

Isabel nodded, forcing herself to remember Aiken, and the way Kol had mistreated him. She unfastened Kol's cloak from atop her own and lay it on the packed earthen floor beside her, as if by doing so, somehow she denied any hold Kol had over her.

Nay, 'twould be a long and miserable night. Indeed, she doubted she would be able to sleep at all.

Kol entered the stable, a narrow structure which abutted the hall. Wind sidled through the timbers, and rustled the straw. Upon their arrival, the stable had been vacant. Only the horses he and his men had ridden stood within. Their gathered warmth shielded him from the frigid cold.

Into the darkness he spoke. "Show yourself."

"I am here."

Kol saw the vapor of the Saxon's breath.

"Have you seen him?"

"Aye."

Kol's blood quickened. Ranulf lived. He craved the moment they would meet again, face to face. He would have his vengeance, and soon.

"Where is he now?"

"He moves from crevice to weald, without revealing the next hiding place to anyone. Even now, I shall have difficulty rejoining him."

"Where was he last?"

"In one of the many caves along the cliffs of Calldarington."

The idea of Ranulf looking down upon the keep, from an unseen vantage point, did not sit well with Kol. Indeed, he had bidden his men to search the cliffs and their honeycomb of caves on more than one occasion.

"And?"

The traitor shrugged. "And sometimes he retreats to avoid your warriors, and disappears into the forests of the west. He seeks a meeting with the Northumbrian, Osbeorht, in hopes of raising an unified army against you. But of late Ranulf had challenged Northumbrian dominion, so Osbeorht hath pleasured in drawing out the delay."

Kol nodded. "Your influence over Ranulf, does it remain intact?"

"At times."

'Twas time to test the traitor. Kol detailed the location.

"You have two days to convince him 'tis a safe haven. Bring him there, and I will be waiting."

"I will make it so."

They stood in silence for a long moment, until the spy spoke again. "The younger princess. She accompanies you, does she not?"

Kol bristled. "You know she does, or you would not ask."

A low, raspy chuckle arose from the blackness. "Such knowledge would drive Ranulf mad, for she is his favorite by far. And what of the boy? What of *your son*? Is he also here, in Leswick Hall?"

"The child remains in Calldarington's fortress," Kol lied. If this man wished for Ranulf's death, he might also wish for the death of Isabel's son, the only male who would carry the blood of the ancient Norsexian line. 'Twas not the first time Kol contemplated whether the traitor was responsible for the attempt upon Godric's life. But he had need of the Saxon for a short while longer. Then the truth would be extracted; the penalty, if warranted, would be meted out.

"Depart now."

"Two days." He heard the whisper of movement, and the shadow merged into night. "Until then."

Kol stood there a moment longer, breathing in the darkness until it consumed him, inside out. Cold air pressed against his skin and soon he felt numb. Just as he should be. He preferred his hatred without the mind-hazing heat of his earlier years, preferred his decisions to be unencumbered by emotion.

He moved between the posted guards, into the rear entrance of the hall. Immediately upon crossing the threshold, the savory scent of strewing herbs curled about him. Warmth pressed into and beneath his garments like comforting hands.

She lay behind the screen, but firelight illuminated her supine form through the gauzy fabric. Too clearly he saw the curve of her hip, the rise and fall of her bosom.

Outside, his soldiers surrounded the hall, protecting him from all those who might attempt to slay him before he fulfilled his final quest. Only he knew that the one who threatened him most lay here. She breathed quietly in her sleep, unlike Vekell and Svartkell, who lay sprawled upon nearby benches, their snores cutting the silence of the room to shards.

Kol unbuckled his baldric and lifted off his jerkin. He dragged a fur to the space between, and lay down to face the princess. Only then did he realize she did not sleep. Her breath, though nearly silent, was ragged and deep.

She shed tears, a young woman alone and amongst captors. The blackness inside him magnified. Did she mourn the tall, golden-haired Saxon they had captured in the forest? Emotions surged within him, a confusing mix of regret, jealousy, and compassion.

He reached beneath the screen and grasped the edge of the fur upon which she lay. She clasped his hand, as if to thwart his claim, but he dragged her toward him, at the same time drawing nearer to her, until only a small space, and a thin veil of linen, separated them.

Firelight edged her in gold, yet because the flames leapt behind her, he could not see her eyes.

"A fortunate man, to have a woman such as you to weep for him." Kol kept his voice low, so as not to wake the warriors who lay nearby. "Is he the boy's father?"

She inhaled sharply. "He could not be."

"Do you love him?"

She shook her head. "I only wish for him to live. His mother and sister have no one else."

Her words resounded in his head. She claimed not to love the Saxon. His heart leapt, but instantly, he struck the hope down. For what did he wish? Isabel's devotion, as he sought to destroy her brother and king?

Yes. That is exactly what he desired.

He curled his fingers more deeply into the furs, and dragged her closer still, until her face was no less than an inch from his. Through the linen he saw the glistening of her tears. Impulsively, he smoothed the pad of his thumb over her cheek, through the wetness. And then across her lips.

Her hand moved beneath the linen and grasped the collar of his tunic. With an urgency he did not understand, she pulled the garment from his shoulder until its absence revealed his bare skin. Her fingertips fluttered across the scar.

He murmured, "I vow, I did not hurt you that day."

"I want to believe." She turned her cheek into his palm.

He traced the column of her neck, and threaded his fingers into her hair.

Savoring the warm fragrance of her hair through the linen, he pressed his lips to her temple. He felt her breath upon his cheek. His mouth brushed hers. She did not turn away. Kol had never experienced such an intense, yet bittersweet pleasure. His body thrummed in reaction to her gentle capitulation.

Unable to resist, he drew the cloth aside. Blood rushed to his head. Soft lips pressed against the corner of his lips.

Too sweet. Too intoxicating.

He exhaled raggedly and lowered the linen between them. "*Nei*, Isabel. I want you too badly, and fear, too greatly, you do not want me at all."

When he sat up, she arose onto one elbow, her eyes bright and dismayed.

He murmured, "None of this matters. Not in the end. Sleep." He stood, pulled on his jerkin, and caught up his scabbard. Stepping into the courtyard, he traversed the slough toward a cluster of his warriors.

Soon, the cold and numbness returned, and he was glad to think clearly once again.

Chapter 12

Though a sea of men surrounded her, she felt utterly alone.

Isabel guided her mare up the rocky path, just behind Vekell. Since the night before, Kol had eschewed her company. How thankful she was for that. Shame flushed her cheeks, a constant reminder of how firelight had combined with loneliness to make her see a man, and a connection, that did not exist. An illusion of the night. But in the daylight she saw her plight with the utmost clarity.

She was a Norsexian princess, held prisoner by a mercenary warlord, one who very likely had taken her innocence two years before. One who presently hunted her brother with an all-consuming desire to kill him. How had she, in her childish yearnings, allowed herself to forget those things for even a moment?

The group she rode amongst broke from the forest onto the mountain road, and joined the large contingent of Danish foot soldiers she had not seen since departing Calldarington the day before. The cadence of the warriors' footfalls echoed off the high jagged cliffs, steady as an un-troubled heart.

Did she witness a march into battle? Why else, Isabel marveled, would such a force be assembled? Fear trickled down her spine. *Had Ranulf been found?*

One thing she knew—they approached Lothair's Ravine.

Her mare staggered against the force of the wind. Though again, she had begrudgingly worn the Dane's fur-trimmed cloak, it did little to smother the cold. In furtive gusts, it crept beneath her hem. Despite the way she'd twisted her hands in her sleeves, her hands had gone numb.

Lothair's Ravine marked the western boundary of Ran-ulf's kingdom. As children, she and her half siblings had visited the marvel with their father. They had sat upon its rocky edge, dropping pebbles and ash twigs into the fath-omless depths. Aldrith had warned them away, claiming the chasm had no bottom. If they fell into the darkness, he'd intoned, they would find themselves in the burning lands of the ogres.

Neither she nor the others had been brave enough to test the truth, although now, she wondered if ogres might be better company than Danes. Especially the tall, dark Dane with whom she had humiliated herself by kissing the night before.

Remembering the shining face of her childhood brother, she wondered, where was he now? She scoured the weather-beaten crags, as if she might discern, by mere will, where he and his surviving officers hid, planning their countermeasures. The alternative was unthinkable. She thought it anyway.

Was he dead?

Wind gusted into her face. Her eyes watered. Her hands gripped the reins.

No. That was not a possibility. Not only was her brother a strong ruler, he was a clever warrior and strategian. He would not fall so easily. Truly, he would be a fearsome match for the Dane. Which is why she still did not understand his disappearance from the battlefield. Ranulf was no coward.

His egress must have been part of a plan. One that, despite leaving her and Rowena behind, would work for the larger good of the kingdom. Perhaps even now, beside some burning hearth, Ranulf united warring rulers into a united front.

Yes, benevolent Lord, she whispered silently. Let that be so.

Since birth, Ranulf had been her protector, a younger mirror of their father. Not only her protector, but the protector of his people. And that role had not come to an end, Isabel assured herself.

Inside her an even greater fear resurfaced. The noble dynasties of the isle were hewn of treachery and blood. Without her brother's protection, she continued to fear for Godric's life. She prayed the Dane's promises were true, and that her child would be safe within the abbey. Her whispered appeals were lost to the wind.

As they neared the crevice, the contingent of warriors she rode among drew aside into a sheltered alcove of rock. Vekell indicated with extended arm she should do the same. Thankful to escape the sharp wind, she sidled up against a steep wall.

All around, curiously, foot soldiers tugged off their boots. To Isabel's horror, their disrobement did not end there. Fur vests and woolen tunics were discarded to reveal naked torsos. She gasped and turned her cheek as braies, too, dropped to the ground.

"You have naught to fear."

Isabel looked up sharply. Kol sat atop his monstrous black animal, reins in hand.

In that instant, Isabel's greatest fear was that he would remove *his* clothing as well.

One furtive glance revealed the warriors had once again donned only their rough fur vests, which barely concealed their chests and loins. Her eyes settled on Kol's shoulders and arms, so completely covered in protective leather and mail. Her mouth went dry. That first night she had seen him almost naked, without his tunic. Even now, the image remained emblazoned in her mind. The hard flex of his muscles and the perfection of his male form defied the scars which marred his skin. She averted her gaze.

Clearly her mind had already settled upon his innocence if it allowed her such musings. Could she allow herself that belief? To condemn someone else. A faceless, unknown Saxon. She looked up, but found him already gone.

Vekell remained clothed beside her. "Your reins, my lady."

He extended a hand. Bemused, she gave them over.

Vekell smiled. "Try to appear distressed."

"Distressed?" She narrowed her gaze upon him. "I am surrounded by a hundred naked barbarians. Do I not already appear sufficiently distressed?"

"*Nei*, a bit more emotion is required, I think." When her expression remained unchanged, he lifted his hand and, with two fingers, pinched the air. Wearing a knave's smile, he threatened, "Perhaps a pinch to your bottom would help?"

Isabel scowled. "You would not dare."

"One day you will adore me, Princess. That I vow." With a chuckle, he led her mount forward, away from the protection of the crag. She clutched the pommel with both hands, unhappy with her lack of control over her mare, and the situation at hand, for she sensed something momentous was about to happen. Excitement charged the air, raising the hairs on the back of her neck.

Surrounded by more half-naked men than she could count, she and Vekell joined a group of mounted soldiers and climbed the final incline to the chasm. All about her she searched. She did not see Kol.

No trees provided a haven from the wind. Only a barren expanse of rocks spread beneath them. Unprotected, Isabel's hair flew free and wild. Across the abyss, she saw movement. Color.

The banner of Osbeorht, ruler of Northumbria.

Though she did not see Osbeorht himself, she spied his regional ealdorman, Thrydwolf. The man sat atop a horse, sheathed in armor. On either side of him spread Northumbrian soldiers, some mounted, most on foot. Many held white shields, indicating their leader's desire for a peaceful exchange.

Isabel turned to Vekell and spoke against the wind. "If I have been ransomed, I will not go."

"No?" Although he shouted, his words were nearly swept away.

"Not without my son."

He leaned from his saddle, closer. "Do not concern yourself." Tugging her reins, he drew her forward, where she would be more visible to the Northumbrians. "My lord would never make such an agreement."

At that moment the wind began to howl at a terrible pitch.

Then Isabel realized 'twas not the wind she heard at all. Her skin turned to gooseflesh. All about her, naked soldiers seethed and shouted. They snapped their teeth and tore at their hair. Some howled like wolves.

Like animals.

The Danish throng, so recently a highly disciplined force, parted down the center, and out from the midst rode Thorleksson. Though a helm covered his face, she knew it was he.

Isabel looked at the Northumbrians. They lined the opposite side of the chasm and she saw a shudder ripple through the army. Thrydwolf, the coward, dropped his sword. The surrounding crags echoed with the humiliating clash of metal and stone. Her attention returned to Kol, trying to see him as he must appear through Northumbrian eyes.

She understood their terror.

He looked like some thing escaped from a nightmare. For a moment there was absolute silence on either side of the ravine.

A blackened helm eclipsed his face. Atop the skull-plate were fashioned two sharp-tipped ears—or horns—she knew not which. The chin piece narrowed to a point. The mask gave him the appearance of a demon, sprung straight from Hell. From his body swung chain mail and furs. With his advance, the air brimmed with the shouts and exclamations of his army. Isabel gasped and sought to calm her mare as several soldiers threw themselves prostrate beneath him, as if in worship. Or sacrifice.

Here were the barbarians of Lindisfarne.

Kol's steed did not misstep once. Vapor curled from his nostrils. He trod over each of the men, his sharp, metal-encased hooves never touching flesh.

Kol rode to the edge of the ravine, a spiked mace clutched low, beside his thigh. He bristled with easy arrogance, a barely harnessed wildness. A man in complete control of a hell-borne army of barbarians.

Suddenly he rode away. His men shrank back, like a ripple of brackish water. Then, turning back to the Northumbrians, he dug his heels into the steed's side. The beast galloped toward the ravine. A scream rose in Isabel's throat. She pressed a hand across her mouth, smothering its escape.

Man and beast sailed across the chasm with otherworldly ease. The horse landed, his muscular haunches bunching with effort. The metallic hiss of chain mail echoed off the stone as did the low guttural grunt of satisfaction from deep within the steed's throat.

A score of mounted Danes followed over the chasm on the backs of their powerful animals. Those unclothed soldiers acting the part of berserkers raced toward the edge as well, as if to attempt the impossible leap in mindless fealty to their liege lord, but were pulled back by their comrades. They snarled and frothed at the mouth like rabid beasts who had scented blood on the air.

Unrest beset the Northumbrian lines. Isabel spied several men lying in heaps on the stone plateau, fainted from mortal fear. Of those brave enough to remain standing, most fell back a step or two when the Danish leader and his warriors moved past.

Kol did not move forward to speak directly to Thrydwolf. Instead, one of his legions approached the king's emissary, feigning the role of translator, she supposed. Isabel could not hear what words were spoken, but all eyes turned toward where she sat.

Vekell murmured, "Make no move but to breathe."

He led her closer to the edge, where she would be most visible to the Northumbrians. For a moment, terrifying images flashed through Isabel's mind. Herself being cast into the ravine, a sacrifice to ravenous, pagan gods.

Beneath his layers of protection, Thrydwolf nodded. Several Northumbrian soldiers brought forth a coffer the size of a small cow, and opened it for Thorleksson's perusal.

Isabel bristled.

Vekell anticipated her question. "'Tis no ransom, my lady."

Nay, Isabel realized. 'Twas payment made by Osbeorht, to ensure the protection of his kingdom from the Danes. At least for a time. Without the help of allies, how would Ranulf regain control of Norsex?

"Cowards!" The accusation burst from her lips. The word reverberated off the stone, and seemed to swirl into the wind. All eyes shifted to her, including the fathomless

gaze behind the mask. Vekell shushed her, but smiled.
Laughter arose from the Danish horde but there was only
silence from the Northumbrians.

Two mounted Danes hoisted the coffer and carried it
between them. They rode in a wide arc, picking up pace,
and leapt in tandem over the chasm. Kol crossed next, followed by the remainder of his men.

The armies diverged. Each withdrew from the naked,
unprotected stone where they had met, into the forest
lands. With a stiff wave of Kol's hand, Danish patrols set
off in either direction to maintain the integrity of the Norsexian border.

Isabel found herself again riding in Kol's party.

She felt numb, as if she had been forced to watch an execution. For an execution it was. Ranulf's chances of a
successful counterattack against the Danes had been
soundly undermined.

All along the Dane had planned this. He had kissed her
last eventide and wiped her tears, knowing that on the
morn he would destroy her world.

She did not need counsel to understand there would be
no heroic rescue of Norsex by a combined English force.
Ranulf had not been on good terms with Osbeorht, but she
had not expected this. A complete abandonment, with a
payment of riches made for good measure. Osbeorht had
turned his back on Ranulf.

All around her echoed the laughter and jibes of the
Danes. They had terrified the Northumbrians with their
false portrayal of a berserker army, and had gained consid-
erable wealth as a result.

She shared her brother's humiliation. This day, Ranulf
had been outmaneuvered by a man who assumed whatever
role suited his current purposes with ease. Is that what he
had sought to do with her last night? To woo her into believing his innocence?

But for what purpose? For the spiteful joy of watching her believe?

Her eyes pinpointed on the back of his head, their aim as true as a finely tipped arrow. He rode near the front of the army, having cast off his demonic garb. Now he simply looked like a man. In profile, she witnessed for the first time, his smile, his laughter, and fought against a begrudging admiration. All about him his men basked in his pleasure, like hounds circling at their master's feet.

Vekell cantered alongside him. The wind carried his words to her ears. "Thorleksson, I have ordered the men to search the nearby areas. If Ranulf is here, we shall find him."

Silently Kol nodded his assent. All around, Danes delved into the forest. Others set off into the rocky bluffs. Like insects foraging for sustenance, they wove in and out of the cliffs, exploring caves and crevices for signs of her brother and his surviving legion.

Isabel assured herself her brother would not be so easy to find. Perhaps he or his men had rested in these caves, but they would not have remained so vulnerable to capture. Aiken had been an exception because of his injuries.

Until well after noonday, she continued the descent along with the others, but after a time came the low signal of a horn. Isabel searched the white bluffs for the source of the sound. Soldiers dotted a rocky plateau and beckoned to their leader.

Kol guided his animal alongside her. "Your mare cannot make the climb."

Stiffly, she allowed him to draw her between his thighs, but only because her curiosity would not allow otherwise. What awaited them at the top of the cliff?

He spurred his animal up the slope. Earth and stone crumbled beneath the steed's hooves to tumble down behind them. Following the lead of his men, they arrived at a cave. Without a word, Kol dismounted and followed a soldier who carried a torch, into the black hole. She remained behind with several other men.

What secrets did the cave hold? Perhaps she was wrong, and it was her half brother, her king. How that thought tortured her. She dismounted. A young warrior moved toward her, clearly unsure whether she should be allowed to enter. She veered past him to delve inside.

Winter light provided dim illumination through several holes in the ceiling. Along the walls there were provisions. Tightly bound furs, bedrolls and earthen flasks. Neat stacks of firewood. Even several crude bed frames. Though at first her heart leapt, believing this might be a hiding place for her brother, upon closer look, she saw dust covered everything.

She had never been here, but she knew about this place. Years before, when Thorleksson had made his first appearance at Calldarington, the burh had descended into a frenzy of terror, certain that waves of barbarians lurked just beyond the horizon, waiting to attack. All through the spring and summer, watch posts had been manned along Norsex's high ridge wall, so the signal could be raised when the first Norse ships were sighted.

Caves such as this one had been prepared as hiding places for entire families, and provisioned for several weeks—because the Northmen never stayed. They came, they plundered, and then they left.

But not Kol. Isabel knew he would not leave until he had shed the blood of Norsex's king. Either that, or he would die trying.

That moment, he appeared out of the darkness, his hands raised to ward her away. "You do not want to see."

"What is it?" Fear sluiced through her. She tried to look around him, but saw only a black void.

"One of your Saxon warriors." He bent, so as not to strike his head on the low ceiling of the cavern. "He is

dead. Most likely he escaped after the battle and succumbed to his wounds."

"Let me see him." Isabel attempted to sidestep him.

He blocked her. "'Tis not Ranulf."

Shadows hid his eyes. Would he lie to her about such a
thing?

"I remember your brother's face. Clearly." He reaf-
firmed, "'Tis not your king."

Isabel said nothing.

He withdrew. "The body will be removed and taken to
the burh so his family can claim him for burial."

Isabel nodded. To the mouth of the cave she returned.
There, wind tugged the folds of the doubled cloaks she
wore and sidled beneath to chill her to the bone. She
rubbed her arms, and wondered if she would ever be warm
again.

Soon the warrior's body was brought forth, wrapped in
cloth. Two soldiers lifted the corpse atop a horse and began
the descent to the burh. She could not help but wonder,
with heavy heart, if Aiken, too, had passed from this life.

Behind her, Kol gave instructions to the remaining warriors to continue their search. Isabel stared out of the cave
as the men mounted. Snow fell from the gray sky.

Do not leave me here with him. Too quickly the sound
of their hoof clatter faded to nothingness.

She tried to ignore the dark presence behind her by staring out over the valley. Darker clouds rolled in from the
ocean, but beneath that dark canopy, Norsex appeared at
peace. Soon, spring would unfold over the earth. Nature
still kept her course, despite human misery.

She closed her eyes, and heard only the sound of Kol's
battle steed foraging nearby.

Finally, when she could suffer no more silence, she
spoke.

"We ought return to the keep. Even if the storm does not

come this far inland, soon twilight will fall, and the descent will become more difficult."

"I think not," he answered quietly.

Isabel turned. Kol stood very near, close enough to touch her, if he so wished. She exerted every effort to keep her voice steady. "But the snow will soon turn to ice."

He did not move. Instead, his eyes persisted with their unnerving steadiness upon her face. "'Tis time you and I ended this thing between us."

Feeling trapped, she backed away, out of the cavern. "There is *nothing* between us."

Snow whirled about her. The wind bore in from the ocean, and flowed across the plateau, singing its tones like a low, sad, lute song.

"Aye, 'tis what I told myself." He followed the few steps, slow of pace, but remained within the cavern. His gaze demanding everything from her. "I have wanted to condemn you, as you have sought to condemn me, but to no avail."

Isabel raised one arm, as if to fend off his words. "I cannot offer acceptance to a man who seeks to murder my king and destroy everything meaningful to me and my son."

He scowled at her upraised hand as if it offended him. "Can you not confess there are feelings between us which have naught to do with Ranulf? Can you not set him aside for even a moment, and acknowledge the truth?"

She saw the flame in his eyes, and as forbidden as such a response was—she felt one spark within her. "As you yourself said last eventide, none of this matters. Not in the end."

"I was wrong. You matter to me."

She inhaled, unsteadily. "Do I matter more than your quest for vengeance against Ranulf?" Would she sacrifice herself to aid her brother? Even she did not know for sure.

He hissed, and looked to the ground. Again, he raised

his eyes to hers. "What matters to me most, at this moment, is that you know I did not steal your innocence." His dark hair merged with the darkness of the cavern behind him. Though he stood his ground, and did not pursue her, she saw the tension roil beneath the surface of him. "I would hear of my innocence from your lips."

Wind shoved at her back, as if compelling her toward him, but she braced against it. "How can I trust in you, the man who seeks to lay waste to my entire world, and the world of my son?" She turned from him, her intent to escape into the whirling expanse of snow.

"Do not turn from me."

She felt the snag of her cloak, as he caught her, and tugged her back, into the cradle of his arm. She stared up into Kol's face, which remained tight at the lips, and square of jaw.

He said, "Stop running away."

She cried out softly when he pressed his lips to hers. Against her mouth he whispered, "You know the truth. I see that in your eyes." Soul-deep earnestness roughened his voice. "I did not hurt you. Would never hurt you."

With a shove, Isabel broke free. To wholly believe in Kol's innocence would be to betray everything in her life which had meaning. Her past, present, and future.

"You may remain here if you like," she said in a quavering voice. "I shall return to the burh."

He called from behind. "Isab—"

A loud crack split the air, followed by a swift, sucking sound.

Thud.

Isabel froze. She waited for the sound of his footsteps. His voice. She heard nothing but the sway and creak of the trees.

The wind strove to tear her veil away. She balled her hand into the cloth, and held it at her throat. She turned, to find Kol supine upon the ground.

She stared at the bottom of his boots. The cavern's shadows engulfed him from the waist up. She crept toward him. Only then did she see the chunk of ice which lay beside his shoulders, as large as a meat trencher.

"Art thou . . . dead?" she whispered.

He did not answer. Of course, he wouldn't if he were dead.

Her heart pled, a bit more strongly than she wished: *please no*. Yet her Norsexian-princess-mind swarmed with the possibilities of the moment. She bent down and touched her fingertips to his throat. Beneath warm skin, a pulse throbbed steadily.

Relief clashed with disappointment.

She should leave him, and flee to Ranulf's side, where her loyalties would no longer be tested. She stared at his closed eyes, at the dark lashes which lay against his cheeks, as if he slept the soundest of sleeps.

Yet, if he awakened, would he punish Godric for her escape? She bit her lip, and looked toward Morke, who stamped nearby in the snow.

She clasped her eyes shut and summoned a vision of the Dane as he had appeared at the edge of the chasm, his face concealed by the blackened mask, the mace clutched ready in his fist. She reminded herself *that* was the man with whom she battled.

She would do what she had to do.

She extended her hand to the horse. "Here, boy."

Chapter 13

His head. How it ached.

Kol peered through slitted eyelids. Above him, a low ceiling of uneven stone wavered orange and black. He attempted to roll to his side. Furs rustled. His arms—his legs—

Were bound.

Bound hand and foot, to a crude wooden frame. With a growl, he tested his bonds. Thin leather straps bit into his skin. *Nei*, not just straps. 'Twas the leather girdle the princess had worn at her waist when he'd seen her last.

He eyed his bonds.

Where was she? With a flex of his abdomen, he wrenched sideways. Beneath him a rope bed creaked. A small fire burned an arm's length away. Ice rimmed a smoke hole overhead. Melted by the fire's warmth, it dripped through the cavern ceiling, to fizzle and spit in the flames.

He peered over the makeshift hearth, outward.

Snow-hazed darkness glared at him from the mouth of

the cave like the cataract-blinded eye of an old man. Night had fallen. Just then the princess entered his line of vision.

"Come along," she murmured.

She tugged Morke's reins, and the steed followed, a large cluster of spindly underbrush in tow. With this, the princess concealed the mouth of the cave. Turning, she fastened his animal to one of the sturdier limbs, covered his back with a blanket, and moved inside.

Bending so as not to strike her head on the low ceiling of the cave, she drew nearer.

"Why have I been bound?" Against his bonds he flexed. Dizziness plagued him. Beneath him, the ropes complained.

She did not answer, but knelt beside the bed. Snow glistened against her dark hair. For the first time he saw his sword on the ground beside her. With both hands she lifted it, and stared into the blade as if it were a looking glass.

Kol swallowed.

She barely managed to hold it aloft. Her arms trembled with its weight. Shadows mottled the delicate skin beneath her eyes. When had she last slept? Beneath his cloak, the one she still wore, he saw the mud-crusted hem of her tunic.

Mud from yesterday morn, when he'd dragged her into the mire of a winter road. A sphere of images revolved inside his mind, remembrances of the way he'd treated her that day. He had taken her child. Today he had ensured her brother would have no military support from his neighboring kings.

All were worthy reasons to find himself bound.

Regardless, he would not abide captivity, the foremost reason being that he cared not for the way she looked at the blade.

Her brow furrowed. Relief ebbed through him as she lowered the sword, though he flinched at its metallic crunch as she lay it upon the earth. Were she not so careless with his weapon!

He held his tongue. Clearly, *now* was not the time for chastisement.

Shallow, quavering breaths left her lips. Condensation misted the air between them.

He asked, "How did I come to be here?"

"That chunk of ice fell on your head." She pointed to a glistening mound near the entrance. "After that, your horse was of great assistance."

Hoof marks dented the earth. He saw the impression where he'd been dragged across the floor. He glared at Morke. Cursed animal. After all the battles they'd survived together. Betrayed for a woman with a soft voice and a persuasive way. She'd not even had an apple to offer as a favor.

A wide plank lay nearby, one she'd likely used to roll him onto the low bed where he now lay.

He spoke in a low voice. "You are ill at ease, which makes me ill at ease. What do you intend?"

Ignoring him, she lifted a dagger, one that had previously been sheathed on his calf. The narrow blade glimmered in the firelight. Slender fingers gripped the hilt, tested its weight. 'Twas not the first time he'd seen her with a blade in her hand, but this time, leather bound his arms and legs, and he found the effect not so beguiling.

He would not remain silent while she decided which part of him to carve.

"Isabel."

He tried to sit, but his bonds held him too closely to the rack and left him no better than a turtle, flipped on its back.

More strongly he urged, "Look at me."

She shook her head. Avoided his eyes. "Please be silent. I shall not listen to you anymore."

Outside, the winter wind wailed and moaned like a

lamenting widow. Isabel leaned toward him, across his midriff. She tugged the furs down his chest.

Cold air touched his bare skin. His scalp shrank upon his skull. She had managed to strip him of not only his mail shirt, but his jerkin and tunic.

All about, the shadows danced and whispered, rubbing their palms together in glee. *Soon to be forgotten.*

"Let us begin." Isabel's voice rang shrill. He saw the rapid blink of her lashes, her deep swallow. "No need to draw this out."

"I bid you, look me in the eye and tell me what you intend."

"You no longer issue the commands. I do." Still, she did not meet his eyes. "And I command you to be silent."

"I did not take your innocence, Isabel." He fisted his hands around his bonds. "I swear to you, Godric is not my son."

Now she did look to him. Her eyes glittered, two vivid jewels of color in an otherwise alabaster face. "Why do you persist in the belief I do not know what you did that afternoon beside the river. I may not remember, but there is proof enough." The hollowness of her tone did not reduce its force.

"Proof?"

"He looks just like you," she snapped.

"Look at yourself. Clearly he takes after you, his mother. Jesu! Your hair is as dark as mine own."

Kol's hands grew icy cold. No longer did he feel the bite of leather into his skin. How could he make her believe the truth?

"Prithee, look at me." He tried to gentle his tone, but 'twas difficult, given the precariousness of the moment. If only she would meet his gaze. With or without her full attention, he would say what he had to say.

"I pulled you from the river and took you to the burh.

There I was captured and you and I both were taken into the keep. *That is all.* Naught else occurred between us."

Clearly his words meant nothing, for she leaned forward and, with another yank, cast the fur off his body. The pelt dangled from the tip of his boot. She drew back, and as she did so, her hair trailed across his chest, teasing him with its scent—something he found seductive even amidst his perilous circumstance. He fought a sudden stab of desire.

Like him, Isabel loved and hated fiercely, and found very little middling ground. What would it be like to have the devotion of such a woman?

"Saved my life," she muttered. This time when she met his gaze, tears rimmed her lashes. "Only to ruin it." She wiped her eyes. "Not that Godric ruined my life. He is my greatest joy, but that does not absolve what you did to me."

"Another man did this to you. Not me."

Again, she leaned forward, but this time to glare into his eyes. Her breath feathered against his lips. "No, *you did.* You took my honor, my maidenhood. My choice."

She waved the dagger in his face, so close he could taste its metallic tang. "There hath been no other man."

"There must have been."

"I shall listen to no more of your lies. You, of all people, understand the importance of retribution. Now I shall have mine."

Isabel grasped the dagger. Despite the cold, her palms grew damp against the ivory.

Between gritted teeth, the Dane spoke. "Godric cannot be my son. Would that he were, for he is the finest boy I have ever seen, but he is not."

Isabel's nostrils flared, impatient to be done with the unpleasant task. "Waste not your breath. Now is not the time for flattery."

"You do not understand." The fine line of his teeth clenched together, tight as a huntsman's snare. "I would . . . consider it God's blessing if he were my son, not by force . . . but—" Breath escaped his nose in heavy gusts. He muttered, "Blessed Lord, give me the words."

With both hands she gripped the dagger. "'Tis difficult to lie to a woman intent on your execution, is it not?"

"I tell no lies!" The words grated from deep within his chest.

Frowning again, Isabel shook her head. Why did she feel so sickened each time she looked in his eyes? Surely the earnestness she believed she saw, deep within that blue gaze, was feigned. How much more evidence of his skill with allurement and deceit did she require?

She would not waste this chance. With trembling hand she reached out and touched his chest, in the exact place where she knew she had to plunge the dagger. His heart beat wildly beneath her palm. She snatched her hand away.

How could she take anyone's life? Even his? She swallowed her fear, and licked away the perspiration that dappled her upper lip.

By killing Kol, she spared her people the tyranny of a foreign conqueror. She gained revenge for the deaths of their sons and fathers. Revenge for herself, and her king. *Remember that.* She lifted the blade.

He thrashed in an effort to break free of his bindings. "I did not father your son. 'Tis not possible!" His abdomen flexed, a plane of smooth, highly formed muscle. The legs of the cot thudded against the earthen floor.

Braving his fury, Isabel raised up on her knees and lifted the blade.

"Will you not listen?" His voice broke. "Why must I say it? I am *gelda*."

Isabel froze, hearing the word, but did not lower the dagger.

"*Gelda*," she repeated.

"I have never sired a child, and I never will." His lip curled with the effort of speaking the words. Not in distaste, she realized, but in abject shame. "'Tis my curse. 'Tis my destiny."

His eyes reflected fury, and to her shock, the sheen of tears. His skin darkened, as if what he spoke brought him great humiliation. He groaned, and lay back, his face averted.

Something inside her foundered. She clenched the dagger, unwilling to relinquish its power.

She whispered, "You would say anything to stop me."

"'Tis the truth," he murmured in a tight voice. "I am accursed, *heljar-karl*, one doomed to die. And I will die forgotten, with no sons to immortalize my name."

Isabel remembered Vekell's revelation that his lord prayed for death. "In the great hall the skald sang of how your mother cursed you. Is this how you came to be . . . *heljar-karl*?"

She barely heard his whisper. "Aye, 'tis."

Isabel renewed her grip upon the dagger. "What a horrible soul you must be, to be cursed by your own mother."

As if some half-healed wound had been torn open, he turned his head and glowered at her. His arms strained against his bonds. Isabel feared he would break free. She scrambled back to press against the stone wall.

His muscular chest rose and fell with the effort of his breath. His voice bounded off the stone. "She cursed me for the simple act of being born."

"Surely not."

His eyes burned into hers. "She despised me because of who my father was, and what he did to her, a helpless slave, against her will."

Isabel thought of her own Godric. She loved him, regardless of who his father was, or how his birth had come to be.

The hilt of the dagger grew sweaty against her palm. "A child is not responsible for the actions of its father."

"My mother believed otherwise. When I was born she

bade the midwife cast me into the snow so I would die."
His jaw twitched. "Vekell found me. He spared my life.
From that moment on I lived in the warrior's longhouse."

"She cursed you as a babe?" How could it be that she
felt pity for him? Yet she did.

"*Nei*, her death curses came later, when I had passed
some twelve winters on the earth. Before that time, no matter how often our paths crossed, she never offered me so
much as a simple greeting."

"What happened, that she would curse you after so
much time had passed?"

He did not answer for a long moment. "As a boy I
revered my sire. After his murder by a neighboring jarl, I
led his warriors to avenge his death. The night our war-
band returned to the village, my mother lured me with tender words, away from the feast . . . only to spew vile
incantations over my head. She died the following summer, mad and alone. Yet through her curses, her evil lives
on in me."

Isabel sat silent.

"Even so, I would never"—his lip curled as if speaking
the words disgusted him—"*force* myself on any woman,
for I have seen the misery it brings. I have lived it."

Isabel pressed her fingertips against trembling lips.
"How can I believe you? If you are not Godric's father—"

Then who is?

In that instant Kol's eyes crucified her. "Then force the
blade through my heart. If I am guilty of what you accuse,
I deserve no less." Slowly he turned his head to stare at the
ceiling of the cavern. "Do it and go. Let me die in peace."

Isabel looked at him, and then at the dagger in her
hands. She closed her eyes, and for the first time, *tried* to
push past the walls that protected her from the horrible
things that had occurred on that day. No memory revealed
itself to her.

There were only raindrops.

His voice.

Stúlka litla.

And peace.

Isabel's eyes flew open, and she stared, through tears, at the innocent man she had almost killed.

In her room at Calldarington, she had a trunk. In the bottom of the trunk, covered by layers of blankets and clothing, she kept a small wooden box. A box which still held a single remnant of the tunic she had worn, stained by his blood.

Her heart had proclaimed his innocence then. Her heart proclaimed it now.

Blameless. He had been blameless from the start. His punishment in her brother's pit had been unwarranted. Her hatred of him, undeserved.

Isabel's broken sigh reverberated through the cavern. She crawled forward. Kol turned his face to her. Confusion softened his features. With shaking hands she cut the bindings from his wrists. She sidled down to where his feet hung over the frame, and slashed the leather cord.

Upon open and upturned palms, she offered the dagger to him. The frame creaked as he sat up. She bowed her head to await his wrath.

Chapter 14

Kol took the dagger from Isabel's hands. He rubbed the sore places on his wrists, and assessed the lump on his head. "Do not bow your head to me, Princess. 'Tis not in your nature. Look up and meet my eyes."

"I cannot." She shook her head. Yet in the next moment, she did look up. The sight of her eyes, wide and unguarded, stole his breath.

"I have wronged you. I almost killed you."

"And yet, you did not." Kol took up the dagger's leather sheath from the earthen floor. He slid the blade inside, and secured it inside his boot. "Why?"

Her face wavered between despair and relief. "For the same reason I freed you from the pit two winters ago. You did nothing wrong."

Kol's heart thundered in his chest. At last, she realized the truth. Elation filled him. Yet Isabel appeared ill. Chills passed through her body. Cold illuminated her skin.

He reached for the pelt, which lay at his feet. "You tremble."

"I am afraid."

Kol wrapped the fur about her. Through some miracle, Isabel had been returned to him. The girl who had spared his life, and treated him with such compassion. Now, he wanted nothing more than to protect her. "Whatever you fear, do not fear me."

She did not pull away from him. Instead she looked up and touched his cheek. With solemn conviction, she whispered, "I no longer do."

He could not believe she allowed the intimacy of his arms around her. A soul-deep contentment spread through him at the feel of her against his chest, growing warmer with each passing moment.

After a time, she whispered, "I am so weary."

"Then close your eyes, Isabel, and sleep."

She turned her face against his shoulder. Her breath touched his naked skin. Eventually, her breathing slowed and her body went pliant. His head ached, and he longed to lie down. Yet he dared not move, lest she awaken.

Though the fire dwindled, he made no effort to put her aside and tend to it. For now, the fire in his chest burned hot enough to warm them both.

Isabel awakened to the feel of soft fur against her cheek, and the heat of a man beside her. Naturally, 'twould be a necessity for them to share warmth, given the frigidity of the night. The fire burned very close to where they lay, but her breath still formed vapor. She tugged the fur over her nose, and shifted ever so slightly to take greater advantage of his closeness.

He exhaled slightly. Surely he slept. But whatever weariness had claimed Isabel had ceased to exist. She felt awakened to her very bones. Inside, she buzzed with a peculiar sort of excitement; one she could only attribute to the man who lay beside her. An innocent and noble man. A man who had fascinated a young woman not so long ago.

She remained very still, not wanting to awaken him. She savored the sensation of being close to a man whose presence pleased her beyond explanation. Though she remained clothed in gunna and kirtle, she felt the hard press of his legs against the back of her thighs. His muscled stomach against her bottom.

If he were asleep, she would be able to take her fill of his features without embarrassment, and without the suspicion that had tainted her image of him for so long. Slowly, she turned to look.

And discovered his eyes fixed upon her.

"Return to your sleep," he said. " 'Tis not yet morning."

"You . . . do not sleep?"

"Nei, Isabel." He did not take his gaze from her. So close were their faces, she felt his breath on her lips.

"Doth your head pain you?"

"Nei."

"Art thou cold?" she twisted to face him. Instantly she regretted the move, for their bodies no longer touched.

"The opposite, I think."

A flush surged to Isabel's cheeks. She felt the energy that coursed between them. It had always been there, disguised by distrust and fear. Firelight revealed the flex of Kol's neck, the thick sinew of his shoulder. Isabel's shy but curious gaze explored the expanse of his chest. Dark hair dusted his chest, and lower, over the firm grid of his torso. The furs foiled any further curiosity.

Two blunt-tipped fingers lifted her chin. His eyes pierced her through.

"Return to your slumber."

Isabel's insides clenched with an anxious sort of excitement. "Forsooth, I am not sleepy."

Why did she not roll away and close her eyes as he'd

asked? She did not know. She only knew she wanted to be close to him. Perhaps closer than they were now.

He exhaled softly, and ran his palm down her linen-clad arm. Her heartbeat tripped into a clumsy rhythm. Breath hovered in her throat, as he eased his hand even lower beneath the pelts to rest upon her hip.

How he fascinated her. Had always fascinated her, even amidst the turmoil of her hatred. She inhaled, seeking to steady herself, to force herself to act with reason, but an exotic scent radiated from his skin, scattering her thoughts like dust motes on a sunbeam. She placed her hand over his.

He is a stranger.

No, never a stranger, not from the moment she'd looked upward into his rain-haloed face and believed him to be an angel. Her soul had recognized him then. Her soul recognized him now. She would stand beside him and find a way to bring peace between him and Ranulf.

His long fingers wove between hers. With a lowering of his face his lips brushed hers.

"Ah, Isabel," he murmured. His arm banded her waist and pulled her against his body. Isabel reveled in the sensation of his hard body, pressed so solidly against her. Down, over her lower back, he spread his hand. A warrior's muscles striated his chest, crushed her breasts. His hand delved into her hair, cradled her skull, as if she were something precious to him.

As he dipped his head, a lock of his hair fell to brush her cheek. Darkly, his shadow veiled them, even from the inquisitive leap and sway of the firelight. His mouth and tongue teased her lips until she offered entrance and met his bold foray with her own. Before, she had feared his power. Now his prowess and strength only fueled the rapture welling up within her breast.

With a low groan he bit, sucked her bottom lip. The

slightest friction of his hand—the shift and hardness of his thigh against hers—

Each touch kindled flames, low in her belly—a sensation so very kindred to anxiety, but different. Delicious and exquisite. Between her legs she felt tight and heavy, all at once. His mouth descended over the arch of her throat. Sharp teeth grazed her skin. A low sound escaped her to mingle with a growl from deep in his chest. Isabel felt drunk, emboldened. She ran her hands over his skin, molded her body to his. Closer. Ever closer. Pleasure surged with every touch, every taste.

Darkly, paradise beckoned, and she succumbed without remorse, without thought for tomorrow.

Had this hunger always dwelt within her? No. Such ecstasy would not be found with another man. She had always been waiting for Kol. His hand fisted in her kirtle and pushed the cloth upward over her stockings. Her thighs tensed, as across the ties he smoothed his palm, a fleeting dalliance against her naked skin. Isabel clenched her hands in the waist of his braies.

His eyes burned into hers. Several harsh, measured breaths left his lips. "Curse me to Hell. What is this I do?"

Shadow and firelight carved his features, illuminated his high, broad cheekbones and square chin.

"Nothing but what I wish for." The confession brought her no shame. She knew he wanted her with a purity of heart she saw in his eyes. Against her thigh, she held his hand.

His cheeks flushed a darker shade. He shook his head. He withdrew his hand from beneath hers.

"A man ill-used you. And the moment you gift me with one bit of trust, at once I—" He gritted his teeth and sought to draw back. But Isabel caught his face in her hands. Darkly turbulent eyes stared into hers.

"You were not that man."

Fleetingly, Isabel saw him—the lonely child, a boy raised without a mother's love. A boy cast away.

Kol's voice rumbled low in his throat. "I will bring no further harm to you. If you knew—" His face hardened, and the warrior returned. "I have committed many terrible things, and fully intend to commit more."

To Isabel's dismay, he sat up. Furs slid to his hips as he swung his legs over the edge of the cot. How quickly he slipped away.

"Kol—"

Light flickered on his back.

He continued, "Truly, I meant no seduction."

Although she had glimpsed the scars that first night in Ranulf's chamber, she could not silence the gasp. Firelight revealed them to be more deep and abundant than she had believed. Savage proof of one man's anger.

Kol hissed and snatched his tunic from the floor of the cave.

Isabel pushed to her knees. From behind, she embraced him, wrapping her arms around his chest. His body grew hard, like stone. For a moment he did not move, did not even seem to breathe.

Then, he thrust his arms into the tunic, but she grasped his wrists.

"Nay." She molded herself against his back, as if she could fill the jagged gashes with her own body, with the sharing of her soul.

She whispered, "Why would you hide them from me?"

Held in the circle of her arms, he sat altogether still. Unyielding as stone.

"Kol, 'tis not pity I feel."

He made no response.

Slowly she released his wrists, and withdrew her arms from beneath his. She smoothed her palms up, over his lower back, where the scars began their ascent. He flinched, his muscles cording tightly beneath her touch.

"Do not," he gritted. He dropped his tunic to the floor and reached back, as if to halt her perusal. Somehow she knew the only reason he did not turn to confront her was because he could not bring himself to face her. Agony radiated from him. Her heart pounded heavily, suspended by a deep agony of her own.

She knew his scars ran more deeply than those she saw with her eyes.

"I know he hurt you," she murmured. She shunned Ranulf's name. She did not want him here, not now. "And I know that pain was undeserved." Her voice went husky. "I would give anything for it not to have happened."

Gently she displaced his hand, more determined than before.

She said, "I know you have never seen the scars. Not all of them." No looking glass would reflect them clearly. She also knew from endless nights passed alone, in the darkness of night, how horrific the imaginings of the mind could be.

"Perhaps you have seen only these?" Lightly she touched his shoulders, where smaller scars feathered his skin. Unlike the rest.

He did not answer.

"Let me tell you what I see." Unflinchingly, she smoothed a path upward, over the marred skin of his muscled torso. Softly she spoke. "They sweep upward. Boldly."

Toward his shoulders she moved. "And outward, across your shoulders." Impulsively she pressed her lips there. He exhaled sharply and shuddered, as if he could not bear her touch.

"What you imagine in your mind must be horrific." She stopped, resting her palms against him. "But do you know what I see?"

"Isabel," he warned, his voice ragged.

The fire crackled in the silence.

"Wings," she whispered against his skin, against the center of his back. The center of his being. "Angel's wings."

His ragged breath echoed through the chamber.

From over his shoulder, his hand smoothed over the crown of her head. She clasped his hand there, turned her cheek into it.

"I am no angel," he murmured thickly.

"You are my sort of angel." In a low voice she added, "What man without scars could fathom me, Kol, when I have so many of my own?"

He twisted sideways, and dragged her onto his lap.

She felt his lips, the slight bristle of his beard, against her cheek. "The night grows colder."

A thrill raced down her back at the touch of his breath on her skin. Furs, drawn by his hand, warmed her. His closeness intoxicated her. She pressed her face against his neck, inhaled his scent. In wonder, she smoothed her hands over his stomach and chest, savoring the feel of his taut, yet supple skin. His heart beat heavily, in time with her own.

"Isabel." Searching, his mouth found hers. His kiss began gently, then grew hungrily urgent. He gripped her hips. His lips never left hers as his hand descended the length of her thigh, to her calf. Strong fingers banded her ankle. Turned her, guided her to straddle him. Never had she been so intimately close to a man, but it felt right. He dragged her closer.

"This is no game you and I play," he murmured. His hands slid over the surface of her stockings, over her thighs. "If you knew everything—"

She did not care about his past, the things he had done while trying to make sense of the way his world had treated him. They would confront the rest upon the morrow. Together.

"Shhh." She kissed him. "I know all I need to know."

His fingers tugged at the ties of her tunic. Calloused fingers parted the linen, grazed her skin. She remained utterly still, cherishing each touch. Her breasts swelled against the neckline. There, atop the exposed, delicate skin, he drew three fingertips.

Reality grew distant. Isabel gave one long, quavering sigh.

With one final tug of the ties, her breasts spilled into his hands. Wide, toil-roughened palms cupped and squeezed. Need surged through her veins. With her legs, she drew him closer.

His dark head lowered. Anticipation tightened her nipples. Isabel felt his humid breath, and then, blessedly, his warm, wet mouth. His tongue slid over one sensitive crest. With her hands clenched upon his thighs, she arched back, offering herself fully to him. His wide, long-fingered hands descended her rib cage, to her lower back, held her suspended.

From outside the hazy brilliance of her pleasure she felt him grip her waist, and then her buttocks.

"Kol," she gasped, feeling that part of him, leather-encased, hard and rigid against her. A heavy throbbing began *there,* between her legs where they touched.

Passion robbed the moisture from her mouth. Never before had she imagined such pleasure could come from simply being close to a man. All she could think about was how to satisfy the need surging so rampantly inside her.

But she did not know how. "Please."

With gentle pressure, he bunched her kirtle over her thighs. Her stomach fluttered as his hand smoothed downward across its delicate skin to press against her pelvic bone. There, he slipped slowly, deliberately between her legs.

Her legs tensed. Her toes pointed. She moaned.

His touch bespoke a confidence with the female body. Certainly there had been others, Isabel realized. A dark

stab of possessiveness tore through her. But she felt his
hand tremble as he touched her. In some way she affected
him. Perhaps as deeply as he affected her.

Strong fingers grazed against a most sensitive place. A
jolt of pleasure shot through her when, with his thumb, he
coaxed apart her folds.

"I need to be inside you."

"Aye," she whispered. "Anon."

Through his teeth he hissed a breath. "I don't want to
frighten you."

"I'm not afraid." She spoke the truth. "I have no memories. Only the images created by my mind. I want you to
be the one to replace them."

The cave whirled as he laid her upon her back. His
darkness and weight settled over her.

"Are you cold?" he murmured, his face flushed and
beautiful. "I don't want you to be cold."

"No. Not cold."

The musty scent of the furs swirled between them, but
provided warmth beneath her buttocks. Her hands collided
with his in their quest to free him from his braies.

Darkness shadowed their bodies. She looked, but could
not see that part of him which demanded her curiosity. She
grasped his shoulders. Between her parted thighs, he descended, wrapping an arm about her. With his other hand
he took hold of himself.

Arcing his body over her, he slid his shaft between her
legs. She felt swollen there, and excruciatingly sensitive.

Torture. Beautiful, perfect torture.

His hand moved between them. Separated her. She felt
a gentle, pressure. His long fingers. He pushed inside. Unable to contain her reaction, she moved against his hand,
clenched her thighs. Her moan echoed off the stone walls
of the cavern. Such intense, exquisite friction. But somehow lacking.

"Please—" She buried her face against his chest,

ashamed by the consuming power of her need. Slowly he withdrew. Between his thumb and fingertip he squeezed a part of her. A tender, hidden pearl—

"Kol!" Stars burst, blinding her with their light. She arched, and at that same moment, felt his thighs brace her, spread her.

"Look," he rasped. "And see how beautiful it can be between a man and a woman."

She did look. Down, betwixt their bodies, light flickered and revealed his member, a thick mast poised above her parted thighs. She saw her own expectant flesh. Her damp, dark curls.

With his hand he grasped, and guided himself. Isabel stared between her mounded breasts, over her bunched tunic. The sight transfixed her. His swollen tip breached her, then disappeared. There came a pressure. She dug her nails into his skin. Around his waist she clenched her thighs.

He groaned. Inch by inch, he pushed more deeply until he was buried inside her, his body pressed flush against her.

She gasped. Sharply he withdrew, almost his whole length. "Do you see?"

She cried out, gripping his sides, feeling the flex of his muscles. For a scant moment she stared into his burning eyes. Then she looked between them again, at their joining. "Aye."

He thrust into her. The surge of pleasure shocked her, stunned her.

He lowered to suckle her breast. When he drove into her, she cried out, nearly screamed. The bed creaked beneath them. Voices—theirs—echoed off the cavern walls. He grasped her ankles and hooked her legs over the side of the narrow bed, spreading her.

Instinct guided Isabel. She lifted her hips, her thrusts matching his. Their mutual fervor grew. Despite the cold air, perspiration glowed on their skin. Isabel could not close her eyes, could not look away. Furs slid down his powerful back, and firelight revealed the shadowy flex of his abdomen, his hips. How beautiful he was. She felt beautiful as well. Her breasts jostled with each thrust. Her nipples glistened with the moisture of his mouth. And lower. She watched the shadowy slide of his sex deep into her. The sight amazed, intrigued her.

Inside her womb, the pleasure grew, surged outward through her limbs. She sought something more.

"Aye, Isabel. Now." His own movement, his thrusts, heightened in pace.

The night burst into a shattering arc of purple and diamonds and fire. Shimmering. Brilliant. Surreal.

Hurtled through the Heavens, eternity parted and granted her a glimpse of her own immortality, spiraling, swirling upward, but entwined with that of another.

Beautiful. So beautiful she cried out when, in a bright flash she spun downward, back to earth, into the arms of the flesh and blood being who clutched her just as tightly, still pulsing inside her, around her, through her.

Kol held Isabel tightly, too tightly. Afraid she would disappear. He pressed his face into her neck, afraid she would see how badly he needed her. Until now, even he had not known how profound that need would be.

For him, the knowledge he could not beget children had transformed the act of sex into strictly a carnal exorcism of his rage. But what had just occurred between himself and Isabel had seared him deep, to his very soul.

He should have told her. Told her everything. But now—now it was too late.

Chapter 15

Morning's light intruded across the stony threshold of the cavern. Kol took up a twig and prodded the remains of the fire. That which had blazed with flame the night before had cooled to ash with morning's arrival. He discarded the stick and stood.

"We must go." He took up his braies and drew them on, hitching them over his hips. "Else they will come looking."

"Aye." From their bed of furs, Isabel watched him without shame, and with a confidence he did not share. She stretched with feline languor.

In the night she had touched every part of him. Learned and fulfilled his desires as no woman ever had. Even now, as she simply lay her gaze on him, the swirling sensation began low in his belly.

He tugged on one boot, then the other. He deserved Hell for what he had allowed to take place between them — and for the pain he would inflict upon her now. Into the early morning he had lain awake, with her sleeping in his arms.

No matter how strongly he wanted it, their joy could not last. His plan was in motion, and he could do naught to change it. When she learned of it, she would hate him even more than she had before. He touched the bump on his head. Could he blame his utter stupidity on the injury?

They had made love under false pretense. She believed him to have a heart, buried somewhere deep inside his scarred body. For a few hours, he had convinced himself of that lie as well. Yet his desperate hope had been an illusion of the night. An illusion that had disintegrated with the first pale touch of morning.

Anger warred with the longing in his chest. Covetously, he watched Isabel bind her stockings, just above her knees. The hardship of the previous days would leave most women smudged and ragged. Isabel's cheeks flushed with springlike radiance. Her hair gleamed like Eastern silk. If only she could be his.

From beneath the dense protection of her lashes, she looked up and offered a shy smile. She sought his reassurance. 'Twas a shame, he could not give it to her. Bending low, he placed her gunna on the cot beside her, and with it, lay his first blow. His voice as cool as the air about them, he said, "I shall await you outside."

Her smile became—not a smile at all. He turned before she might perceive his regret.

Outside, he knelt upon the snowy earth to examine Morke's fittings. He had only himself to blame for the torment he felt. He'd let her inside his walls. Walls which protected him from the most dangerous of his enemies: hope.

He heard her soft step upon the stone behind him. "'Twould be safer to make the descent on foot. If the animal slipped on the ice—"

"Of course," she agreed in a quiet voice.

He nodded brusquely. "Good."

With a tug of Morke's reins, he set off across the narrow plateau. Her footsteps followed behind, light and quick. 'Twas not long before she placed herself beside him.

"Wilst you send a message to Ranulf once we arrive in Calldarington?"

The mention of Ranulf's name awakened the savage part of him.

"'Twould be difficult when I do not know Ranulf's whereabouts." He stared straight ahead. A sardonic edge whetted his voice. "Perhaps thou dost know?"

Beside him, Isabel stumbled over a low spot in the path. He fought the urge to catch and steady her.

"You know I do not." From beneath the dark fall of her cloak, her slender white hand appeared. She swiped a dark tendril of hair from where it pestered her cheek. "I merely wondered if a messenger would be sent to find him. Perhaps a Norsexian warrior. Someone he trusted."

The hope in her voice sickened him. They had made love, and now, as a result, she fully expected to negotiate a peace between the two men in her life. Simple as that.

He stopped. Behind him, Morke had halted without so much as a command. "And what message would you have me send?"

Wind caught his hair, and blew it back from his face. Isabel turned to him slowly, her face white with realization.

"You still intend to kill him."

She stared. Waited. Kol maintained his passionless guise. Though her misery tore him apart, he could offer her no comfort now.

"Kol!" she cried, then pressed her hands against her lips. She seemed to summon whatever calm she could, before lowering her arms, again, to her sides. "The conflict betwixt the two of you was founded upon a misunderstanding. You realize that now."

The heat of Kol's agitation boiled over. Her words, in effect, negated all he had told her of her father's request for his military alliance. 'Twas as if she outright accused him of lying.

"I have already told you Ranulf's hatred for me doth not exist solely out of concern for you."

"What else is there?" she demanded.

Kol responded with silence.

"Kol, answer me. What else is there? Do not look at me thusly, as if we are strangers. From the first night, you have hinted at villainy in Ranulf which exceeds the punishment he bore upon you in the pit. Yet you have never presented any justification for your accusations."

Kol did, indeed, feel like a stranger, looking at her, and clenching the reins to his horse.

Her short laugh cut him like a blade. "I see. Already you deny me. And so quickly."

Kol spoke what he knew to be the truth. Even if she did not realize it yet. "*Nei.* 'Tis you who will deny me."

He walked away, toward Calldarington.

She shouted at him, "Why would you say that?"

He turned, crushing the shallow crust of snow beneath his heel. "Are you prepared to turn your back on Ranulf?"

"Why would I?" She lifted her hands, imploringly, and stepped toward him. His heart reacted so strongly to her nearness, he had to take several steps back to bolster himself against her pleading eyes and earnest tongue.

Still, she spoke. "Aye, Ranulf's torture of you was wrong. You were innocent. But he punished you because he believed I had been attacked. That is all. There is no more to the story, no intrigue or secret motives."

Kol shook his head. "Your father summoned me, and it was to thwart a threat from within his household. That threat was Ranulf."

"It could not be."

Hostility soured his tone. "That you continue to hold him in such vaulted esteem infuriates me. *Would that you knew the Ranulf I have known.*"

"I cannot believe the Ranulf you conjure even exists. You demonize him to further your conquest." Isabel brushed past him, her eyes trained upon the path they would take.

Kol spat, "You know, he watches you."

Isabel froze. Instantly, an invisible burden seemed to weight her shoulders. Clearly, he had struck some chord within her. "What did you say?" she rasped.

He felt both strengthened and ashamed by the words he continued to speak. He wielded them to hurt her. "Through a hole, in your chamber wall."

Kol shifted his stance, and traded the reins to his other hand, yet he kept his eyes fixed on her, perversely eager for her reaction. In a low voice, he repeated, "He watches you."

Isabel's face lost all emotion.

An uneasy chill scored Kol's spine. He dropped Morke's reins, and tilted his head to stare into her face. Sick at heart, he uttered, "You show no surprise."

Isabel's lips parted, yet no words came forth.

He accused, "You show only shame when confronted with this revelation?"

Isabel could barely catch her breath. She could not speak of this with Kol. Not with *anyone*. Fingers trembling, she pressed the sleeve of her cloak to her mouth.

Kol lunged and grasped her shoulders. "What is there between you and Ranulf? God, Isabel, confess the truth now."

She barely felt the strength of his hold on her. The shock of his words numbed her too greatly. She stared into his eyes, horrified by the disgust she read therein.

All at once he released her, and backed away. Cold and heat washed over her in alternating waves. She could not bear to have him believe something so foul as an incestuous relationship between sister and brother.

"Ranulf is not my brother."

Kol's eyes widened. "What did you say?"

"Ranulf and I share no blood." Isabel clasped her eyes shut. She betrayed Ranulf by speaking the secret aloud, a weight which crashed down like a huge boulder upon her chest.

"Tell me everything." He stepped back, as if distancing himself from not only her, but any emotion he felt toward her. The snow on the ground reflected in his eyes, making them the color of a frozen sea.

Isabel felt feverish. She smoothed cool hands over her cheeks. Somehow the words came.

"When Ranulf's mother came to my father in marriage, she already carried another man's child. 'Twas a secret she held until the day of my half sister, Rowena's, fateful birth. The queen confessed everything to my father before she died."

Kol's features remained hewn of stone. He did not take one step toward her, nor away. Behind him, Calldarington perched on its promontory ledge, distant and uncaring. "Continue."

She took one low, bracing breath. "Ranulf himself did not know of this until he grew to be a young man." She walked toward a nearby tree and leaned against it for support. "One day while hunting, he lost control of our father's favored stallion, and ran it into a narrow ditch. The animal's forelegs were broken. As Father slit the suffering beast's throat, he spoke in anger, and revealed to Ranulf he was no legitimate son."

Kol drew in a low breath, his eyes assessing. "But by all accounts, your father, and even the Witan of Norsex, held Ranulf in high esteem and as duly named heir."

She shrugged. "To my knowledge, the matter was never spoken of again, and remained a secret held between Ranulf and Aldrith. I do not believe my father ever knew Ranulf had revealed the truth to me. Any paternal affection aside, my father sired no more sons. No more male heirs.

'Twas essential Ranulf's claim to the throne remain unquestioned. For all our sakes, even my father's."

Kol's fingers curled against his palms. He shook his head, as if to clear his mind of her words. "That does not make it allowable for him to spy on you through a hole in the wall, with lust in his heart. In the eyes of the Christian church, he is your brother."

Isabel bristled. "I know of no peephole. The door—it has always been there, from the time the upper hall was built by my father. Ranulf has never made use of it. I cannot believe he would be guilty of such a transgression as watching me without my knowledge, yet—"

"Yet what?"

"I confess, as I grew to womanhood, I sensed—" Isabel flinched inwardly, knowing once she said the words, she could never take them back. Still, in some way she felt relieved to say them. She'd had no one to confide in. "I sensed Ranulf's interest. I suppose, I told myself he was simply lonely. You see, long ago 'twas decided Ranulf would not marry. My father survived attempts by the families of both his first wife, and his second wife, my mother, to wrest his throne from him. Ranulf made clear, from the outset of his rule, he would extend no claim to rivals through marriage. Since then, to my knowledge, he hath remained devout, and devoted to his celibacy. If he has taken lovers, I never knew of them."

Kol strode forward to grasp her chin, roughly, forcing her gaze up into his. "Tell me the truth, Isabel, for I will have no more lies between us."

Isabel trembled beneath the onslaught of his continued accusation, one which sickened her, "He never touched me. Never. I would not be able to live with that."

"Why can you not confess it? It becomes all too clear." Kol released her, his eyes agleam with feral heat. "He is the father of your child."

Isabel's stomach turned. "Your accusations disgust me.

Do you believe if that were the truth, I could abide living alongside him in Calldarington? Nay, Ranulf is not the missing piece to my unfortunate puzzle. He would not have committed such a sin against me." She pressed the flat of her palm to her chest, where her heart beat at a troubled pace. "In my heart, I know this to be true."

Kol clenched his hands into fists. "You continue to defend him, knowing his lust for you."

This time, 'twas Isabel who gripped his arm. "His lust for me, if it ever reached such a proportion, was confined to his heart. I swear it. He has been nothing but a brother and king to me, and a protector to my son."

"I cannot fathom this," Kol muttered, pulling away. He strode toward the ledge overlooking Calldarington.

She lifted her hands. "What would you have me do, Kol? I am a princess of this realm who bore a fatherless child, a son with no future but that which his king deems to bestow upon him."

Kol remained silent, his back to her.

"What do you think I should have done? Upon sensing Ranulf's interest—for remember this, he never revealed any desire for me through word or deed, 'twas only a suspicion of mine. A feeling. Should I have taken my son into the forest to live in exile for the rest of our days, eating roots and berries for sustenance?" Her arms fell to her side. "That only happens in children's tales."

He caught up Morke's reins from the ground, and leveled his hard gaze upon her. "I will ask you only once more. Are you willing to turn your back on him?"

"He is not the evil you avow." She pled, "Do not force this choice upon me."

"Are you willing?"

She whispered, "I am not."

Without another word, he moved to descend the ledge.

She called out to him, trailing along behind, "Do you not understand my position in all this? Do you not understand I have trusted you with a secret that could undermine Ranulf's claim to the Norsexian throne?"

Kol held up a hand, but did not slow his steps. "'Tis clear no reasonable discourse will come from this."

In a fit of temper, Isabel kicked her boot into the crusted snow, and sent a clump flying. "Reasonable discourse cannot come from amidst unreasonable accusations."

The remainder of their descent was made in silence. The closer they grew to the burh, the greater Isabel's anxiety grew. Now she had not the loyalty and love of her people, nor of Kol. She had not even her son to return to. And worst of all, she had betrayed the confidence of the man who, despite the underlying tension between them, borne of an unspoken attraction, had never behaved as anything but a brother.

Upon passing through the perimeter Isabel sensed an excitement in the settlement. Smiles lit upon the faces of Kol's men. Warriors dragged large planks piled with trunks and bundles from the harbor, toward the burh.

A Danish officer called to Kol. "My lord! The rear boats arrived this morn."

Kol nodded. "'Tis good. All are safe?"

"Aye, my lord."

Rear boats? Isabel turned to scan the distant harbor. Indeed, a small cluster of Norse vessels dotted the coastline.

"What of the others for whom we await?"

"We have neither seen nor heard word of their approach."

Isabel followed close behind Kol, through the throng of men, until the keep's shadow darkened the ground.

A small multitude clustered upon the stairs. There were so many, their faces unfamiliar to her. Norse women, children, and booming-voiced, ecstatic men. She needed no scholar to advise she witnessed a reunion of warriors with their families. If she understood Kol's mention of "others," there would be more to come.

Many turned to smile and greet their lord as she and Kol drew near. Without a word, Kol handed Morke's reins away, and walked toward the keep. Isabel hovered at the side of the large beast, ankle deep in the mud of the churned-up road. A soldier led Morke away in the direction of the stables.

Truly, she knew not where to go. She felt even more like a stranger to Calldarington than before. What did the appearance of the Norse families mean? Would they depart once their leader's quest for vengeance had been satisfied? Or did they seek to settle here?

She felt betrayed. First, by Kol's attack of words on the hillside, and now this. An influx of foreigners would affect her Saxon people in many ways, great and small.

A male voice spoke from behind. "My lady."

Recognizing the voice of a friend, Isabel turned. Father Janus stood beside the road, on a high, flat piece of earth.

He smiled with relief. "I had hoped to find you well. When you did not return last eventide with the others—" He smiled again, but tightly, and lines etched his forehead.

Isabel walked toward him, arms extended. "I am well, Father. Despite everything. And you?" He grasped her hands.

"As well as the situation allows." He nodded. "The Danes have left our church intact. Fortunately their leader is a believer of our faith."

"Aye. That alone is a blessing." Just the thought of Kol made her chest grow heavy. She glanced toward the hall.

"Last eventide, the Danes summoned me to the pit to minister to Aiken of Leswick."

Isabel clasped her eyes shut and prayed Father Janus would not inform her of the Saxon warrior's death. With unsteady emotions, she asked, "And how doth he fare?"

"When I arrived, the Danish physician had already cleansed and dressed his wounds. God willing, he will live."

" 'Tis good," Isabel sighed with relief.

Father Janus tucked her hand into the crook of his elbow. "I heard dear Godric hath been taken to the abbey?"

"I do not wish to think of it. I believe him to be safe and well tended by the sisters, but what of his future? He is still but a babe, and if Ranulf does not return, who will be his protector?"

"We cannot purge the uncertainty from our lives." Father Janus shook his head. "Perhaps a return to your everyday habit would bring peace to your days. I will say Mass for you now, if only you will come with me to the church?"

Though in the past, Isabel had taken her Mass in the keep's private chapel, she could not bring herself to go there now. Not when she might cross paths with Kol.

"Aye, I will go with you."

Together, she and Father Janus walked the short distance to the church. She nodded at each passerby, thankful for Father Janus's escort, for she still remembered—too vividly—the attack upon her in the streets of Calldarington. Even so, she savored the scents of normalcy about her, for they represented the survival and good health of her people. Roasting meat and baking bread. Evidence that despite the violence and unrest of their times, life continued on.

Father Janus led her up the stairs and pushed open the door. Once inside, he carefully closed and secured the portal behind them.

Isabel looked toward the altar. The last time she had come here, Kol had knelt there. Now the nave was deserted. A sense of peace settled over her, as if the turmoil of the previous days had not touched the protected space between these walls.

Father Janus led her down the center aisle. Though she expected him to don his chasuble, to drape his stole around his shoulders so they could begin, he did not. Instead he drew her to the side of the altar.

At once, Isabel detected a change in the air, as if an unseen force possessed the room about her. One glance at the priest's face told her he felt the presence too. Fear deepened the lines of his brow.

"Wait here," he whispered, as if the words stole his breath.

"What is it?"

"Silence, child. Forgive my impertinence, but please simply wait as I have instructed."

He disappeared into the shadows, but returned almost immediately. But no, Isabel realized. The figure emerging from the darkness was not Father Janus at all.

Chapter 16

Ranulf," she whispered.

For a moment he simply stood, appearing just as astounded by her appearance as she was by his. He wore the same garments he'd worn when she last saw him, on the field of battle. From beneath his shirt of mail, his linen cuff hung, torn and soiled. His cheekbones protruded, and his hair and beard had grown unkempt.

'Twas almost as if a stranger stood before her.

But the man who hastened toward her wore the eyes of her brother—aye, *her brother*, for Ranulf was nothing less, even though they shared no blood. His broad-palmed hands touched her cheeks.

Tears glazed his eyes. "I feared you slain. Do they not know you are my sister?"

She took his hand. "Yea. They guard me closely, but I have not been harmed."

"But dishonored?" Emotion roughened his voice. "Isabel, I could not bear knowing I had again failed to protect you."

"I have not been dishonored." Her face flushed hot, re-membering, in a flash, the passion she had shared with Kol.

"You lie to spare me a brother's anguish." He searched her face, attempting to deduce that which she would not confess. "I vow it, Isabel, I shall avenge thine honor with my sword."

"Nay, Ranulf." She shook her head. "'Tis the truth I speak."

"Then why do you weep so bitterly?"

Only then did Isabel become aware of the dampness of her cheeks. "Because I am so gladdened to see you alive." *But in my heart I betrayed you, at least in part, for the Dane.*

Relief softened his features. When he pulled her to him, she rested her forehead against his chest. She *was* glad to see him alive. But if she truly honored her brother and king, how could she have forsaken him? She had revealed Ranulf's darkest secret to his most dangerous enemy.

She had loved Kol in the cavern, and along with love there had been trust. Had her trust been wrongfully bestowed? Elsewhere in the church, incense burned. Heavy and florid, the scent sickened Isabel. Only a full confession would relieve her afflicted conscience. "Ranulf, I must—"

"And what of Rowena? Is she also well?" He held her by the shoulders and peered into her eyes. "I would have the truth from you, sister, in all things."

Isabel clasped his hands. "All too quickly the Dane tired of her tears and banished her to the abbey to pass her days with the sisters."

Despite the tension of the moment, Ranulf barked out a short laugh. Since childhood, their sister's rampant emotions had made her a trying sibling.

The smile fell from Ranulf's lips. "I had thought never to see you again. No matter what happens in the days to come, knowing you are well is my life's greatest reward. I hope you would not keep the truth from me. Once before, not so long ago, I reacted badly, and without understanding. Now I strive to be a better man."

His earnestness pained her. *Confess to him.*

"Ranulf." She held his forearm. "You must hear what I have to say."

"There will be time to talk later. Now we must go."

Another voice joined their whispered exchange. "Aye, for we are in danger each moment we remain." A man stepped forth from the shadows, his face partly shielded by a cowl.

Isabel's pulse bounded. "Stancliff. Hermione said you fell during the battle. That you were dead."

Stancliff reached to take her hand. Dark circles shadowed his eyes. He kissed her palm. "Do not tell Rowena. Not yet. I prefer to reveal myself when the time is right and our future is secured."

"But you *must* allow me to tell her." Isabel had known no greater joy in the previous days. Rowena's betrothed had survived! Perhaps in some way, her half sister could now forgive her.

Ranulf warned softly, "Nay, sister. Our incursion must remain secret, and as you well know, our sister suffers from the most careless of tongues."

He was right. Rowena held secrets like a sieve held water. Ranulf's gaze shifted to his man-at-arms, as if he dared him to dissent.

Stancliff merely shrugged. A sly smile spread across his lips. "'Tis a sad pity, but a weakness I shall readily forgive when all this is past and I can hold her in my arms once more."

"When all this is past?" For the first time, Isabel realized several more Saxon warriors hovered in dark crevices of the chancel. Doubtless, more waited outside to escort their king to safety. No matter how great their collective strength and cunning, her brother and his men must have had help from the citizens of the burh, to secure this meeting with her. "Have you some strategy to bring our oppression to an end?"

Ranulf nodded, his eyes sharp. "Aye, Isabel, we mount an offensive." At Stancliff's signal, he led her toward the rear of the church. "'Tis only a matter of time before Norsex is regained from the barbarian."

A sphere of fire formed in her belly. *The barbarian.* The barbarian with whom she had lain the night before. Ach! No matter how badly he had hurt her this morning, she knew Kol was no barbarian, but a man noble and proud, who had suffered a horrible injustice. But while Kol had been wronged, when she looked into Ranulf's eyes she could perceive none of the depravity which Kol accused. She felt such confusion. While she supported her brother's claim to the throne, she would feel no satisfaction if Kol were defeated.

The warriors emerged, weapons held at the ready, to disappear, one by one, through the rear doorway. Stancliff followed them, but paused to hover beneath the bent timber archway.

Though she knew this was not the time nor the place to question her king, she could not remain silent. "Will the Northumbrians lend their forces? I witnessed with my own eyes how they offered Thorleksson payment in exchange for peace. Would they dare break their agreement with him?"

Ranulf's nostrils flared. "I have no need of the Northumbrians, nor their treacherous king. For an age they have coveted Norsex. They hover at the border to watch our destruction, like vultures, ready to tear apart our carcass once the Northmen have had their fill."

She clenched the cuff of his tunic. "Then how do you foresee victory? Our surviving forces are few."

"Such details have not escaped my notice." His voice

sharpened. "But as I have said, we will discuss all of this further, once we have returned to a safer place."

Stancliff signaled to his king that it was time for them to depart. Isabel felt her skin go cold. They intended to take her with them.

"Where dost thou take me?" Isabel asked in a low voice, watching as Ranulf accepted a dark bundle from Stancliff. 'Twas a rough peasant's tunic. This he draped over her more finely woven cloak.

"You shall return with us to Caervon. 'Tis there we mount our defense."

Isabel stood like a child, allowing the hood to be fastened, but inside her a battle raged. "What of Rowena? And Godric? He too is held at the abbey."

Without offering any sort of answer, Ranulf led her beneath the archway. He no longer met her eyes.

Isabel pushed his hand from her arm. "Nay."

She retreated from him, pushing the cloak from her shoulders. "I cannot leave as long as my son remains imprisoned. I shall not risk his life by making my own escape."

"Isabel." His tone reprimanded her. "You prick my patience. Come with me. I command you to do so. When the attack is made, I cannot guarantee your safety."

"'Tis not my safety for which I am concerned, but that of my son. Any escape I would make would endanger not only Godric, but Rowena as well." Her gaze veered pleadingly to Stancliff. "Dost thou not see?"

Stancliff spoke softly. "Trust your king, Isabel."

Isabel's heart grew hard. Too many men demanded her trust, when she had so little left to give. Oh, she *trusted* that their intentions were good. But someone was wrong in this entangled conflict. Was it Kol or Ranulf?

In her desire to know, she blurted, "He claims our father summoned him to Norsex."

Ranulf's face grew stark. "Summoned him? Obvious

lies. Why would our father invite a mercenary force into our midst when none was necessary? Our *fyrd* performed sufficiently, and well, in our border disputes."

"Thorleksson says the threat came from within."

He snapped, "And I see you have chosen to believe him." Amidst the anger, she also saw hurt, as if he sensed some part of her had already betrayed him.

"My liege, we must go," Stancliff urged.

'Twas as if Ranulf did not hear Stancliff. His eyes continued to hold Isabel's. "We both know what he did to you."

No. The denial flew to Isabel's lips, but from behind them came a hard rattle of the doors at the entrance to the church.

Ranulf snared her arm in a painful grip. "If I am defeated and slain, your son will not live to become a man. Our enemies will come from all sides, to purge our blood from the earth. Do you truly believe you alone can protect him from that fate? Come with me now, and we will see to Godric's deliverance in the days to come."

Male voices sounded from the nave.

"Go now, brother," Isabel implored. She twisted her arm free. "Before you are taken."

"Damn you, Isabel." Ranulf's hand flexed upon the hilt of his sword, and for a moment she feared he would remain to engage the Dane in battle, here upon the tiled floor of the altar. He retreated into the darkness. "We will encamp in the northern forest until morning. Remember your noble line. Your duty to your kinsman."

Kol stood in the alley beside the church, waiting for Isabel. He did not intend to interrupt her private Mass with Father Janus. Yet she had spent the past two days in the wilds. She required fresh, warm garments and food. Despite the emotional distance he had cleaved between them, he would see her well tended. 'Twas essential for the princess to remain strong and healthy for herself, and for her child, in the coming days.

A short distance away, Vekell and Ragi bartered over some bit of goods with a Saxon merchant. Vekell shook his head, and shifted stance, clearly on the losing end of the bargain. Kol smiled, dimly. Was he wrong to believe his people might eventually be accepted here?

This morning it had pained him to hurt Isabel. He sorely regretted his words and actions, for they had cut her deeply. But their inevitable parting would be easier if she harbored no gentle feelings for him. He would rather she feel the sting of betrayal now, than when Ranulf was slain.

Kol looked to the sky. The noonday was near past. At this moment, Svartkell and thirty Danish warriors waited in the forest near Leswick for the traitor to appear with Ranulf. Would that he were with them, but his unanticipated night with Isabel had precluded his involvement. Despite all that had passed this morning—he could not say he was sorry.

A peasant, draped in a colorless cloak, walked past the alleyway. The man glanced in Kol's direction, his face framed by a hood, before continuing on. *Familiar.* Kol straightened, and gripped his sword pommel. He'd seen the man before. Perhaps amidst the rage of battle.

Kol took the corner and searched the muddied road, yet Calldarington's winter shadows seemed to have swallowed the man.

The hairs along Kol's neck stood in awareness. Instinct compelled him up the steps of the church. Only to find the doors barred against entrance.

"Vekell," he called. "Ragi."

Within moments, Father Janus stumbled alongside him, his voice raised in clear warning to whomever might hide in the chancel.

"My lord. I am not prepared to offer the sacrament at

present, as I am required posthaste at the bedside of an ail-
ing citizen."

Vekell blocked the priest's path. Kol advanced toward
the nave. His sword sang a whisper when he pulled it from
its berth.

Father Janus pled, shrilly. "Would it please you if I
came to the keep's chapel this eventide, before vespers?"

At the altar, Isabel whirled, her eyes wide, her cheeks
flushed. Instantly, *Kol knew.*

Fury lent calm to his voice and his thoughts. "My lady."

Ragi strode past. "There are footprints. A good many of
them."

The old warrior pushed open the rear door, and
searched the muddied lane behind the church.

Kol approached Isabel, circled her. "You have seen
him."

Vekell cursed softly.

Isabel shook her head. "Nay, I came to the church to—"

In that moment, the flame he'd jealously guarded, hidden deep inside his heart, flickered and died.

"Do not *lie to me*," he shouted. Isabel flinched, as if his
words struck a physical blow.

His voice barely rose above a hiss. "Come."

He led her past the moist-eyed Father Janus, down the
aisle and out of the church doors. To his consternation,
countless Saxons hovered silent and watchful along the
edges of the muddy road.

"To the keep, Isabel."

She took one step down.

A man's voice called from the crowd, "Thou art our
lady, Princess Isabel!"

Isabel stopped her decent. Kol's gaze swept out to see
what Saxon might have offered such an encouragement.
Did they not all despise her for setting him free, and for al-
legedly bearing his son? He did not think it his imagination
she now stood taller and prouder beneath her winter cloak.

"Continue," he growled.

Isabel's cloak fanned behind her as she finished the stairs, and took the road toward the keep. Vekell and Ragi provided escort, their swords still drawn.

"Free our lady, Danish scourge!"

"Norse poison!"

Kol felt a strike against his chest, and with it a chink of metal. Someone had cast a stone at him! At learning of Isabel's meeting with Ranulf, he had felt a numbing anger. At this act of Saxon defiance, his temper erupted.

He bellowed, *"Do not test my benevolence."*

Before his eyes, the crowd disbursed, granting him some level of satisfaction. Nostrils flared, he drew to Isabel's side and chided, "It seems your fickle subjects seek to embrace you into their fold."

She kept her eyes on the keep, yet her lips formed a pleased—*nei,* smug—little smile. "They can be no more fickle than you, Dane."

She increased her pace, and left him standing alone in the road. Kol lunged in pursuit, but halted himself. He had wanted this. A reason to set her free of the bindings of his heart. *Let her go. Let her go forever.*

From a distance, a horn lowed in announcement. Up the road, Isabel whirled round. How beautiful she was, Kol thought with intense longing, even with the smile fallen from her lips.

"What was that?" she demanded.

He set off toward the stable. Over his shoulder, he called, "Go to the rampart. Soon, you will see."

Isabel gathered her heavy skirts in one hand, and climbed the rampart stairs. A hard ocean wind swept her hair from her face.

Riders emerged from the weald, making their way toward the burh. Several hundred of them. Mail and weaponry glinted in the morning sunlight. Standards whipped the sky. The world around Isabel grew frenzied.

Beneath her feet the walkway vibrated as the great wooden gate creaked down to impact the earth. Warriors lined the walls. Others grouped in the courtyard.

Panic hummed in her blood. Had Ranulf's attack come so soon? Had Kol anticipated it? At once, she realized she was not ready to learn the final resolution of things, no matter what it might be.

Frantic to catch one final glimpse of Kol, she followed him, maneuvering through a solid column of warriors and weaponry, up steps and over walkways to the foremost promontory of the earthen wall. A banner rippled at the forefront of the advancing horde, but at this distance, 'twas only a slash of featureless gold.

From below came the sound of horses' hooves upon the weighty planks of the gate.

Her breath caught as Kol rode through the opening, carefully nudging through the crowd of citizens who, at first sign of an attack, sought the protection of the keep's high walls. Goats bleated and children cried.

Kol had donned a shirt of mail. Light reflected off the sword scabbarded at his side. His hair fell free, uncovered by any helm. Fingers of apprehension scored Isabel's spine. Never mind his cursed destiny! Why would he face his enemy so recklessly? He could be killed.

The advancing force grew closer. The rapid step of the foot soldiers echoed an even cadence across the valley. Again her eyes narrowed upon their banner. She saw it now, a two-tailed fish upon a vert and argent background. Only one man flew such a banner.

Ugbert of Wyfordon.

Ranulf's salvation had arrived in the form of their uncle from the north.

She searched the field for Kol, but a second faction of riders drew her attention as they burst forth from the forest to join the first. Amidst the men she saw the flowing mantle of a woman upon a white horse. 'Twas her half sister, Rowena.

Ugbert's contingent halted, still a goodly distance away. Silence filled the narrow valley, broken only by the steady pulse of the ocean's waves.

No orders rang out, no horns were blown. No battle cry arose.

Instead, Kol and his officers rode to the forefront of the Danish forces. Instead of halting to take his place there, Kol continued on. Isabel's gaze traversed the open field and saw a single Saxon who rode toward Kol.

Was that man Ugbert, himself? She could not tell from this distance. What she did observe, however, were gloved hands raised—

In greeting.

Clasped in alliance.

Understanding thundered inside the confines of her mind. Thorleksson and her uncle.

Allies against Ranulf. Allies in betrayal.

Chapter 17

Kol rode alongside Devon, son of Ugbert. "Your men may encamp along the north side of the burh."

"Very good." Devon smiled. A squat, robust man, he sat much lower in his saddle than Kol. His eyes roved over the earthen walls, and the timber keep beyond. "You did well, Thorleksson. Not a timber out of place. I trust your rewards were pleasing?"

"My men are satisfied."

"Aye, our Saxon women accommodate, do they not? I hope you have enjoyed more than one during your stay. Take several with you when you go, with my warmest wishes."

Kol did not answer, for Isabel appeared. The princess walked along the rampart as he and Devon rode beneath the gate. Not once did she look at Kol. Instead, her eyes tracked her cousin. She descended the stairs like a beautiful, dark peafowl, her mantle fanning out behind.

"What of Ranulf?" Devon queried, oblivious to the dag-

gers being lodged into the side of his head. "I see no severed head upon a pike."

"He lives."

Devon's congeniality fell away. "He is supposed to be
dead so my claim will go unchallenged. My father will not
be pleased."

Kol's attention remained on the princess. "Your father's
pleasure or displeasure does not concern me."

Devon's fat, shining lips parted in dismay. But then, just
as quickly, his face smoothed into a smile. "Ranulf's a cunning goat. Not an easy foe to capture. I do believe I shall
enjoy hunting him."

Kol's gaze slid over the toad of a man who rode beside
him. Did the mail conceal a robust stature, or rather, the
corpulence of an overindulgent swine? If there was a neck
within the stacked, thick jowls, Kol saw no evidence of it.

"Neither you nor your father made mention of Aldrith's
daughters."

"Daughters." He frowned. "Ah, yes. Two, I believe?
The youngest got herself with child by some heathen some
seasons back. Ranulf couldn't seem to marry her off after
that." He smirked at Kol. "Tried your luck? She may have
a liking for your kind. Is that not the Norse ideal? Treasure,
acclaim, and the hand of a foreign princess?"

Kol frowned at Devon, wishing he'd fall off his horse
and land on his head. Isabel awaited them upon the keep's
stairs. There, Rowena dismounted with the assistance of
one of her warrior escorts. She ascended the stairs to stand,
without word or greeting, beside Isabel. Kol swung down
from his saddle. Devon did the same and started up the
stairs.

The sight of Isabel apparently froze his joints in their
sockets. He glanced at Kol, then back to Isabel. "Cousin?"

She nodded, almost imperceptibly. Her eyes never
strayed from his face.

The Isabel who stood upon the stairs was not the same

Isabel who had warmed Kol's bed the night before, soft and pleasing. This woman's eyes glittered, hard as jewels, and glinted their displeasure at Devon.

The fool laughed and extended his arms, climbing the next several steps, as if to embrace her. Isabel stiffened, her face an unmistakable reflection of her fury.

A spectacle on the steps of the keep would serve no useful purpose. Kol interceded, in a low, cautioning voice. "My lady, please show your cousin to the great hall and see that he is made comfortable."

She laughed, a bitter sound that echoed off the limestone steps. "Forgive me, sir, but I believe you mistake me for the lady of the keep." She glanced to Kol. "I am naught but a prisoner here."

Devon tilted his head, and smiled upon her as if he were a doting parent. "Now, now. Things have not been so bad, have they? You look well, and now that I am here—"

"I shall welcome no traitor into my brother's home."

Devon's conciliatory attitude vanished instantly. "I regret hearing such words from your lips, cousin, when my good favor determines each aspect of your future." He smiled. "As well as that of whatever bastards you have managed to bear."

Isabel's glance toward Kol was sharp, yet fleeting. Rowena brushed past Isabel to collapse into her cousin's arms. "Cousin. Thank our Lord you have arrived."

Isabel shot a glare of incredulity on the back of her sister's fair head, and stormed up the stairs into the keep. Kol caught her just inside the doors. She spun around when his hand touched her arm.

"What have you done?" she hissed.

Kol ignored the stares of curious onlookers, and herded her into a corner for privacy. Isabel yanked her arm free. She pressed herself flat against the wall, and swept her garments close, as if she could not bear for him to touch even her hem.

Kol would change nothing he had done—other than perhaps not waste his time again on Ranulf's feckless traitor. Still, he wanted her to understand. "When I left Calldarington two winters ago, I swore vengeance upon your brother. What better vengeance than to turn a man's kin against him, and allow them claim to his kingdom?"

Isabel's cheeks flushed red. "Is that what you sought to do with me? Woo me, make love to me, and turn my loyalty against my brother?"

With the memory of their night in the cave so fresh in his mind, her words wounded. His heart, not his mind, reacted with a fierce—yet unexpected—confession. "I *made love* to you because *I love you*."

Kol went rigid, his reckless words ringing in his ears. Isabel, too, appeared shocked, as shown by her wordless lips and paling skin.

An immense creaking of wood and metal cleaved the moment, and the hall's great doors swung open. Devon marched in. The pale-haired princess walked beside him, smiling, her hand on his arm. They and their numerous attendants surged in a boisterous mass toward the hall.

Isabel hissed low, "If you *loved* me, you would not make me and my son chattel to a fool such as he."

She shoved his arm aside, and disappeared up the stairwell to the privacy of the upper hall. In her chamber, Isabel cast off her soiled garments. Cold air bathed her naked skin, subduing the waves of heat which rolled through her. Her legs trembled. Kol's hoarse confession resounded in her head.

Because I love you.

Liar. He did not love her. Love crossed all boundaries. Defeated all hatreds. How dare he say he loved her, moments after presenting her with such a betrayal? 'Twas only a matter of time before Kol revealed Ranulf's lack of birthright to Devon.

Another man's voice arose in her mind.

If I am defeated and slain, your son will not live to become a man.

On the stairs, Devon had alluded to her son's tenuous favor. Isabel grasped the clay pitcher from the table, and poured fresh water into a shallow basin.

Our enemies will come from all sides, to purge our blood from the earth.

Vehemently, she grasped up a length of linen, wet it, and began to scrub. The cold water shocked her skin, and cleared her mind.

Remember your noble line. Your duty.

She had a choice to make—but really, there was no choice at all. In her mind a plan took shape. She dressed quickly. On her bed, she spread a clean winter cloak. Upon this she placed mittens and woolen stockings, and rolled everything into a tight bundle. Without bothering to plait her hair, she crossed to the door—

Only to turn back again, and walk along the center wall. She pressed her hands across the timbers, her fingertips searching the mortar until she found it. The hole.

In a quiet voice, she whispered, "There had best be an explanation, Ranulf. And you had better live long enough to provide it to me."

Isabel left the room. Below, the hall thronged with warriors and their families. 'Twas easy for her to slip with her bundle, unnoticed, from the keep's side door.

A thin layer of snow dusted the back courtyard. She hurried toward the garden, sparse with winter offerings. There, she concealed her things. She would join her brother's forces tonight, but not before she set her plot into motion.

Would her plan work? She could only pray it did. The outbuilding where the keep's meals were prepared each day lay just a stone's throw away, and she hastened toward it.

To her dismay, upon her entrance several faces turned toward her. Unfamiliar faces.

"Greetings," Isabel blurted.

It appeared that already, some of the Norse women had found their way to the kitchens. They opened baskets and sniffed jars, assessing the stocks. Isabel's gaze veered past one woman's skirts to focus on a low cabinet.

She did not seek to kill. Not like the fiend who had sought to take her child from this life. She sought only to inflict a dreadful level of discomfort. To lay her enemy low, and subject to capture and defeat.

There, pushed back against the wall, separate and apart from the other items of the kitchen, she saw the narrow clay vessels she sought.

"I have come to join you—" She forced a smile to her face. "In preparing a feast of friendship and welcome."

Kol paced the length of the stall. "You see, only when I spoke the words to the princess did I realize the truth of them."

He bent to peer down the center aisle, to ensure no one had entered the stables. Satisfied his privacy remained intact, he rounded back toward his confessor.

"When I set my revenge into motion, I did not know she was Aldrith's daughter. Devon, the oaf, suited my purposes perfectly. I took great pleasure knowing Ranulf's kingdom would fall into the hands of such a fool. But now . . . now the lives of Isabel and her child are at stake."

Kol nodded, rubbing his thumb along his lower lip. "I know what question you ask: how can I simply sail away after all that has occurred? After all, I have lived with this hatred for so long, it is more like blood than emotion."

Morke offered only sympathetic silence and brown eyes.

Kol scowled. "I have gone mad. What sort of fool finds counsel in his horse?" He shoved the gate open so hard its peg dug a clean furrow into the earth.

Vekell stood in the center of the aisle, his expression damningly innocent. "My lord."

Kol scowled in mortification. *"What."*

For once, Vekell's eyes did not shimmer with mirth. They reflected something far more complex. "That night, when I discovered a helpless babe in the snow, I preserved his life with the intention that he would live."

Stiffly, Kol answered, "I do live."

"Nei, you breathe. Yet do you live?"

Silence spread like an ocean between them.

Kol looked to the rafters. "I think 'tis easier for me to speak to the horse."

"You have remained ever constant in your leadership, Thorleksson." Vekell backed away, toward the stable entrance. "The men will follow you, no matter what your decision."

Isabel stepped away from the kitchen entrance, her insides churning with excitement. Berry juice stained her hands, visible proof of her clandestine undertaking. She rubbed her palms against her skirt, but the stains remained. She felt a coward's satisfaction: pride for what she had accomplished, but relief she would not be present to see the terrible results. Shivering, she hurried into the garden.

"Princess."

Her heart lurched. Vekell trotted down a shallow garden furrow, his long braids swinging at either side of his face.

Arriving at her side, he looked to the sky. "'Tis nearly nightfall."

Though he did not smile, his tone seemed gentle enough. Isabel avoided meeting his eyes. She did not wish to feel regret for what she had done.

"Aye," she answered cooly. "'Tis."

"My lord requests your attendance in the hall this eventide."

Anger flared, taking the edge off the cold evening air. She felt instantly reassured she had done the right thing. "I will not welcome Devon of Wyfordon into my brother's hall. He is naught but a traitor to me."

Vekell shrugged, and stamped the earth, shifting from one booted foot to the other. "Perhaps my lord hath something else in mind?"

Something besides welcome? Curiosity compelled her to ask, "Prithee, tell me what that might be."

"Even I do not know with certainty what my *stallari* will say before he says it."

Her bundle lay just a stone's throw away. Isabel fixed her attention on the spot to remind herself of her duty. "I do not see why my presence is necessary. Whatever announcement your lord intends, I am sure it will portend only misery for myself and my son."

"Why not hear for yourself?"

Isabel pretended to consider his invitation for a moment. If only he would leave, so she could make her escape!

"Truly, I am weary from the previous days' journey. Please tell your *stallari* I prefer to pass the eve alone in my chamber."

Shoulders proudly squared, she crossed to the next furrow, intending to return to the kitchen where she suspected he would be too cowardly to follow. As soon as he left the garden, she would return and claim her things.

Vekell's gloved hand closed firmly, yet gently, upon her forearm.

"I see." She glared through narrowed eyes. "This invitation to attend the feast was no invitation at all."

Kol lifted his goblet.

"More mead, my lord?" Rowena ascended the platform, wine pitcher in hand. She appeared pleased to have been returned to her place as lady of the hall. As custom dictated, she had welcomed her cousin and each of his Saxon warriors, symbolically filling each man's cup. Now she hastened to fill Kol's.

"Mead, Isabel?" he asked of the silent beauty on the bench beside him.

Isabel vocalized no answer, but the cutting gleam of her eyes told him he ought to shove his goblet up his nose. She sat rigidly, her hands crossed in her lap, as if she could not bear the slightest touch of either of her neighbors on the feasting bench; Kol on the one side, Devon on the other.

He sighed, and nodded to Rowena, hoping the mead would take the edge from the coming moments. He would reveal his amended intentions to Devon—and lay his heart bare to Isabel. Would she accept or reject him?

Either way, he felt certain of the decision he had made. In the past he had always tried to do right. In the situation of Norsex, *right* had simply evolved from one set of possibilities into another. Yet there could be no guarantee how the parties involved would react. He remembered Isabel and her knives, crouched upon his bed. A certain amount of anger would not be so terrible, as long as her sweet surrender followed quickly thereafter.

In the far corner, upon his woven pallet, the skald sang Kol's praises. *Kol the Fearless. Thorleksson the Brave.*

Legs tensed, Kol prepared to stand, yet several kitchen maids appeared with large trenchers, piled high with berry tarts. He growled low in his throat, frustrated by the delay. Yet he would wait until there were no distractions.

Beside him, Isabel bent her head. "Might I return to my chamber?" Her hands twisted spasmodically in the skirt of her gunna.

"You have eaten nothing. Art thou ill?"

She whispered, "Mayhap."

He could not allow her to leave. A maid placed a trencher before them. The tarts' berried centers glistened dark and sweet. Isabel paled. Devon reached across, jostling her roughly, to grasp a tart in each of his pudgy-fingered hands. Both disappeared simultaneously between his plump, shining lips.

"Delicious," he pronounced. Purple juice streamed over his chin to disappear into the folds of his neck. "I shall have another."

The princess stared at her cousin with an expression very akin to horror. To Kol, she murmured, "Verily, I wish to leave."

She truly looked ill. Kol softened. "Perhaps thou art merely fatigued? Last eventide, thou hadst little sleep in the cave."

Isabel's cheeks flushed deeply.

"I intended no jibe, Isabel. Prithee, remain here beside me for a short while longer."

"I have no wish to hear your announcement, whatever it might be."

Kol breathed evenly. He would not allow her to undermine his confidence in what he intended to do. All around, the gathered Saxons and Danes enjoyed the tarts. Kol selected one for himself, and lifted it toward his lips. The skald plucked his harp and sang of Kol, the Destroyer of the Wicked.

Beside him, Isabel grumbled, "I might suggest a few different verses. Why not Kol the Betrayer of Women and Children? Or better yet, Kol the Big Norse Louse."

Kol exhaled through his nose, and lowered the tart to the table. Lord, how she provoked him—in all the right ways. Rather than inciting his anger, her words—spoken low and from wine-red lips—enticed. His entire being buzzed with pride and pleasure simply because she sat at his side.

Now was as good a time as any, he supposed. He nodded to Vekell. The warrior set down his tart, and wiped his mouth. Standing, and with raised arms, he shouted, "Silence. Our lord wishes to speak."

Anticipation charged Kol's veins. He stood, knowing that in the coming moments, Isabel would know his heart, and he would know hers. He closed his eyes, and recalled their closeness in the cave the night before. Isabel's love would be a much sweeter and more meaningful gift than vengeance could ever be. Finally, he understood he displayed no weakness in accepting such a gift.

There came the sound of someone retching.

Kol's eyes flew open.

Devon groaned loudly.

Everywhere he looked, grown men and women began to rise from their benches. They doubled over and clasped their stomachs. Some ran from the hall, while others became ill where they stood. Beside him, Isabel pushed up from the bench. Something in her wide-eyed expression compelled him to take hold of her wrist. Her hands—the hands she had buried in her gunna, bore purple stains.

In that instant, he knew. *The tarts.*

Between clenched teeth, he ground out the words. "What did you put in them?"

Isabel's eyes narrowed. "Baneberries. Toadroot. Bugbane. I know not the exact mix of things. I only know 'tis what the cooks used to use to warn the hounds away from the kitchens."

Incredulous, Kol looked out over the writhing multitude of the hall. A sour-sweet scent permeated the air. "You sought to poison them all?"

"Aye," she cried. "You, my cousin, and all who support you."

Fury torched his cheeks. Could she not have given him one chance? One chance to set things right, for all concerned? Did she believe so little in him?

On a nearby bench Vekell held his head in his hands. He groaned loudly. At his feet lay one of the tarts, half-eaten. Kol thought he saw a glimmer of regret in Isabel's features. In a quiet voice, she said, "'Twill not kill them."

Ah, but in this moment he wished to kill *her*. Kol grasped her arm, and pushed her toward the door. "Get thee to your chamber. *Now*. Do not show yourself until I come for you."

"Nay." Isabel dragged her feet. The regret now lay plain upon her face. "I will stay and help."

She started toward Vekell. Kol intercepted her before she could touch the warrior.

"Do you truly believe anyone will want your help once they know it was you who poisoned them?" With his eyes, he shot her a black warning. "Now do as I say. Get thee away from us."

Chapter 18

Isabel fled beneath the archway, but instead of going to her chamber, she pushed out the doors, and ran down the stairs into the courtyard. The cold air did nothing to cool the fire in her veins.

She should feel triumph. Instead she felt guilty and *angry* all at once. But why should she be condemned for attempting to thwart an enemy's claim on her brother's kingdom? For seeking to escape her captor? As if she had betrayed a trust.

"Isabel!" Kol's voice rang, raw with fury.

For a moment, Isabel stood frozen. If he dragged her inside and punished her in front of everyone, she would likely scream like a fool, or worse, burst into tears. Her emotions had never felt so out of control.

There could be no turning back. She would flee into the darkness and make her way to the forest, where she prayed Ranulf waited as he had said he would.

Several outbuildings dotted the inner face of the rampart. Rather than take her chances in the open, she could hide behind the structures as she made her way to the garden, where her bundle waited. She caught up her skirts and ran.

"Isabel!" Kol's roar shattered the tranquility of the courtyard. Startled from their nightly perch, a flock of birds took flight from an evergreen near the steps.

Let him shout. Let him curse her. She would not feel regret for what she had done. Her only lament was that he had escaped the sickness. She took refuge in the darker shadows alongside a narrow hut, and quickly found the doorway. Over her shoulder, she saw the shadow of a man ascend in gigantic proportions against the moonlit side of the keep's wall. If she ran across the clearing, he would see her.

She pushed inside, intending to hide until he passed. For a moment, darkness disoriented her. A pungent scent tightened her throat. She stood motionless, her back against the door, until her eyes adjusted.

From just outside came the crunch of gravel. Her heart pounded faster.

In search of a better hiding place, she took one step inward, her hands outstretched. Something crunched beneath her slipper. She froze. Had the sound been loud enough to hear from outside? With one hand she smothered a sneeze. The smell. What *was* that smell? She heard no further footsteps.

She bent forward to touch the floor. Walnut shells? And the scent—yes, 'twas alum. With this knowledge, and the adjustment of her eyes to the darkness, Isabel recognized her sanctuary. Along the wall, there would be narrow clay vessels, standing in orderly rows, filled with the dye master's precious madder, leaves of woad, and, yes, bowls and baskets full of crushed nutshells, all used to dye the keep's textiles.

Behind her the door opened and she felt a hard smack to her bottom. She pitched to the floor.

"Ow!" Shells stabbed into her palms. Her head thumped a copper dye vat.

She whirled around, her hand pressed to her brow. Kol stood in the doorway, the night a blue black eternity beyond his shoulders. He carried a small torch.

"You—" She rubbed her forehead. Now that he had found her, how would she escape? The thought of remaining in his presence even one more day was unbearable. "Trough slime!"

"You . . . poisoned . . . my . . . men," he gritted. He lunged through the portal.

"Oh!" Isabel scurried behind a waist-high copper kettle.

Kol tossed the torch onto a small fire grate in the center of the room, then walked toward her, weaving between several dying hooks, which swung to and fro from the ceiling.

"Not only my men, but a goodly number of thine own Saxon people." He sidestepped as if to come around.

"Devon's men? Traitors! All of them." Isabel sidled away, in the opposite direction.

"Why do you flee, Princess?" He grasped the edge of the pot. "Art thou frightened?"

Isabel lied, working through the limited possibilities for escape. "Not of you, Norseman."

He leered. "You should be."

Before she could blink, he tipped the vat onto its side. Isabel gasped and jumped back. Liquid splashed her hem and surged over the tips of her slippers. Kol circled the overturned kettle, his boots crushing the scattered shells and sloshing through the dye.

Isabel snatched a bowl of walnuts from the windowsill. "I warn you."

"Warn all you like."

She flung the bowl. Kol swatted it. Nuts hailed down, and then, with a thunk, the bowl. Isabel scrambled beneath a linen-draped drying frame. Spilled dye moistened her palms and knees. Heart pounding, she crawled toward the door, but instantly the cloth evaporated. With a creak, the frame flew up and away and crashed against a wall. Cold air bathed her skin. For a moment she sat as still as a cornered mouse, her eyes on the barely visible tips of two large boots.

Her hair spilled wildly over her shoulders. Forcing calm on her overwrought heart, she smoothed the errant tresses behind her ears. Surely Kol would not murder the very woman he'd made love to the night before, even if he had set her aside immediately thereafter.

Emboldened, she stood. "You have no right to terrorize me." She jabbed a finger at the center of his chest, in the exact place where she'd placed her lips the night before. She blinked away the thought and continued her declaration. "You and your men deserved to be poisoned, just as they have poisoned Norsex with their presence!"

She shook her fist in the air, cursing providence. "If only you had eaten a tart like the rest." Wide-eyed and with affected voice, she cooed, "But I suppose you have been too busy plotting with my oaf of a cousin to feel any sort of hunger."

Kol leaned forward, placing himself in such proximity to her face she could have kissed him—if she had so wished. Her entire body tensed.

"Dearest Isabel," he murmured, his voice as smooth as summer-warmed honey. "I was prepared to kick thine cousin's loathsome ass back to Wyfordon before you took matters into your own hands."

At his words, shock numbed Isabel's limbs. She turned her face aside. "I want only for you to leave this kingdom, for thou art wholly unwelcome."

"I was not unwelcome last eventide."

Isabel pressed her hands to her ears. "Do not speak to me of last eventide."

Isabel sidled behind a long table, toward the door. In

one sweeping movement, Kol upended the table. As it crashed, Isabel screamed and pressed back flat against the wall.

"You cannot escape." To her ire, satisfaction mingled with the anger she saw in his eyes.

"That remains to be seen." Isabel tugged a dyeing hook free from the ceiling, and held it ready.

Kol's attention pinpointed her, like a beam of withering heat. Her palms dampened around the narrow handle of the hook.

"Tsk, tsk, sweet Princess." His voice was but a rasp in the utter silence betwixt them. "Have your past failures at physical aggression taught you nothing?"

She swung the hook. He moved to catch it, but still, Isabel heard the sound of torn cloth.

"Oh." He looked down at the front of his tunic, and up again. *"Mistake."*

Angrily she swung again. He caught the hook, wrenched it from her hand, and dropped it to the floor. He pushed her to the wall. Against her cheek she felt the solid press of his jaw, the score of his beard against her skin. In short gasps, she inhaled his breath, and remembered, instantly, the scent and taste of him. In that moment her body and soul teetered on the cliff of dark and all-consuming desire.

Kol stared at her, his eyes glittering in the dark. His lips grazed hers with the slightest contact.

She turned her face aside. "Release me."

"Never." He teased her with each breath, each movement. Invited her to kiss him. She commanded her lips not to respond, not to press against his, but the draw grew strong.

She shoved against him. "Faithless tripe, you betrayed me—"

His lips crushed hers.

With a gasp, she wrenched away. "What are you doing?"

Their eyes remained open, wary upon one another.

"Ending this." His hands crushed into her hair. As his mouth pressed against her neck, Isabel gripped his shoulders. He spoke the words against her skin. "I'm sick to death of wanting you."

"Your alliance with Devon." She twisted her hands in his tunic, a warning. "I cannot abide it."

"The alliance is ended." He grasped her skirts at her thighs, and dragged them higher, so that she felt the night chill swirl around her ankles and knees. "'Tis your fault alone, he doth not know it yet."

Ended? Isabel had no chance to savor the relief spreading through her veins, because Kol's mouth claimed every shard of her shattered attention. Her leg slid up his, and hooked behind his calf.

"What of Ranulf's secret? His lack of birthright?"

"Devon knows nothing, nor will he."

His beard grazed her skin. He smelled spicy and male and alive.

"And your quest for Ranulf's death?"

"My desire for you exceeds all else."

When he kissed her she did not stop him. She no longer had the will. His hands gripped her hips, and he pressed the ridge of his arousal against her belly. His knee spread her thighs.

He bore her against the wall. Hot and wet, his mouth moved over her throat. He whispered words, Norse utterances.

His hand gripped the neck of her gunna and tugged it down. Boldly, he palmed her breast. Isabel arched, his words spinning through her mind. She felt her skirts dragged to her waist. Cool air washed over her thighs, betwixt her legs, to cool the heated part of her. He stroked her with an urgency that fueled her need. Her legs failed, but he held her against the wall.

In possession of her body, he slid one finger, and then two, inside her warmth. She gasped. Such pleasure, *there*. Pleasure and tight, hot tension radiating outward through her arms and legs to her very fingertips. But almost instantly his fingers left her.

He sank to his knees before her, holding her skirt at her waist. Isabel shuddered, as reverently, he placed a single kiss at the apex of her thighs.

"I should hate you," she whispered.

"You don't." He kissed her there, and tasted her.

Isabel gasped, fisting her hands in his hair. "Then you should hate me. 'Twas my intent to fell you and your men with the poison, then inform my brother of your weakened state."

"But not now."

"Nay," she confessed brokenly. "Not now."

When she thought she would faint from desire, he dragged her down, onto his legs, bracketing her into the corner, her thighs spread to either side of his waist.

"My love," he whispered into her hair. "My only love."

Her heart surrendered at hearing the words. She smoothed her hands over his hips, beneath his linen shirt and over the tautened skin of his torso.

He fumbled betwixt them, freeing himself. Roughly he readjusted her, spread her with his fingers. She felt his member press against her, then gasped at the sudden tightness, the stretching of her body. He moved beneath her, slowly, encouraging her to take up the rhythm. One hand swept over the small of her back, then downward to cup her buttocks.

Abruptly he stopped and cursed. "These nutshells are death on my knees."

Despite the tension of the moment, Isabel giggled. Kol's scowl softened, but only by a degree. With a growl he twisted them around. He grasped a length of heavy linen. Flinging the cloth across the floor, he lowered her without ever disengaging from her body. Spilled dye seeped through linen to dampen her skin.

Kol thrust into her. The muscles corded in his arms as he braced himself above her. His blue eyes glowed in the firelight.

"You are mine." He lifted one dark, glistening hand and touched her skin, painting her with the dye. Through barely parted eyelids, Isabel watched. He marked her with dark hand prints. Claimed her. "Mine."

She wrapped her legs around his waist, bringing him deeper.

Forever. She could make love to him forever.

Even as the pleasure of their mating made her cry out, a bittersweet agony weighted her heart. Along the edges of her conscience, the events of the past and the dread promise of the future, hovered, demanding she recognize them.

Reality shattered in a frenzy of light and movement. Isabel cried out in her climax, her body overcome by a maelstrom of force and light. She arched, mournful and joyous at once, wanting to remain joined with Kol for eternity.

Kol grew rigid, then arched into her with such a shout and force, she was left breathless, her own body taut with pleasure, relishing each strong pulse of him inside her.

He lowered himself slowly, gently, and kissed her, his hair teasing her skin. Against the side of her neck, he groaned. After a long moment, he said, "I believe what we need now are four walls and a bed."

"Yes." She yearned to be alone with him. They must claim whatever private moments they could. She had no illusions about what difficulties daylight would bring.

He rolled off her, and lay on his back, his braies still bunched at his knees. With a slight lift of his hips, he tugged them up. "Since we cannot seem to keep our hands from one another, we shall have to come to some sort of an agreement."

"'Tis more than that, is it not?" She pushed her skirts down and looked to him. "What we share is no simple lust."

"Aye," he answered quietly. His cheekbones appeared more pronounced, his profile stark. "'Tis much more than that."

He turned onto his side, so their eyes met. She found herself face to face with her lover from the cave. His expression hid nothing from her. "You and your son wilt be protected."

Isabel looked to his chest, for at this moment she found it easier to stare at woven cloth, than into his eyes. Wedlock might never be possible between them, but she would not deny her love for this man again. "I hold myself open to the promise of the future."

One could not forget the primary barrier to any happiness between them. Could Ranulf and Kol resolve their differences through peace? He reached for and lifted her chin, returning her gaze to his.

"What are you thinking?"

"That I cannot conceive of how all the shattered pieces of my life will converge to become whole again—but you give me hope."

"Hope," he repeated softly. "Be patient with me, for I have lived a lifetime without it."

She had to ask. "What will you do about Ranulf?"

Again Kol rolled to his back, to stare at the rafters. He pressed his lips together as if the words did not come easily. "I would hear his reasons for submitting me to such torture . . . and attempt to judge him with open mind."

She lifted to her elbow and looked down into his face. The blue intensity she saw there left her disarmed, yet at the same time, reassured of his feelings for her. That he would attempt to set aside such deep-seated hatred to give her peace touched her deeply.

"'Tis all I have hoped for."

Kol took her shoulders and pressed her back to the floor. He rolled to crouch above her in an display of male prowess which thrilled her even in the aftermath of their lovemaking. Against her neck, he whispered simply, "Trust me."

Tears beaded the corner of her eyes. "I do. I will not sway again."

He did not speak again, other than to smile almost sheepishly and say, "Your garments are ruined."

"I have few left, thanks to you."

"I cannot claim to feel remorse." He planted a kiss on her lips, and, with leonine grace, drew back into a crouch to fasten his braies. Dye stained his elbows and knees. Isabel confirmed, when she sat up, the back of her gunna dripped with the stuff. Kol stood and went to inspect the drying racks, and returned with a yellow tunic.

"The fit might not be the best." He tugged her garments over her head. Calloused hands grazed her hips, the sides of her breasts. She shivered.

Bending low, he kissed her. Arousal lit his eyes. She gripped his shoulders, her response instant, as if their recent coupling had only partially satisfied a need.

A low sound came from his throat. He took up the yellow tunic. "Put this on, and let us find a more satisfactory place to continue this night."

When she had dressed, he took her hand and pushed open the wooden door. Isabel followed. He halted suddenly, and she bumped flat into his back.

All around, men clamored accusations and curses. Moonlight reflected off raised clubs and spears. Isabel clenched Kol's tunic.

"Stand back," Kol ordered them. His arm snaked back to shield her. Her heart thumped.

Isabel gained a partial view of her foes by peering around Kol's side. Vekell stepped forward, his skin ashen, his eyes glassy. Stains marred the front of his tunic.

At Isabel, he pointed a long, shaking finger. "This plight is your own, Princess. Wrought by your own hand when you made those wicked tarts. Curse you, wom—" He pressed a hand to his lips, and gave a hearty belch. After a moment he bellowed, "Woman! Were we not patient and kind in our dealings with you?"

Isabel cringed inwardly.

Vekell continued his diatribe. "Like fools, these men worshiped you for saving the life of their lord, when all along you plotted foul miseries, such as this, against them?"

Kol lifted a hand to his captain. "No good will come of this."

Isabel clutched his arm. "No. Let Vekell speak."

Silence fell over the hoard.

Vekell cleared his throat. "'Tis our right to demand she be punished for her crime." His scowl swept from Isabel to Kol again. "And we don't mean whatever method of punishment you sought to employ in that little hut, Thorleksson."

Isabel's cheeks went to flames.

"Aye!" shouted the men.

"Just punishment is what we seek."

Kol responded, "I see you hold your weapons ready. She killed no one. I shall agree to no execution."

Vekell wiped a hand across his mouth, and swallowed hard, as if he battled a resurgence of the sickness. His voice cracked as he said, "'Tis no execution we demand."

Ragi appeared at Vekell's side. He, too, appeared unsteady on his feet. Berry seeds dotted his gray beard. "We had a goodly bit of time to discuss the matter as we waited here for the two of you."

"Aye, our decision is made," Vekell agreed.

Ragi waggled his club at Isabel. "Three days in the keep's prison!"

"Three days?" scoffed Kol, amidst the raucous cheer of the crowd. "The princess is of noble birth, and is unaccustomed to—"

"I consent to the sentence." Isabel broke free of his protection to stand before the warriors. "Three days in the keep's prison. I deserve at least that, for what I have done."

"Isabel," Kol warned.

"Make no attempt to dissuade me." She considered the faces of the men who gathered there, and met their eyes, one by one. "Prithee, accept this as my offering of peace to you. By giving myself over to your punishment, I announce to all my desire for a lasting accord between our peoples."

Ranulf would be horrified to hear her say such things, but she could no longer claim the sins of his past as her own. She would strive to bring peace to this land.

Isabel extended her wrists to Vekell and Ragi, prepared to be bound, but all the fury seemed to have left them. They stared at her upturned palms, bafflement upon their faces. They looked to Kol.

Chapter 19

T is what you wanted, is it not? She hath agreed," he muttered low, through clenched teeth. He refused to meet Isabel's eyes.

His manner unsure, Vekell took Isabel's wrists and led her toward the hall. Behind them the crowd lurched and swayed in pursuit. Once inside, only Vekell and Kol descended the carved stone steps with Isabel, past a guard, into the pit. Torchlight wavered against the walls.

"This way." Vekell tugged her toward a small cell.

"No," Isabel said. She peered into the darkness of the central corridor. "Prithee, take me there, to the furthest room."

"Isabel?" came a voice from the pitch, Aiken's.

"As always, I seek to please." Vekell guided her over the uneven earth, past the other cells.

"What do you do with her?" shouted Aiken through the small opening in his door.

As they passed, Isabel said, "I am well, Aiken. Fear not for my well-being."

She glanced to Kol to be sure he still followed, and found his eyes dark, his lips twisted into a frown.

When they reached the end of the corridor, Isabel stared into the darkness of the cell, the same cell where she had found Kol two winters before. Kol stood back several paces, the memories of that night, and the pain he had suffered, etched on his face. Isabel forced down her fear and moved inside.

Vekell did not slam the door, he simply closed it with a gentle push. Though she waited for the metallic turn of the lock, it did not come. Isabel saw only Vekell's jaw through the slat. She sat in absolute pitch.

His lips moved. "Be well, Princess."

The crunch of his boots signaled his departure. For a long moment she sat, wondering when Kol had slipped away. Perhaps the memories had been too vivid.

She heard his breath and knew he still stood there. She leapt up, and pressed herself to the door. "Kol?"

He stood there, his face shadowed. "Why did you agree to such terms? I could have stopped them."

"No." She shook her head, and slipped her hands through the narrow slat, where he grasped them. Warm and strong, his hands soothed her fears.

"Do you doubt their fealty to me?"

"This is not about your leadership of your men. 'Tis about the future of our people. I made a mistake tonight. I must acknowledge that, and be held accountable."

She read the anguish in the taut frame of his jaw, the press of his lips.

"We both have scars, Kol. You healed mine a great deal, last night in the cave." She squeezed his fingers. "Perhaps my imprisonment in this cell, and what it symbolizes, will heal some of yours."

"Isabel—"

She pressed her fingertips to his lips. "You shall bring

me a blanket and a lantern, and swear Godric will be returned to me as soon as I am released."

He closed his eyes. "Aye, he shall. I promise you."

"These three days shall pass quickly."

Suddenly he reached through. Cupping her jaw, he pulled her face toward his and kissed her ardently. Sweetly. Then he tore away and strode down the corridor.

Isabel sank to crouch against the door.

A moment later, Aiken's voice emanated from the shadows. "Oh, Isabel. What have you done?"

"You do not sleep, my lord?" Vekell appeared from the recesses of the night-darkened hall.

Kol sat against the wall beside the entrance to the pit. "I cannot, knowing she is there."

Vekell lowered himself to sit on the stones beside his lord. "Nor can I."

"Hath your sickness passed?"

"Aye. And so hath my anger." The warrior's wiry brow arched with devilment. "After much thought, I have decided 'tis you who are to blame for all that occurred this eventide."

Kol's eyes widened. "Me? How am I to blame?"

"If you would have come to your senses earlier, none of this would have occurred." Vekell grinned. After a pause, he softly added, "Isabel hath owned your heart from the start."

Kol nodded. Denial no longer held comfort for him. "What you said in the stable was true. I want to do more than breathe. I want to live. Somehow she understands me, and makes that possible."

It felt good to make the admission. To be capable of love. He felt stronger for it, and at peace with whatever the future would bring. The acknowledgment of his love for

Isabel—and her son—defied his mother's hateful curses in some way.

"'Tis a lesson for us all." Vekell leaned close. "As for Isabel's lesson, I have conferred with our hearth companions and all agree one night in the pit is sufficient punishment."

Kol's breath caught in his throat. "Truly?"

"*Nei*, not truly." Vekell chuckled. "But the Saxon maid who owns *my* heart is furious with me for imprisoning her mistress, and so, with my own selfish interests at stake, I have convinced the others to be lenient in their judgment."

Kol could not believe his ears. In all their time together, Vekell had never shown a preference for one woman over any other. "What maid is this?"

"Her name is Berthilde, and she makes me believe I could spend the rest of my days in this place."

Beneath the surface of Vekell's gentle admission, something momentous had occurred. Destiny closed thickly around them both. It felt like goodbye. Yet a new and exciting world opened before them. He knew not how long he would be allowed to spend there, but a single day with Isabel would be enough.

He squeezed Vekell's shoulder. "Go to your Berthilde, then."

"And you . . . claim your princess from her cell."

Light flooded Isabel's slumber. Berthilde's face beamed between the bed curtains.

"Awaken, Princess. There is not much time."

"Not much time?" Perplexed, Isabel lifted herself to one elbow. After several hours in the pit, sleep had finally claimed her. Why did she awaken in the comfort of her own bed? "Who brought me here?"

"Thorleksson."

"That cannot be." Isabel frowned her displeasure. "I

agreed to two more days in the pit. I thought he understood. 'Tis wrong of him to spare me my just punishment."

Berthilde held up one of Isabel's gunnas to the light, and examined it for flaws. She smiled over her shoulder, eyes twinkling. "Your freedom hath been negotiated—"

Her voice trailed off, but Isabel thought she heard her say *in a most enjoyable manner.*

"Negotiated how?"

Berthilde blushed. "Much in the same way you got those big blue handprints all over your body."

"Berthilde!" Isabel shrieked. A quick peek confirmed she lay naked beneath the bedcovers. Kol's hand prints still covered her skin.

"Now, hurry. I hath allowed you to sleep far too long." Berthilde bustled about, glowing with joy. "You must wash and dress quickly, for he hath requested your attendance at the noonday meal."

"What doth he intend?" Isabel wondered allowed. She had interrupted whatever announcement he'd intended the evening before.

"I cannot say. He told me only to keep you out of the kitchen."

Vekell seated Isabel at her cousin's side. Devon barely spared her a glance, so intent was he on demolishing a leg of mutton. Or perhaps he ignored her in anger. After all, he, too, had been a victim of her berry tarts.

"More food," he shouted over his shoulder, spraying Isabel with particle-laden spittle. She retrieved a square of linen from the table and wiped herself clean. It took every bit of strength she had to keep the disgust from her face.

She glanced at Kol, unable to prevent herself from drawing comparisons. Kol was infinitely superior to Devon in masculine grace and manners. Her heart swelled with pride. How had she ever thought to call him a barbarian when there were men such as Devon in the world?

A serving maid brought Devon another trencher of meat. Isabel heard the girl's gasp, saw her try to pull away. Isabel realized her cousin had thrust his hand beneath the girl's tunic skirt. He boldly clasped her buttocks in full view of anyone who cared to see. Before the girl could escape, Devon pulled her into his lap, and bestowed upon her a greasy, open-mouthed kiss.

"Stop that," Isabel hissed.

Devon froze and, fixing his bulbous eyes upon her, growled, "You have no say in what I do. No say in *anything*."

Kol's voice cut between them. "Not now, Saxon. You and I have much to discuss." Just as quickly as the girl had been captured, she was freed and held behind Kol's protective arm. The Norseman's icy gaze was riveted upon Devon, but Devon continued to glare his fury at Isabel.

After a long, tense moment, Devon shrugged, lifted his goblet, and gulped the mead; it streamed over his cheeks and into his beard. Slamming the goblet to the table, he exclaimed, "Of course. Of course."

He beckoned to one of his men, and in moments, a large chest was presented in front of the dais. When opened, a mountain of gold coins glimmered within. Devon ripped another mouthful of mutton with his teeth. "The twelve horses we discussed, they are also yours to keep."

Anxiety turned Isabel's stomach. Just the thought of living beneath Devon's cruel hand rent her internal peace into a thousand fragments. She looked to Kol.

Trust him, she counseled herself.

Kol spoke not a word. He merely stared at Devon, his eyes fathomless and cold. For the first time, Devon seemed to sense discord in the air.

"A glorious undertaking, Thorleksson. Just as my father instructed." He smiled hopefully. "Please use my men freely to assist in preparation of your departure. I'm sure you will want to leave posthaste now that I have arrived."

"My task here is not done."

Kol nodded to Vekell, who stood at the bottom of the dais. Vekell strode toward the hoard of gold, aglow in the firelight. With his foot, he kicked the lid shut. The metallic clank echoed throughout the now-silent hall.

Kol announced softly. "I and my men have decided it is within our interests to remain in Calldarington."

"There is no need. I will find Ranulf, and finish him myself."

"'Tis you who are finished, Saxon."

Beside Isabel, Devon's face drained of blood.

"What did you say?"

For the first time he seemed to remember Isabel sat beside him, for he swung his head in her direction. "What did he say?"

She took joy in leveling her gaze to his and speaking words she knew struck fear into his heart.

"Apparently the Dane intends to remain. Dost that not fit well with your plans for Norsex, cousin?"

Over Devon's shoulder she met Kol's eyes. Warmth flowed through her.

Devon sat as if paralyzed, clutching the glistening haunch in one hand. His lips, shiny with grease and spittle, worked but produced no translatable objection to Kol's announcement.

Kol eased back into his chair, but his lips held their hard line.

"I demand—" Devon began, but his demand transformed into a croak. He cleared his throat. "I demand you speak your intentions."

Vekell stepped forward from beside the trunk. "Dost though not understand your own spoken tongue, little man? My lord dost speak it well and clearly."

"Aye, I understand," Devon spat acidly, his gaze swing-

ing between the two giants. Petulantly, he threw the bone
to the floor of the hall. The portion landed at Vekell's feet
with a meaty thud. Instantly, the Norse giant's eyes smoldered golden and hot.

Devon stood from the bench, but turned to Kol. "I understand all too clearly. Thou dost seek to void our pact.
What I wish to know is whether this voidance is under-
taken in the name of continued vengeance against my
noble cousin Ranulf, or rather in aggression against myself
and my father's authority."

Devon's corpulent form partially obscured Kol from
Isabel's view, but she heard his response. "Perhaps all of
these things."

Devon stamped his foot. "I should have known you
could not be trusted. Cursed mercenaries! Thieves and barbarians, the lot of you, as faithless as a common whore."

"Ah." Kol's laughter held no warmth. "Then you are
amongst equal company, Devon of Wyfordon."

Devon remained standing, while all others on the dais
continued to sit. The stance gave him no authority. Rather
he seemed the fool at a feast. A drunkard who'd drawn attention to himself with boorish jokes and inappropriate
stories.

His chest rose and fell. His face twisted into a grimace,
and he announced, "I demand a gesture of good faith from
you, Norseman. One which will convince me of your
benevolent intentions toward myself and this kingdom."

"I believe 'tis not so much this kingdom or any benevolence which concerns you," Kol said. "But rather your
longevity in a place where you seek to assert yourself as
regent."

"You knew that from the start and had no qualms before." Her cousin's meaty fist slammed down upon the
trestle. Several Norse warriors edged toward the dais.
Devon eyed them warily. "Thou shalt guarantee your good
will toward myself and my father. I demand this."

"You make demands of me, a barbarian ruled by animal instinct and lust for blood and treasure?"

Isabel's hair stood on end, watching the two men quarrel over the leadership and future of a kingdom whose monarch still lived. Slowly she surveyed the great hall. 'Twas filled with Kol's fiercest warriors. The newly arrived Saxons appeared dwarfish in comparison.

Devon shook his head. "With me arrived a legion of men, sworn to protect their lord and the kingdom of Norsex with their lives. I will assert my claim."

"You shall?" Kol questioned lightly, examining his goblet. "There is another with stronger claim."

Isabel sat uneasily in her chair. She knew he did not speak of Ranulf, and could think of only one other legitimate contender for the throne.

Devon stiffened, his fist clenched. "Another? I demand to know his name. Have you taken up with this usurper against me?"

Kol's voice lowered. "He was here all along."

"Name him."

"Godric of Norsex. Named heir to Ranulf, according to the remaining members of Ranulf's witan."

"A bastard child!"

Kol answered easily, "Lesser kinship hath secured greater thrones."

Isabel exhaled sharply.

Kol shifted his gaze to her. As rigid as a tree on a windless day, Devon stood. Only the pulse in the side of his neck evidenced the life coursing through his veins.

"You would throw your lot in with a child king?" he taunted.

"I merely name the players in this game."

Devon's face was that of a man at the end of a slippery rope, with only jagged rocks waiting far below. Finally he asked, in a low voice, "What is it you intend?"

"The boy will be protected and raised with the expectation he will rule this kingdom upon his coming of age. Saxon and Norse warriors will comprise his guard."

Isabel swallowed hard, fighting the surge of tears. Kol knew of her fears for Godric, and had chosen to champion her son's future.

But what of Ranulf's place in such an arrangement? Would Kol negotiate beneficial terms for her brother?

Beside her Devon growled. "And what of my ambitions?"

Kol answered lightly. "You may remain as an advisor to the future king of Norsex. 'Tis no paltry appointment."

"As temporary regent?" suggested Devon.

"*Nei*. You shall be appointed ealdorman." Kol nodded, his brows raised. "Aye, 'twould be sufficient, I believe, for a man of your aspirations."

"I decline. 'Tis not enough."

Kol leaned forward, his demeanor instantly threatening. "Then resume your place as your father's hearth hound, for you shall have no rule in this place."

Devon's lower lip rolled out, and in again, as he puffed. "Even if I accept this role as ealdorman"—he shook his head—"I still do not trust you. What would prevent you from slitting my throat as I slept? I demand a display of good faith."

"Your demands begin to chafe," Kol muttered tightly.

Devon sat heavily onto his bench. "My life is the one at stake. Bind yourself to me in some way or I will not lend my support to this child king. Indeed"—nervously, he looked around the great hall—"while I may not have sufficient forces to defeat you, I would sacrifice the entire legion to weaken yours, so much so that the Northumbrians . . . or even Ranulf . . . would find it easy to swoop in and defeat you, and claim Norsex for their own."

Kol leaned forward in his seat, as if he would leap from

it and assail Devon. "You would sacrifice so many lives simply to soothe your vanity?"

Devon's upper lip trembled. "I would."

After a long silence, Kol asked, "If my word doth not bind us, what shall?"

Isabel looked at her cousin. His brow furrowed in thought, he searched the room, as if to find the answer to a question. His eyes settled upon an area just below the dais.

There Rowena stood, wine pitcher in hand.

"You must wed a Norsexian princess, a woman who shares my blood and the blood of our future king. Only then will I accept your proposal without contest."

The silence of the room seemed to swell. Indeed, it pressed painfully into Isabel's ears. *Her sister Rowena?* Kol would refuse. She waited to hear the words.

Kol's lips parted. "I agree to your request."

Isabel's stomach turned over. Had he truly agreed?

Isabel's half sister flushed. Peering up the dais toward the Danish lord, she smiled.

"But I must insist," Kol added, "upon the Princess Isabel as my bride." He looked past her cousin, to her, and smiled—much too boldly, given the current tension in the room.

Before everyone, he claimed her as his own. Isabel could not remember ever having experienced such a thrilling, marrow-deep contentment. She felt embraced, to her very soul.

Devon's frown cut into his jowls. "The Princess Rowena is the eldest. 'Tis she who should be chosen."

Rowena blinked, and looked between the two men, clearly hopeful. Kol's gaze never left Isabel.

Vekell stepped forward. "My lord hath made his preference clear." One shaggy brow slashed upward in challenge.

Devon shrugged. "So be it." He grasped a chicken leg

and shook it at Kol. "But the wedding shall take place on the morrow."

Vekell grinned and shouted, "Feast into the night, gathered legion, for tomorrow our lord takes his bride."

Chapter 20

Y our sister seems a bit displeased by last eventide's outcome." Berthilde pressed her lips together, but her eyes twinkled.

"Shhh," warned Isabel, tying off a knot.

They sat in Isabel's bower, on opposite sides of a small table, and worked to repair the embroidery on the gunna her mother had worn the day she'd become Aldrith's queen. Isabel would wear the treasured garment when she married Kol. Her heartbeat still quickened each time she thought of the ceremony to come. Love did not come easily in her world. Even if death separated her from Kol upon the morrow, she would cherish the memory of this day forever.

If only Ranulf could make a peaceful return, and once again become part of their lives, her joy would be complete.

She regretted her son would not be present for the wedding. The night before, Isabel had revealed to Kol all that Ranulf had told her in the church; specifically of Ranulf's plans to attack Calldarington and regain his throne. Because of that threat, and the unsteady loyalty of Devon's forces, they had decided Godric should remain in the safety of the abbey.

Upon the speaking of the final vows, Kol would issue an offer of reconciliation to her brother. She prayed Ranulf would see the honor in bringing peace to Norsex, and allow their two peoples to live side by side in harmony. If Kol could forgive the terrible thing done to him, could Ranulf not also compromise?

Rowena huffed in a chair beside the window. Draped across her lap was the ivory kirtle Isabel would wear that day. "I despise embroidery. I despise each of these awful leaves and berries."

In the next moment she gasped. "I have pricked my finger. Surely 'tis an omen this wedding should not take place."

Berthilde stood and hurried to claim the kirtle. "Wicked girl! You have stained the garment out of spite."

Rowena grimaced at Isabel. "'Tis not fair! I am the eldest sister. I am greatly offended he hath chosen you over me. Perhaps you warmed his bed, but I should have been his bride."

Isabel's cheeks pinked. "Rowena—"

Berthilde interrupted, "Do not soothe your sister's vanity." Gravely, Berthilde took Rowena's arm and assisted her from the chair. "'Tis time you return to your bower. You shall not ruin the happiness of this day with your petty jealousies."

"I do not consider the rule of this kingdom to be a petty matter." Rowena flounced toward the door. "'Twas my right, as eldest sister, to marry a man of importance. 'Tis I who should stand at his side."

Isabel rested her needle on the tabletop. "What if, by some chance, Stancliff lived, and returned to claim your hand?"

"Stancliff? Alive?" Rowena's gaze narrowed upon her, as if she sensed some truth to the scenario Isabel proposed.

Isabel shrugged. "Would you wish to be married to the Dane if your true love returned?"

"Little sister, I am not so ruled by my heart as you— which is exactly why I should be the one accepting the Dane's promises today. I would tell Stancliff a woman of my worth must align herself with the victor for the sake of dignity."

Isabel nodded, her lips pressed together. "I see."

Rowena smiled, but the corner of her lip twitched. "The courtyard at noonday. I shall be there." Sardonically, she added, "With ribbons and flowers in my hair."

"Thank you, Rowena," Isabel said.

At the close of the door, Isabel returned her attention to stitching the final cluster of leaves onto the sleeve.

Berthilde sniffled.

Isabel drew the needle through the linen, and squinted to be sure the stitches remained consistent.

Berthilde sniffled again.

Isabel looked to her maid. To her dismay, tears streamed down her cheeks. "Prithee, Berthilde, what troubles you? Why do you cry?"

"She is horrible to you."

Isabel shrugged. "She is spoiled. I cannot allow that to ruin my wedding day." She smiled, with the expectation her maid would respond in kind. Beneath the table, she tapped her toes against the floor. She wore a wedding gift from Kol, a new pair of scarlet slippers. He had also painstakingly polished her mother's jeweled dagger and returned it to her, so that she might wear it in her girdle during the ceremony. "Perhaps soon, 'twill be your wedding gown we stitch. You have feelings for Thorleksson's captain, Vekell, do you not?"

Berthilde bit her lip and nodded. "I do."

"'Tis good. Such unions will engender the peace between our peoples." Isabel tied the final knot on the cuff, and cut the thread. "The Norse have made clear their willingness for peace. We should not fear them."

"'Tis not the Norse whom I fear, my lady."

Isabel's smile faded. "Who do you fear?"

"Your brother, my lady. Ranulf." Berthilde's voice thickened. Her face crumpled, and tears squeezed out from between tightly closed eyes.

"Hush, friend." With the cuff of her own sleeve, Isabel reached out to swipe the tears away. "Why would you fear Ranulf? Has he not been an honorable king to you? To all of Norsex's people?"

"Aye, that he has." She angled her face against Isabel's palm, as if she sought to hide a terrible guilt.

"Then why do you tremble?"

"For he hath not been an honorable brother to you."

Isabel sat the needle upon the table. She took up the thread, and carefully wound it onto its spool. Her mouth dry, she asked, "What do you mean?"

Berthilde wrung her hands in her skirt, and looked to the ceiling. Tears streamed over her cheeks. "Ranulf was my king. He commanded I remain silent. I was so frightened." She met Isabel's eyes. "As your friend, I should have told you long ago."

Instantly, Isabel's attention narrowed to a point. "What should you have told me, Berthilde? You must say it now."

"That morning . . . after you had confessed to helping the Dane escape from the pit, Ranulf summoned me to his chambers."

In a leaden voice, Isabel urged, "Go on."

"He ordered me to put sleeping herbs in your wine."

Outside Isabel's window, a cloud moved across the sun, diminishing the springlike warmth of the room. She shivered. "Sleeping herbs?"

"He was in such a fury over the Dane's escape. I had never seen him in such a state, nor ever again since."

Berthilde swallowed, and pressed the flat of one palm against her chest, as if attempting to quell the rapid beat of her heart. "So at his command, I did, indeed, boil the herbs for your evening wine."

In truth, Isabel did not remember much about that time in her life, and had attributed the lacking memories, her lethargy, to distress.

Berthilde twisted her sleeve. "At that age you were so full of mischief. You wandered about the keep, and even the burh after dark. I just wanted you to be safe. To behave."

Isabel's heart grew very heavy, but at the same time there was a peculiar relief at hearing a possible explanation for what had happened to her. Could this time of unbroken sleep have been when the attack upon her occurred?

Isabel said, "I would have liked to have known, but still, you torture yourself over this. At times Ranulf's concern bordered upon tyranny. What you did at his command, is no terrible admission."

Berthilde sobbed, "Nay, my lady. That, alone, is not." She pressed her hands to her eyes. "But I fear what I tell you next will not be so easily forgiven."

Isabel grew a bit more anxious at hearing this, and seeing the maid's near-frantic nature. "Tell me, then. I must hear this confession and decide for myself."

"Several nights after the Dane's escape, you were still confined to your chamber. The king had instructed the Lady Rowena to continue sleeping belowstairs to ensure your unbroken rest and continued recovery. After I saw you had fallen asleep, and wouldst not awaken until morn, I left the keep to visit my sister in the burh. Her babe was to be born at any time—"

"'Tis well. I would have wanted you to go." Isabel patted her arm.

"My lady, please listen. I would have you hear my confession."

A long moment of silence passed as Isabel stared into her maid's stricken eyes. "Proceed as you will."

Berthilde swallowed heavily. "When I returned I found Ranulf at your bed."

At hearing this, Isabel could barely gather enough breath to speak. Any words felt strangled in her throat. "What do you mean at my bed?"

Berthilde looked toward the bed, as if remembering. Tears streamed from her eyes. "He crouched just inside the bed curtain, peering at you as you slept. And when he heard me enter, of course he withdrew. Whilst I was fully prepared to believe he had come to ascertain your good health for himself, he became very angry. He ordered me to keep silent about ever having seen him."

Now tears glazed Isabel's eyes as well. "Surely that is all that occurred."

Berthilde hiccupped. "But my lady, there were other nights I went to the burh. What if he is Godric's—"

"Do not say it." Isabel turned to the window.

"I am so very sorry, my lady." Isabel felt Berthilde's hand upon her shoulder. "Like everyone, I assumed the Dane guilty. If I had thought Ranulf—well, I would never have remained silent if I had even considered—"

Isabel closed her eyes against tears she felt determined not to shed. Would she ever know what had happened? Only a confrontation with Ranulf would provide the answers.

Isabel reached up to grasp her maidservant's hand. "'Tis well between you and I, Berthilde."

Berthilde answered, weak of voice. "Your kirtle is finished. The noonday approaches."

"Aye, let us prepare. Today I shall be married." She would not allow Berthilde's dark revelation to destroy what peace Kol had brought to her life.

At noonday, Isabel made her way to the courtyard, accompanied by Berthilde and Rowena. Each woman wore her finest gown. Blue sky spread above them, a brilliant canopy. Though, thankfully, the day was more springlike than winter, the air still carried a very noticeable chill.

Isabel felt a tug on her sleeve. "Sister, wait."

Rowena pursed her lips, then said, "I should not have been so churlish this morn. I suppose I can't have every-thing my way." She smiled, and adjusted Isabel's head veil. "Go into this marriage, knowing I wish you every happiness."

To Isabel's surprise, Rowena embraced her.

Berthilde urged softly, "My lady, your betrothed awaits."

Kol saw Isabel search the garden, and its multitude of gathered faces. Her gaze alighted upon him. Love glowed within her, so powerful that in that moment he felt forgiven by God and all of humanity for all the sins he had com-mitted during his time upon the earth.

Father Janus stepped forward. Kol saw acceptance, if not outright approval, in the priest's smile.

"Shall we begin?" the man said, taking his place upon the steps of the chapel.

"Aye," Isabel answered, moving toward them.

Devon sidled up alongside her. Kol nearly laughed aloud, for with a souring of her lips, and a narrowing of her eyes, she rested her hand upon his arm and allowed her cousin to escort her to the waiting ceremony.

When the crowd had settled, and the only sounds to be heard were the chirping of birds and the distant swell and crash of the waves, Devon cleared his throat and, through scowling lips, announced, "I, Devon of Wyfordon, offer my lady cousin, the Princess Isabel of Norsex, in mar-riage."

Isabel wiped her now-freed hand against her skirts and, with a renewed smile, reached for Kol's. One look into her eyes, and he forgot about Devon and Ranulf, and gave his undivided attention to his bride.

"Do you take this woman, Isabel of Norsex, to be your wife, in the name of the Lord?"

Kol squeezed Isabel's hands. In a low voice he said, "I take thee, Isabel of Norsex, to be my wife, in the name of the Lord."

Isabel repeated the same vow, at which time, Father Janus blessed a ring with holy water.

Kol took the ring, and considered it with a gravity he'd never felt before. "I never thought to find love," he whispered to Isabel.

"Get on with it, then," urged Vekell, and laughter arose all around.

"In the name of the Father." Kol placed the ring upon her thumb. "The Son." Gently, he moved it to her index finger. "And the Holy Spirit." He slid the band onto her long finger, where the gold gleamed in the sunlight.

Father Janus began the blessing, but from the rampart came the bellow of a watchman.

A horn bayed, low and distant.

From outside the courtyard walls arose the collective battle cry of an army. Kol's blood froze. Beside him, Isabel's expression of serenity evaporated into one of fear. The guests scattered.

"Come," he ordered. In haste, he guided her from the garden into the courtyard.

Rowena followed, "What happens? Doth Ranulf attack?"

"My lord!" came a shout, drawing his attention away.

From outside the walls arose cries of fear from the burh, the wailing of children.

"Remain here until I return." Kol ascended the wooden rampart.

Ragi strode toward him. "'Tis Ranulf, my lord. And there is a mercenary force to match our own."

Kol stared out over the lands surrounding the burh. A hundred men, perhaps two, materialized from the forest. Destiny would grant him not even one hour of peace? Looking down the stairs, he met Isabel's eyes, and saw that she understood. They would have no opportunity to extend an offer of peace to Ranulf. Their conflict would be decided in battle.

He descended the steps. Before Isabel could protest, he brushed his lips over hers and turned her over to the care of a young soldier. "Take your lady to the keep's innermost pit, and defend her unto death." To Isabel, he said, "With God's grace, I will see you again."

"Surely 'tis Ranulf!" A smile curled on Rowena's lips.

"How quickly your loyalties change!" Isabel snapped.

"Me?" Rowena gave Isabel's shoulder a sudden shove. "Confess your own sins, sister."

Isabel's heartbeat steadied. "What I feel is no sin, but love. Even if Kol dies today, my loyalty will forever remain with him."

The warrior led them down darkened stairs, into the prison.

An acrid scent filled Isabel's nostrils. "I smell smoke."

A hiss of metal sounded. The warrior groaned and collapsed to the earthen floor. Before Isabel could kneel beside him, a multitude of hulking giants appeared. Grime and filth caked their skin, and merged to their yellowed teeth. Around their bodies were draped matted animal pelts.

Rowena screamed. Isabel pulled her dagger.

"Lower the blade, my lady," instructed a voice from the darkness. "Your salvation has arrived."

Chapter 21

Stancliff strode from the darkness, his helm lifted to expose his face. He extended one leather-clad hand. The other clenched a bloodied short-sword. "Come, I will take you to safety. Your brother awaits."

"Stancliff," cried Rowena. "My love, thou dost live!" Rushing forward, she threw her arms around his neck. Isabel stood rigid as Stancliff kissed her sister, hard and thoroughly. Clearly the heat of the battle kindled his ardor.

In the next moment he ordered them both to follow him into the darkness. His hand circled Isabel's wrist firmly.

Isabel thought to fight against him, to struggle, to remain and stand with Kol, no matter the outcome. But after what had been revealed to her by Berthilde that morning, her desire to confront Ranulf quieted that impulse.

She had to see Ranulf. She had to know the truth. She allowed herself to be taken.

All of a sudden, a man's arm reached out of one of the cells. Through the slat, Isabel recognized Aiken's features.

"Release me," he insisted. "I must take up the sword and fight alongside my Saxon brethren."

Without hesitation, Isabel pulled from Stancliff's hold and hastened to retrieve the keys which hung on the nearby peg. While her fealty lay with Kol, she wished Aiken no ill. Within moments he stood in the corridor alongside them.

Stancliff urged, "Let us get to the outside. We are not safe inside the keep."

Aiken limped along beside them as they made their escape. To gain entrance to the keep, her brother's forces had hacked and burned their way through the sealed hidden tunnel. The haze of charred timber hung heavy in the already darkened cavern. Stancliff drew her close, in the same way he held her sister, and guided them through the ragged hole toward the light and the ongoing battle.

Stancliff pulled Isabel and Rowena into a crouch below a hedge, and advised, "We will cross the field, and go into the forest."

Aiken shouted, "If 'tis God's will, I shall see you again in this life. I choose to remain here, to fight."

Stancliff tossed him a *scramsax*. Before Isabel's goodbye could be spoken, Aiken had disappeared into the foray.

Stancliff urged them forward, toward the battlefield. Warrior giants rushed to provide them with escort.

"Who are these men?" Isabel asked.

"Mercenaries from the north."

At Isabel's gasp, he answered, "Aye, Northmen, and far more ruthless than Thorleksson's."

All around them, men waged violence. Weapons crashed upon flesh and wood. More than one terrified cry fled Isabel's lips as they wove their way through the melee, thickly defended by the Norse soldiers on all sides.

Stancliff hastened them away from the ocean harbor, to ascend a jagged crag which swept upward into the sky beside Calldarington. Atop the plateau, they moved into the trees. Soon the sounds of carnage became dim. Stancliff took them north, as Isabel had suspected he would, and urged them up the steep incline that would take them to the caves.

The ground sloped steeply beneath Isabel's feet. She and Rowena both slipped at times, but Stancliff guided them to the top. After traversing a narrow embankment, he led them toward the mouth of a cavern. At the edge of the precipice, Saxon officers clustered around her brother. Together they observed the distant battle and conferred on strategy.

A warrior ran past the newcomers, his helm bloodied. Falling to his knees before the strategians, he announced, "The assault has succeeded. We have penetrated the keep."

Her brother, solemn-of-face, nodded and lifted his gaze to her. She saw the gleam of his eye, and the hard slant of his lips, and realized something terrible simmered inside him. She was given no chance to consider that further, for Stancliff led her and her sister past several guards, into the cavern.

Without warning, Isabel felt herself shoved forward, hard. She nearly fell to the stony floor, but did not. She whirled, nettled by Stancliff's unexplained roughness. He still held Rowena by the arm.

"Stancliff?" her sister cried. She pressed at his hand, clearly desperate to pry it from her arm. "You are hurting me!"

"And thou didst not seek to hurt me, beloved?" With a growl he pushed her toward Isabel. With eyes full of fire, he glared at them both. "Answer to your king."

"Aye." A voice growled out from behind him. Isabel tensed. Stancliff moved aside, and there stood Ranulf, his mail argent in the faint light. "Answer to your king."

Isabel held her tongue. Her sister did not. "Ranulf. Dearest brother, my king." She hastened forward and fell to her knees. "God will grant you victory against the pagans. I have prayed it would be so."

"When did you pray this, sister?" Ranulf did not bend toward her; rather, he lowered a dispassionate gaze to the crown of her head. Lightly he trailed a finger along her cheek, but his eyes held no affection. "As you stood beside our traitorous cousin, Devon of Wyfordon, to witness the marriage of the Dane to our sister? A man you wished for your own husband?" He hooked his finger into the circlet of flowers and tore it from her head. Rowena gave a little scream and, holding her head in her hands, sobbed.

"Aye, I have spies. Your disappointment in our sister's match was duly noted." With his boot, Ranulf ground the petals into the dirt.

His hot gaze lifted to Isabel. "And you—"

Isabel stepped back.

"Leave us," Ranulf bellowed.

Stancliff stood rigid at the entrance. He considered Isabel, his face as dark as Ranulf's. "My lord, we are in the midst of a battle for control of Norsex."

"I'm aware of the situation." Ranulf's gaze never left Isabel. "Leave us now."

Stancliff lunged past Isabel to claim Rowena's arm. He yanked her to her feet and led her from the cavern.

Ranulf turned his fury to Isabel. He strode forward, violence in his eyes, but Isabel kindled a rage of her own. She would waste no time defending herself when 'twas Ranulf who should be put on trial.

She backed away from him, ensuring she remained out of his reach. "Tell me this true, *brother*. Are you the father of my son?"

Ranulf ceased his advance mid-step. As if she had stolen the breath from his lungs, he blanched. "What?"

"Answer me."

After an eternity, he whispered, "God, no."

Isabel swallowed hard, but forced the foul accusations from her lips. "I know of the peephole." Her voice quaked.

"Of your visits to my room while I lay rendered helpless by sleeping herbs."

Shock rounded Ranulf's eyes, as if he'd been run through with a spear. "I never touched you."

"Do not lie to me." Isabel rushed forward. She had to see his eyes, to see if he lied or spoke the truth.

But to her shock, Ranulf fell away, into a sudden crouch against the cavern wall, as if he could not bear the weight of her accusation. "God's blood, I swear, never."

It stunned her to see the great warrior-king defeated by a few words from her lips. Her voice took on a shrill pitch. "If you are innocent, then why do you cower so?"

"How I struggled to purge my desire for you. How I prayed to God for succor, but he abandoned me to that sin." Ranulf's eyes gleamed with desperation. He covered his mouth, as if it held a thousand secrets. But at once, he arose to his feet and came toward her. "But I never dishonored you. *Never!* My love for you exceeds my passion, and I honor God's commandments, at least in my actions, if not my heart. Tell me, sister. Is this why you have turned from me?"

She pressed back against the stone wall. Never before had she been more afraid than in this moment. Ranulf appeared mad. Isabel flinched when he lifted a hand to her cheek. Instantly that hand clenched into a fist as Ranulf disallowed himself from touching her.

"Of course," he whispered flatly. "You must find me disgusting."

"Aye, that I do. In the eyes of the church, and in my heart, you were my brother."

In sudden violence, he pressed her against the stone wall. "If I am already condemned for my sins, why should I not go forth and commit them?"

Isabel tried to shove him away. Her breath escaped in short gasps. "Take your hands from me."

"I desire you, Isabel, as a man desires a woman. For so

long I have yearned for you, knowing we could never be together."

"You disgrace yourself," Isabel cried, turning her face. Her blood curdled as his kiss slid wet and cold upon her cheek. She shoved him back far enough to escape, if only momentarily, toward the interior of the cave.

Ranulf stalked her. "God hath turned his back upon me for my sins, and I no longer fear his punishments. Why should I, when I already suffer them, day by day?"

Seeing Ranulf's weaponry carefully aligned along the wall, Isabel grasped up a small mace. "Release me."

"Do your best. I surely deserve death, for the things I have done."

From Isabel's mind swept forth an image of a smiling child brother, a brother who had sat upon their father's lap, and who had once played with his toy soldiers, so much like Godric did now. She could not forget him. Emotion choked Isabel. "Nay, Ranulf. 'Tis not too late. Let us go to Father Janus. He can help you."

Ranulf prowled along the far wall of the cavern, moving slowly toward her, trailing his hand along the gray stone.

"Always, Isabel, I loved you. Waited for the time when perhaps I might see the same light in your eyes as I felt in mine own. I knew we could have no lawful union, but perhaps in secret. It made no sense for either of us to marry elsewhere, when doing so would invite covetous relations, powerful men who would wish to claim Norsex for their own. We could have loved one another in clandestine splendor, and guarded our father's legacy."

"No."

"I loved you so much, loved this place so much. And when I thought it would be taken from me—"

"Taken from you?"

Ranulf stopped. He whispered, "I killed him."

Isabel's blood went cold. "Killed who?" Already she knew the answer.

"I killed our father."

A scream clawed inside Isabel's throat. But she subdued the urge, knowing her hysteria might drive him over the edge.

"Why?"

"You already know my secret, Isabel. I was no true son." He shook his head, sadly. "I tried so hard to please him, to become the son he'd always wanted. But in some way I must have displeased him. I loved him with all my heart, but he was going to cast me out and name another heir."

"No. He would never have done that. Father loved you. Even if you were not his true son—" Isabel *remembered*. Her father had adored Ranulf, had believed without question Ranulf would lead Norsex into a cloudless future.

"Then why did he send for that cursed Dane?" He spat his next words, his face twisted with envy, "Your beloved mercenary?"

Invited.

"That's right, Isabel. By honest mistake, I intercepted father's missive to Ugbert. In it he revealed to his brother his intention to subdue *the usurper*—" Ranulf's hand shook as he lifted it to wipe the sweat from his upper lip. "That's what he called me, Isabel, 'the usurper.' "

"Ranulf."

"He was already dying, Isabel." As if in concert with this statement, Ranulf's eyes went dead. "I merely helped him along."

"To secure your place as heir."

"Aye." A resurgence of fire lit his eyes. "And no one knew. No one. No one but the Dane, you see."

"Kol did not know."

"Aye, he did," Ranulf almost sobbed. He smeared his

hands across his cheeks, distorting his own image. "I saw the condemnation in his eyes when he looked at me."

"Is that why you tortured him?"

With a guttural moan, Ranulf clenched his fists over his eyes. "Every time he looked at me, I could feel that he *knew* my sin, knew of the patricide which ate at my heart."

Isabel watched as he paced, as he ranted his fears for her to hear, fears he had held inside for so very long. "I was going to gouge his eyes out the next day, for they haunted me in my bed the entire night. But in the morning he was gone. Set free. By you."

Isabel hovered against the wall of the cave, knowing Ranulf would not allow her to leave this cave with knowledge of what he had done. She would die here.

Slowly, he walked toward her. "He was going to take it all away from me, Isabel."

From outside the cave came shouts, the crisp report of arrows striking against stone. Suddenly Ranulf lunged at her. "I will kill you before I will let him have you."

So distracted was Isabel by the sounds from outside the cave, she failed to escape his sudden grasp. She screamed as he lifted a blade above her.

A hand stopped the downward plunge.

"Ranulf!" Stancliff's voice was hoarse above them. "My God, what are you doing?" With a curse, Stancliff dragged Ranulf away. Isabel raced toward the mouth of the cave.

There she stopped. Up the mountain stormed a multitude of men. Saxon and Danish. And there, at the forefront was Kol. He wore no helmet. His hair flew wildy about his head, tossed by the force of his movement and the wind. All around him fell his opponents, victims of his fury.

Suddenly he paused, and looking up the crag, met Isabel's gaze. She raised her hand to him—

Only to be torn from the earth, a tourniquet crushing her abdomen. She gasped, unable to breathe.

A huge Norseman, one of Ranulf's mercenaries, carried both herself and Rowena toward the tree line.

"We are safe. He has orders to protect us," gasped Rowena, her lips nearly blue from the Norwegian's crushing hold.

Further into the forest they moved. Around her, the world veered and jostled, and finally Isabel lost all understanding of exactly where they were.

The mercenary hurled them to the ground. Isabel rolled to a stop against a tree trunk, as did Rowena beside her.

Isabel's skin crawled, hearing the Norseman's low laughter. *Why* did he laugh so? She realized the answer quickly enough.

Like a bear seeking prey, the soldier reached out a meaty paw and grabbed her sister. In one quick movement, he tore the front of her tunic. Rowena screamed.

Frantically, Isabel searched the ground for any sort of weapon. She cringed, hearing Rowena's screams, and again, the sound of rending cloth.

Desperately her hands grasped a huge stone, too large for her to lift. Again, she heard the laughter from deep within the man's throat. This time, instead of inspiring her to tremble in fear, she trembled with rage.

She would not allow her sister to be defiled by this foul beast. One defiler of women upon the earth was one too many, and if she had to exterminate them all, one by one, she would begin now.

With sudden strength, Isabel bellowed, and lifted the stone into the air, above her head.

Upon the ground, the beast grasped her sister's hands over her head and sought to part her thrashing legs with his knee.

Isabel staggered beneath the weight of the stone. The beast, intent on his prey, remained oblivious to her presence behind him. A smile curved Isabel's lips.

Steadying herself, ensuring her aim, she catapulted the

stone in a downward arc. It landed on the Viking's head and rewarded her ears with a satisfying crunch. Rowena screeched.

The stone bounced off the fiend's skull and rolled to the side, while the mercenary collapsed onto her sister.

"I'm here, Rowena." Isabel scrambled to pull her sister from beneath the unconscious hulk. "He won't hurt you."

Rowena continued to scream, even as Isabel dragged her away. "He was going to . . . going to—"

"I know. I know. But he won't now."

"Is he . . . dead?"

"I don't know." Isabel glanced toward the giant. "I think so."

"I can't bear to look at him." As if to emphasize her disgust, Rowena screamed again.

Unable to take any more screaming, Isabel moved to block her sister's view of the man. "Calm yourself, sister. We must think of what to do."

Suddenly, Rowena's eyes widened. A shadow fell across them.

Rowena screamed.

Pain ripped across Isabel's scalp, as if her hair had been torn from her head. Above her, the sky moved in short, jagged bursts. He dragged her by her hair. Pain shot down her spine as jagged stones gouged her skull and back. Desperately, she dug her fingers and heels into the earth.

He stopped and crouched above her, his lip curled into a wicked smile. Blood trickled from his forehead, down his nose, and dripped onto her cheek.

This time it was Isabel who screamed. Though she knew her strength to be futile in comparison to his, she curled her arm and rammed her fist into the side of his face.

Shockingly, his expression went blank. He tilted to the side, and collapsed. Isabel shoved the senseless heap from her shoulder and leapt to her feet. Oh, God, the stench of him. It was all over her.

Frantic, she searched the small clearing for Rowena, but realized she had been left completely and utterly alone with the downed Norseman.

Rowena had run away, leaving her here to fend for herself.

At her feet the man stirred, groaning. Isabel did not tarry another second, but lunged into the thicket. She ran. Beneath her feet the spring foliage crunched and rustled. The sound of her breath echoed off the trees.

"Rowena!" she shouted. "Rowena!"

She paused, listening for a response, but there was none. Not even the sounds of the battle penetrated this deeply into the forest. Isabel heard only the furtive clickings of insects, the rustling of foliage. Bird songs. Nature held herself oblivious to the spilling of human blood.

Behind her arose a bellow of rage, and a startled flock of birds.

Clasping her hands over her mouth, she fled into the thickest part of the undergrowth.

She did not call for her sister again.

Chapter 22

Isabel!" Kol bellowed into the darkness. He had not paused for even an instant after felling the final challenger, before crashing into the forest in search of her.

Ranulf fled north, but Kol did not care. Nothing mattered anymore. Nothing but Isabel. He had to find her. He had seen the mercenary take her and her sister into the forest.

Even now dusk fell in a thick, smothering blanket across the land. How long would he be allowed to follow the trail left by the Norwegian giant?

He forged ahead, tracking the beast. In time, he could no longer perceive the crushed grass, the bruised leaves or broken stems. Fear clenched itself with an iron vise around his heart. If Isabel was dead, he could only hold himself and his pride to blame. For so long he had pursued his vengeance, scorching his way across the earth and stamping out those he deemed unworthy of a life he would not be allowed to live himself.

He should have lived, he should have loved, regardless

of the brief time he would be allowed. Now his time upon the earth, and all its violent glories, faded to nothingness beneath the knowledge his bride might be dead.

Kol fell to his knees and stared up through the trees, into the purple sky of twilight. Had it taken her death to bring him to final redemption?

He halted, perceiving a sound. A low groan. Male.

His nostrils flaring, he lifted his sword and held it ready. But the man, when he found him, offered no threat. He lay crouched, his head in his hands. Blood matted the man's hair, as well as the ground beneath him. A large stone lay nearby, it too circled with blood.

Then he saw them. Shreds of cloth, their weave fine, their color, delicate of hue. Pieces of a woman's tunic. Kol swallowed hard and circled the man. For Kol, the twilight turned red. Blood red. With a foot, he shoved the Norseman to his back.

Through rage-clenched teeth, Kol hissed, "Where is she?"

"Danish bastard." The Norwegian's lip curled. He attempted to spit on Kol, but managed only to spray red hued spittle upon himself.

Nostrils flaring, Kol extended his sword. "My enemy, this death will be the easy one. For if I find you have hurt her I will follow you into your Hell and slay you a thousand times more."

He finished the warrior.

Turning, he peered at the circle of forest around him, his eyes keen for any sign of Isabel's path of escape.

Blood stained the grass, and there, the trunk of a tree. Inside his chest, his heart quaked. He crashed through the forest, his heart growing colder in tandem with the chill of the descent of night. Though his body performed instinctively with the stamina of a warrior, he grew increasingly soul sick. He had seen the wickedness of men firsthand, the consequences of human deviance. Too vividly he remembered these horrors, and could not prevent his mind from placing Isabel's image in their midst.

"Isabel!" he bellowed his anguish into the colorless purgatory which surrounded him.

He wandered. For an eternity, it seemed.

From somewhere came the murmur of water over stones, smooth and demulcent. He pushed toward the sound. Overhead the sky mimicked the river's path, a midnight swathe of blue, revealed by the treeless riverbed. Beneath his feet the wet river stones clicked and slid. He stumbled the last few steps, as an excruciating thirst built like a ball of flame within his throat. Kneeling, he plunged his hands beneath the surface and drank, and drank.

Finally, realizing his thirst would never be satisfied, he stared down into his hands. The water slipped through his fingers, ran in fine rivulets down his forearms, to paint streaks of black in the dirt and blood.

Inside, his soul screamed its loss. He crouched, wanting to retch. For so long he had battled to remain within this life. But without her he did not care whether he lived or died.

He heard a sound. Or thought he did.

He stood, straining to hear above the rush and splash of the water. Stone scraped upon stone. The hair on his neck arose. Crouching, he lifted his sword, and drew back away from the river.

The sound came from—he closed his eyes and tilted his head to better perceive its source—upriver. He looked north, across the expanse of the water.

From the darkness emerged a slender figure. Low, hiccuping sobs met his ears, mingled with the din of the river. The woman stumbled on the rocks and, for a moment, knelt, as if she had no more strength left in her.

"Isabel." Was she real or had she joined the shades of his mind?

The water crashed against his shins as he stormed into

the river, never taking his eyes from her, afraid to blink for fear she would disappear.

"Isabel," he shouted from the abyss of his soul. His voice cut through the night.

Her head snapped up. Her face shone white amidst her dark, wild curls.

She pushed up, stumbled on her hem. "Kol!"

She fell into his arms. Stains mottled her tunic. Blood, he could smell it. Did Death follow her, just beyond the range of his sight? He did not look into the trees, afraid he might see an otherworldly being, flanked by his demons, stalking her.

She belonged to him. Death would not claim her. No one would take her from him. Never again.

Who could have thought he would be brought to his knees by his love of a woman? Frantically, his hands moved over her, searching, but he quickly realized there were no wounds, no evidence of violation.

She cried, "There is so much blood." Her hands gripped his arms. "You are wounded."

"I am well," he murmured into her hair. "Now that you are returned to me."

Devon was dead, by the hand of a Norwegian mercenary, and he did not know where Rowena had been taken. He did not care. Isabel had been returned to him, and he vowed never to let her go again.

The cries of the wounded punctuated the silence of the burh. Black smoke merged with the low fog. Those who were able, crawled over the debris of war and searched for fathers, brothers, and comrades. In the coming hours they would tend wounds or hold vigil. Or say prayers for their dead.

The sight of the destroyed burh would have over-whelmed Isabel if not for Kol. He led her through the de-

struction, a steady hand at her back. Thatched cottages
smoldered. Flames cast eerie, wavering light against the
mist.

Isabel took in the horror through a sheen of tears. "I
would not have thought my broth—" She bit down on the
word. She had almost called him *brother*. But never again.
"I did not think Ranulf capable of this. These were his own
people."

Kol stepped over a fallen timber, and guided her across.
She knew he had seen much worse during his lifetime.

Somewhere a child cried for a father who most likely
would never return. "Even if he were not a true son of
Aldrith, the people were not to blame."

"The most dangerous men are those who act in desperation." Kol spoke softly. His blue gaze, true and steady,
settled upon her face. "He will not return to Calldarington
again, Isabel. Not alive. I swear it."

"I see now, that is the way it must be."

"My lord!" A voice pierced through the darkness.
"Thorleksson." She believed it to be Svartkell. The smoke
was so thick she could not see the warrior, although he
could not be so very far away.

"This way," Kol murmured, taking her forearm.

At that moment a figure lurched from the darkness. Isabel recoiled, but the man slumped at her feet. "My lady.
Help me."

Though the man lay facedown, the muffled voice was
Saxon.

"Thorleksson!" Svartkell called again.

Isabel urged, "Go to your men. I will stay here and see
what help I can offer the wounded."

"You should not wander alone."

"'Tis my duty to tend to them. They are my people,
more so now than ever before."

Kol considered the man at her feet. "I will return for
you posthaste. Do not move from this place."

Isabel nodded. When he was gone she bent to the prostrate figure. "Friend, reveal to me your wounds, so that I may help."

"Princess." The slumped figure straightened, grew broad and solid. Beneath the deep hood of the man's mantle she saw only darkness where a face should have been. Fear took hold of her. She pulled back, but a hand snared her.

"Do not fear." The man pushed the hood to his shoulders. "'Tis I."

Her sister's betrothed sat before her, his face muddied and nearly unrecognizable. Though she felt no loyalty to her brother or his officers, she knew this man had been just as deluded as she about the nature of her brother. "You must go, Stancliff. Your life is in danger here."

"Perhaps I should spare your Dane the trouble of killing me." He cursed beneath his breath. "I am tempted to kill myself for giving my fealty to such a madman as Ranulf."

Isabel blinked in disbelief. Stancliff had always been Ranulf's most stalwart supporter. "You have turned from him?"

"He hath deceived me, my lady." He rose to his knees beside her. His face was weary. "How long has he known he was not Aldrith's true son? He could have confided in me. I would have supported him regardless. Blood alone does not guarantee a throne, not on this wicked earth. But now . . . he has gone too far."

"Rowena," Isabel gasped. "He has harmed her?"

"God protect her, I do not know. He has gone mad, I swear it. He will not let me so much as see her, let alone speak with her. He intends to imprison her at Caervon."

She grasped his shoulder. "Come. Let us tell Thorleksson. He will rescue her."

"I pray it." He peered at her through the fringe of his hair. "God has led me to a difficult decision, but one into which I place my whole heart. I have come to give my fealty to Thorleksson."

Isabel stood. "I will take you to him."

"Wait." Stancliff held her fast. "There is a reason for my secrecy. There is danger——"

"Danger?"

He licked his bottom lip. His hands were gentle as he took her forearms in hand, holding her, preparing her for some revelation. "You must be strong."

"What is it?" Inwardly, she braced herself. "Do not delay, tell me now."

"'Tis Godric." In that moment, the world stopped around Isabel. His next words seemed spoken from the bottom of a well. "Ranulf has taken him from the abbey."

"No." She shoved him. Her words sounded muffled to her own ears. When her legs failed, Stancliff held her.

"Isabel, Ranulf is out of his mind with hatred for you since learning of your marriage to the Dane. He killed those who stepped in to protect the child."

"Please, no!"

Stancliff closed his eyes, as if blocking out a terrible vision. "Isabel, he hath confessed to me the siring of Godric."

Isabel wrenched free of him, and took several paces into the dark before bending at the waist. Her stomach heaved. She could not breathe.

Behind her, Stancliff said softly, "Now that he has Godric, he will not rest until he has you as well. He swore to me——"

She swung round to face him. He clamped his lips closed.

"What? What did he swear?"

He took a deep, steadying breath. "He swore he would release Rowena to me if I brought you to him."

"That is why you came here." Isabel stared at him in horror. "Such wicked games my false brother plays."

Stancliff rubbed a hand across his brow. "I would not do it. No matter how much I love her, you are as dear to me as a sister. We will find another way."

"Kol would never allow me to go to Caervon without him. Tell me, doth Ranulf know you have turned from him?"

"Nay." As if shamed, he looked to his feet. "I do believe he expects me to bring you to him."

Isabel lifted her fists to her cheeks. "If Kol charges in to rescue Godric, I fear Ranulf's madness, and what he might do to my child in his fury and determination to keep him from me."

"Aye," Stancliff conceded. "As do I."

Isabel made her decision. Though she loathed any deceit against her husband, she would do anything to save the life of her child, even if it meant giving her own. "Come. We must find horses so that we may travel to Caervon now."

"But lady!"

Isabel drew herself up, and aligned her shoulders. "As daughter of Aldrith, and princess of this kingdom, I command you to do as I say. You will take me to Ranulf."

Stancliff closed his eyes, then nodded. "I shall do as you wish."

Together they hurried toward what remained of the stables. From the haze, a tall figure emerged. "Isabel."

'Twas Kol. Isabel's heart fell, for how would she save her child now? Already, he had seen her.

Isabel quickly formed another plan. She gripped Stancliff's arm, praying he would follow her lead.

"Husband. Ranulf's adviser has come to offer you his fealty."

Kol peered through the smoke, his eyes riveted to Stancliff's face. "Has he, now?"

Stancliff stepped forward to kneel at Kol's feet.

Isabel spoke again, before Stancliff could ruin her intentions. "Stancliff hath brought word Ranulf holds my sister and—" Isabel's voice failed her. Did she do the right thing? Could she, alone, save her child? "And Godric as well, at Caervon."

His face devoid of suspicion, Kol sidestepped Stancliff, and moved to her side. "Isabel." He pulled her to him.

Guilt nearly overwhelmed her, but she could see no other way. "What will you do?"

"We will depart for Caervon posthaste."

Isabel nodded. 'Twas what she'd hoped for. "Ranulf doth not know of Stancliff's change of loyalties. You may use him as messenger."

Early the next morn, as the pyres still lit the sky, they departed for Caervon, and arrived there just as evening turned the afternoon sky into a deeper blue.

Kol walked through the trees, into the clearing. Warriors had been posted to protect the encampment through the night. All about him, his men clustered, and lit fires. Among them were Saxon men who had sworn fealty to Kol after witnessing the violence their usurped king had wrought upon Calldarington's innocent citizens in the name of vengeance.

His gaze found Isabel, who sat beneath a tree mending a sword gash in his tunic. Tomorrow morning he would wear the garment beneath his mail when he met Ranulf on the field of contest.

Moments ago, he had sent the Saxon, Stancliff, to Ranulf, under the continued guise of a loyal thane, to deliver terms. At first light, Kol would meet Ranulf on the field at Caervon. They would fight to the death, for the kingdom of Norsex, and for the lives of Isabel's sister and son.

Father Janus traversed the far side of the clearing. He met Kol's eyes and nodded, before disappearing down a darkened trail.

Perched on a branch of an oak, a single raven cawed and lifted its wings. Kol narrowed his gaze. "Cursed bird."

The animal tilted its head and regarded Kol with dispassionate black eyes. The same raven had flitted alongside the trail, alighting upon trees, and swooping overhead, as Kol and his assembled forces had traveled to Caervon. He had heard the whispers of his warriors.

He would die on the morrow.

Kol lowered into a crouch before Isabel. She looked up. Tears glazed her eyes, as if she knew their time together grew short.

"Come with me."

In silence, Isabel folded his tunic, and accepted his hand. He led her from the clearing, down a narrow trail which ended against a cluster of oaks.

Father Janus awaited them there, cloaked in his vestments. "Your husband hath reminded me of the untimely interruption of your wedding."

Emotion tightened his chest. "Father Janus assures me we are married, but still, I wanted—"

"Yes," Isabel whispered. "I want the same."

Father Janus lifted his hands. "Then please, cross the threshold into God's church." He indicated the bowed arches overhead. Kol and Isabel followed the priest to where he had spread a cloth on the grass. Together they knelt upon it. The warmth in Isabel's eyes almost made Kol forget the blood and soot on her wedding garments, and the raven, which even now, perched in the tree above.

Father Janus led them in Mass and Communion. When they finished, the first stars glimmered in the heavens.

"Now you may bestow upon your bride the Kiss of Peace."

Kol bent and pressed his lips to Isabel's. Against his mouth, he felt her smile. "Husband."

"Wife."

To Father Janus, Kol said, "You will forgive us for not lingering?"

Father Janus appeared only mildly shocked. "Of course."

Kol rested her hand on the crook of his arm, and led her toward the encampment, to a tent which stood larger, and apart from the rest. Dragon heads perched at the crossed timbers, their lips drawn to reveal their fangs.

His men kept their distance. Some smiled. Others shouted encouragements. Kol pushed open the flap, and Isabel went inside. Warmth curled around him in teasing, seductive coils. A light haze filled the room, a product of the small fire in the center of the earthen floor.

A bed stood partially hidden behind a heavy curtain, its beams carved into flourishes and ravens. His armor hung nearby. His weaponry glinted in the firelight, polished and laid out in an orderly row.

Bliss and despair washed over him, all at once. He had but one night to impart to Isabel a love which would last beyond death.

She drew him to the chair beside the fire, and lowered to her knees. Upward, over the leather of his boots, she ran her palms. With a gentle tug, she loosened the laces, and the boots, and slid them off.

"What a fine wife you are," he whispered. When she looked up, he saw her anguish.

'Twas clear she, too, believed tonight would be their last together.

"Only for you, my lord."

He reached for, and touched her hair. Her eyes glowed.

"Do you see the small case, there beside the bed? Bring it to me."

Isabel stood, and retrieved the narrow box. When she returned to him, he pulled her into his lap. He pulled her close against his shoulder, never wanting to forget her softness, the smell of her skin. He would take those memories with him to Caervon at daybreak, and they would be his strength. Even in death.

From the case he produced an ivory comb. "Your hair hath always intrigued me."

"Truly?"

"Aye." He lifted a silken lock and drew the comb through. "Your hair, and your scarlet slippers."

Isabel rested her head against him, and lifted her feet. She still wore his wedding gift. "Do you know what intrigued me about you?"

"I am afraid to know."

"Everything." She laughed, not without sadness.

He pressed a finger alongside her chin, and brought her around for a kiss. A brief, chaste sort of kiss, yet inside he smoldered.

"Let us go to bed. I will hold you."

She sat up straight. "You wish to *sleep*?"

He let out a low breath. "No, I do not wish to sleep." He set the comb aside. "But I know your heart is with your son, as it should be. I would not wish to—"

She pressed her fingertips to his mouth.

From his lap she stood, and turned, her back to the fire.

"My heart is also here, with you." Her voice wavered on the last word. "I became a bride yesterday, and I choose to make love to my husband this night, so that he will face tomorrow with my love as his shield and strength." Slowly she unfastened the closure of her gunna, and allowed it to fall to the floor.

He stood, but did not move toward her.

Isabel dropped her kirtle and tunic, and stood naked before him. Her eyes gleamed so darkly he no longer saw the color in them.

She reached. "Come, husband."

"Isabel—" His voice caught.

She whispered, "You asked that I trust you. Now I ask you do the same."

Chapter 23

Isabel awoke to darkness, and a frantic realization. Blessed Lord, she had fallen asleep. Had she missed her chance to slip away?

Nearby, the fire turned to ash. She turned toward Kol, but found only an empty pillow. Voices came from outside the tent. Naked, she crept from the bed to listen.

A voice, Vekell's, said, "You will best him. I have no doubt *you will prevail.*"

For a long time, there was only silence. Kol finally said, "If I die—"

Vekell laughed, an uneasy sound. "The Norse have abandoned Ranulf. His forces dwindle to nothing."

"My destiny awaits me, there on that field. You sense that truth as well as I. We must discuss settlements for the men and their families."

Vekell laughed no more. In a quiet voice, he answered, "What would you have me do?"

Isabel backed away. She would hear no more talk of

what would occur when Kol was dead. The time for her departure had come.

In haste, she donned Kol's woolen tunic. After pulling on his too large boots, Isabel shuffled to where Kol's mail shirt and helm perched on their stand.

Neither Kol nor his men would allow her to leave the camp, yet no one would question the movements of their lord. Even if her ploy gave her only a moment's lead, she could outrun them and surrender herself to Ranulf, and by doing so, spare the lives of everyone she loved.

She paused only long enough to kiss her scarlet slippers and place them side by side upon Kol's pillow.

Though she struggled beneath the weight, she donned his armor. From his weaponry, she selected a sharp, long-bladed knife. Into the rear panel of the tent, she thrust its tip, and dragged it down through the sturdy fabric. Heart pounding, she entered the shelter where Morke stood awaiting his master's command.

Kol strode through the camp with Vekell at his side. "—and you will return her safely to Calldarington. From this day on, your duty is to Isabel, and to her child."

Vekell grimly agreed. "Aye, my liege."

Kol gauged the time by the paling hue of the morning sky. "I suppose I should prepare."

"I will wait for you here, my lord."

Kol walked toward the tent. The fragrance of spring scented the air and the earth about him felt new. How he yearned to remain in this life with Isabel.

He stared at the tent. How would he say goodbye to her?

He had no time to ponder the question, for, from behind the tent appeared a rider in mail and helm. A warrior? The rider grew close.

He saw himself.

An unsteady, suspiciously smaller version of himself. *Atop his horse.* The rider snapped the reins and thrust Morke into a full-out run. Kol's hair whipped about his face as the rider sped past.

The air carried her scent.

"Isabel," he roared. Dirt thrown up from the horse's hooves showered all around him.

"Stop her," he shouted. But already she had flown past his men, who stood looking perplexed at the rider. They turned confused looks upon him as he shouted again.

Isabel rode Morke at high speed down the narrow path. She knew the way to Caervon. She had been there before, years ago, with her father. 'Twas an ancient stronghold, abandoned long ago. Leaves whipped around her, branches snagged in Kol's mail shirt.

She grasped the pommel of Kol's saddle. It was a struggle to remain upright beneath the weight of his helm and mail.

They would follow her. She just had to make the clearing.

She could waste no time. She must allow Ranulf to see her immediately, to realize her willingness to be taken prisoner. She grasped the chin piece of the helm and lifted—

"Oh—" Pain speared her shoulder.

She plummeted, amidst the scrape and clash of mail, to the ground. Overhead the sky shone a radiant blue, through the narrow aisle of trees. Breath escaped her.

She twisted, rolled. The scent of earth covered her. She faded in and out of awareness.

"Don't touch her," a man's voice commanded. Isabel did not want to awaken to see who spoke. The darkness protected her from the pain. Someone lifted her. A sharp jolt shot through her left side.

Moist lips pressed against her cheek. ". . . my love . . . thought you were he . . ."

Isabel tried to open her eyes, but her lids were so very heavy.

". . . should not have interfered . . ."

So familiar. Even his scent called to mind hazy, vague recollections.

"Soon we shall be together."

Someone rolled a huge boulder onto Isabel's chest. Isabel's eyes flew open to find no boulder, only a balding, berobed man, who sat on the floor beside the pallet where she lay. He held a length of linen and leaned over her.

"Greetings, lady princess." Gently he lifted her into a near-sitting position, and deftly secured the linen beneath her arm and shoulder. "I am the medicus. You will survive the wound, but you must rest."

"Wh—who—" she croaked. Her mouth had no moisture.

The man lifted a crude wooden goblet to her lips. "Drink."

As soon as the liquid soothed her parched tongue, she asked, "Who brought me here?"

The man seemed not to have heard. Calmly he turned from her, placed several small tools into a leather case. That done, he stood and left the room, closing the door.

The room around Isabel slowly became clear. She lay in a partially ruined tower. That she knew from the circular shape of the chamber, and its high, pointed rafters. Through great, sagging holes in the roof, she heard birds call to one another. Tree branches and leaves littered the floor, as well as the trestle at the center of the room.

Men's voices came from outside. "Tis the only way to ensure your victory, my king."

The door burst open. She saw the back of Ranulf's head as he turned to argue with the other man.

"I do not like it. I will fight by my own skill, my own strength. If God deems me worthy, he will see that I prevail."

"God would not wish that Danish bastard to have your kingdom. 'Tis yours by right." Stancliff pursued Ranulf into the room. "Take it." In his hands he held a sword. The weapon glinted in the sunlight.

At that moment Ranulf realized she did not simply occupy the pallet on the far side of the room, but watched, fully aware.

He rushed forward and fell onto his knees beside her. "God, Isabel." He took up her hand. "At least God has seen fit to answer one of my prayers."

Isabel stared down at the crown of Ranulf's head.

When he looked up, she saw the tears that brightened his eyes. She saw his plea. *Forgive me.*

Aloud, he said, "Can you believe that Danish pig had you shot in the back?" His hand shook as he extended it toward a trencher at the side of the pallet. From it he lifted a shattered arrow shaft. "Today I will kill him for it."

Dreamlike memories sprouted from within . . . *should not have interfered . . . my love.*

Realization flowed over her like a wave of scalding water. She forced herself to take slow, even breaths. She knew full well no Danish arrow had pierced her shoulder.

Stancliff had led the ambush against her, believing she was Kol.

But why would Stancliff seek Kol's death when he had sworn him fealty? By his interaction with Ranulf now, it became clear to Isabel he played each man against the other.

"Why did you escape the Dane?" Ranulf leaned to adjust the pillow beneath her head, giving her a direct view of Stancliff.

"Because I realized I wish for the same outcome as you," Isabel lied, staring hard into Stancliff's eyes. "I wished to prove my loyalties before the contest."

Stancliff stood rigid and silent. He still held the sword crosswise in his hands. After a moment, a smile crept to his lips.

She turned her cheek to the pillow, unable to look at either man. "I am so tired. May I see Godric now?"

"Godric?" There was a short pause, and somehow Isabel knew what Ranulf would say before he said it.

"He remains at the abbey. I shall send for him posthaste, once the contest has been won."

Isabel knew she could no longer avoid Stancliff. Lord, his eyes bored holes into her very skull. She knew he watched, waited for her reaction to Ranulf's ignorance of Godric's whereabouts. All along he had plotted against her brother, and desired her for himself.

Godric's life could depend upon her reaction.

As Ranulf stood, Isabel smiled at Stancliff, a small, secretive smile. *Let him believe they were co-conspirators.* 'Twould buy her time to decide what she must do.

Relief broke across Stancliff's face. His skin, which had been pallid, flushed with warmth.

When Ranulf turned back to them, she purged the smile from her face.

"I must go now and prepare." He straightened proudly. "Isabel, if you should wish to watch, this window overlooks the field where I shall defeat the Dane."

"My lord," Stancliff interrupted with clear urgency. "The sword."

Ranulf glanced at Stancliff as if he were a bothersome, but necessary, fly.

"All right," he muttered tightly. "I shall carry the sword."

Stancliff held it out, his eyes aglow. "Careful. Touch only the hilt, and here, the midsection of the blade."

Isabel's stomach roiled with the understanding that the blade had been poisoned to give Ranulf an unfair advantage in the contest.

Ranulf did not take the sword. "Friend, if you would take the sword belowstairs and wait for me. I would like a moment with Isabel."

Isabel's skin crawled. Surrounded by murderers and liars, she wanted only to scream. But what if Stancliff held Godric elsewhere? That is, if the child were not already murdered by his hand.

Surely not, she calmed her fears. Certainly Stancliff knew if he hurt her child 'twould only engender her hatred. She prayed Godric remained safe at the abbey.

Stancliff's lips tightened. 'Twas clear he did not wish to leave the two of them alone. "Of course, my lord. As you wish." He glanced out the window. "But make haste. Already the Danes line the field."

"Let them wait," Ranulf snapped. "I will be there anon."

"Yes, my lord." Stancliff held the sword carefully, and pushed backward through the door, leaving them alone.

Isabel sat up from the pallet.

"Lie back, sister."

"Ranulf, you must listen to me. Stancliff has betrayed you."

Ranulf's brows creased downward and a half smile quirked his lips. "What is this you say?" Suspicion edged his tone.

"Stancliff told me you held Godric hostage and would kill the boy if I didst not surrender to you."

"No." Ranulf pulled away. "That is impossible. Stancliff has been my closest ally since boyhood."

"I would not lie to you, Ranulf, I—"

"Yes, you would." Ranulf shoved his fingers through his hair. "You despise me for . . . for what I did to Father."

He peered at her with shadowed eyes. Suddenly he

strode forward and pulled her from the pallet. She cried out as pain scored her shoulder in jagged rows.

He forced her to look out the window. Instantly she saw Kol emerge from beneath a large tree on the south side of the field. He wore no mail, or jerkin. Only a linen shirt. A leather strap held his hair back, and his face appeared angular and fierce.

His eyes fixed upon the window, where Ranulf held her. To her surprise, Aiken stood amidst Kol's gathered legion. Was the Saxon prisoner or friend?

Beside Isabel, Ranulf hissed, "Watch me kill your lover. When he is gone, you will have no choice but to turn to me." He thrust her onto a stool beside the window.

"Ranulf!" Stancliff's voice, sharp and disapproving, called from the door. He strode forward and looked at Isabel.

"Isabel, you should not be out of your bed."

Ranulf's eyes flashed. "She will remain at the window, and she will watch me kill the Dane. Only then will she begin to forget." He backed away from them both. "I won't be back until he is dead."

He whirled and departed. The sound of his boots faded down the narrow stair.

Stancliff drew closer to her side. "'Twill all be over soon, Isabel."

"Aye, it will." Isabel cautioned herself against hysterics, but she had to ask, "Stancliff, my son—"

"He is safe. Well guarded and well fed. You will see him before nightfall." He smiled with utter arrogance.

She had need to *see* Godric, to know Stancliff spoke the truth. "At the abbey or—"

"I must go." He smiled hopefully. "Ranulf will want me there when the contest begins."

"Of course." She forced her own smile, one that could have been nothing more than wan. "I will wait here. For you."

Isabel turned toward the window, her heart racing. Kol still stood at the edge of the field, staring at her window. She must warn him of the poisoned blade. Could he see her? The sun moved high overhead, and surely she was lost in shadows.

Ranulf rode out from beneath the wall. He glanced up at the window, his lips turned down in a grimace. If only he would believe her, that he had been manipulated by Stancliff.

How long had Stancliff played his wicked game? At the north edge of the field Ranulf dismounted. He stopped and rested his face against the side of his saddle, as if praying for strength.

He turned to a Saxon beside him and extended his hand for the sword. With a swish of chain mail, Ranulf lifted the blade, examined it. The metal glinted in the sun.

Isabel remembered Ranulf's strength, his prowess. Even if Kol managed to inflict a fatal wound, in all likelihood, Ranulf would achieve his goal.

Just a scratch of the poisoned tip could kill Kol.

On the far side of the field, Kol took up his own sword, and turned to meet his challenger. She saw his eyes search for, and find, the window where she stood.

He thrust his sword into the air and shouted, "Remember me!"

Isabel opened her lips to scream a cry of warning.

A large hand clamped down on her mouth. "I knew it. I knew you would try to warn him." Stancliff's breath blew hot and fetid against her neck. "Faithless bitch."

She grew faint from pain as he applied pressure to her wounded shoulder.

"Watch. Watch as your Danish lover dies."

Held captive against Stancliff's chest, she could do nothing but. Ranulf and Kol sat atop their mounts, on opposite sides of the field. Each man shouted, and thrust his heels into his animal's sides. The steeds stormed toward one another. Spears were lifted—

Isabel screamed against Stancliff's hand. He wrenched her closer, his arm immobilizing hers so she could not move. Isabel slumped in Stancliff's arms. He sensed her surrender, for his hand slid from her lips, to her neck.

"That's it, my sweet. Soon we will be together."

She screamed. Loudly, fiercely, fighting and kicking. Caught off balance, Stancliff rocked back, falling to the floor with her in his arms.

Her wound screamed with pain. Blood darkened her kirtle. Yet she leapt to her feet, kicked away his clawing hands. She leaned out the window, only to see both men afoot and staggering. Wounded?

She shouted as loudly as she could. "The sword! Poi—"

Chapter 24

Amidst the shouted encouragements of his warriors, Kol rolled up from the ground. Ranulf's spear had knocked him from his borrowed horse, but inflicted no wound. He glanced over his shoulder to see his own spear lying shattered, but Ranulf stood, and appeared to favor no wound.

Vekell thrust out Kol's sword and shield. "Destiny be damned! Take the day, my lord!"

Grasping both, Kol swung round, and advanced on his enemy. His mind held only shadowy memories of the man who had tortured him in Calldarington's fortress pit. He'd preferred to believe Ranulf was weak, and too cowardly to fight without aid of an army beside him. But the man who came at Kol now, with sword raised, matched him in size and skill.

The clearing fell silent, but for the crush of their boots upon the dry grass. Ranulf swung, and the ring of sword against shield-boss signaled the continuation of the contest.

A scream—Isabel's—pierced Kol's concentration.

Ranulf's eyes darted toward the window, revealing a concern which perplexed Kol.

Desperate to spare Isabel any harm, Kol shouted to his opponent, "You care for the princess, I see you do. Release her and the boy, and we shall meet in peace to negotiate terms."

"The boy?" Ranulf shook his head. "Speak no words to me, Dane. Only die." The Saxon lifted his sword above his head, but froze as a strangled scream carried over the field.

Fury raged from Kol's lips. "Damn you. Why doth she scream? What do they do to her?"

Kol leveled a murderous blow. Ranulf deflected it with disconcerting ease, his fair hair clinging to the side of his face. "'Tis a *Viking* arrow in her shoulder, not a Saxon one. Do not accuse *me* of causing her pain."

"She is wounded?" Instantly, he lowered his sword. Desperation eclipsed all else. "Send my physician. He is there at the corner of the field."

Ranulf snapped, "Her wound hath been duly tended."

"Then why doth she scream in such pain? Who tends to her now?"

"She is attended by mine own captain," Ranulf snarled defensively. "Now, concern yourself only with my sword, for it sings your death with my every blow." He crouched, as if to attack.

Suspicion spread through Kol like plague. "Your captain? The man called Stancliff?"

"Aye." Ranulf shifted his grip on the pommel of his sword. "Cease your delay, coward. Let us finish what should have been finished two winters ago."

Kol's blood pounded so hard in his head, it smothered the roar of the Saxon and Danish warriors who lined the field. "You must stop him. He is traitor to you and I. He hath played us against one another."

With an angry roar, Ranulf turned to stalk away. He

whirled, and extended the point of his sword toward Kol. "Lies!"

" 'Tis his plan that we destroy one another."

At that moment, another scream came from the keep.

Kol looked to the sky and uttered a desperate prayer. "God, take my life, not hers."

"What is this you pray?" Ranulf circled Kol.

"She is my wife." Kol threw his sword to the ground. All around, his men shouted in protest. Stepping toward Ranulf, he said, "I swear on all God's saints, 'twas no Viking arrow which did her harm but a Saxon ambush, because your captain believed her to be me. If we delay any longer, Stancliff will kill not only Isabel, but your son as well."

"Godric is *not* my s—" Ranulf took several steps back. "Oh, God. 'Tis all so clear now."

Though exertion reddened his face, a certain calmness appeared to claim him. Only then did Kol see the blood seeping from the Saxon king's side. His Viking spear must have pierced the Saxon king's armor at the onset of their contest.

Kol approached Ranulf, his voice low so that no one else could hear. "I know you love her, and Godric. Come, let us put aside our hatreds and save them. Together as allies."

With purposeful slowness, Ranulf drew his blade across his leather-clad thigh; and, turning it to the other side, did so again.

For the first time, he met Kol's eyes. "Tell Isabel . . . 'tis a wedding gift from her brother."

Before Kol could react, the Saxon attacked.

Rolling, Isabel kicked Stancliff in the center of the chest. He grabbed her leg and yanked her from the wall. He pulled himself on top of her and ground her shoulders into the floor.

"You will forget him."

"You're mad!"

"No, I just go after what I want."

"You were betrothed to my *sister*!"

"Second choice is no choice at all." He fisted a handful of her hair. " 'Twas you I wanted. Always. Perhaps because I knew he desired you, and would never allow himself the pleasure. But Ranulf refused."

"No."

"Aye, it's our story, my love."

"No!"

"Ranulf knew you set the Dane free, and spoke his suspicions to me. Always the little hellion, sneaking about at night, getting into trouble. If the burh learned the truth, they would burn you on a stake."

Isabel gasped, his weight crushing her.

"So he had your maid put herbs in your drink to make you sleep at night. I know, you see, for I mixed the herbs myself. I must confess, I've found a knowledge of herbs — and poisons, for that matter — to be quite useful. Nightshade worked very well on your father."

Isabel gasped, her hate burgeoning tenfold.

"But you . . . you were so pretty, in your bed. I just wanted to look, but your skin was so perfect, so soft—"

"You disgust me!" Isabel hissed. "I was defenseless."

"But always intended for me."

He leaned down, as if to kiss her. Isabel wrenched an arm free and tried to claw his eyes, but he held her.

From behind him came a scream. "I shall kill you myself!"

Rowena brought down a large pot on Stancliff's head. At what point had she entered the room? In the moment Stancliff fell, Isabel scrambled away and returned to the window.

"Isabel!" shouted Stancliff.

"Foul traitor," Rowena shrieked. "Murderer!" *Clonk.*

Isabel knew not what occurred between Rowena and her faithless betrothed after that, so focused was her attention on the field below. For a moment she saw nothing but a blur of movement. So many warriors, clustering. Where was Ranulf?

Her heart stopped beating.

Where was *Kol*?

The throng parted. Vekell knelt, and just beside him—

"No!" she screamed. *"No!"*

She tore at her hair, and shut her eyes, but saw nothing but the image of Kol's body, lifeless upon the field, his warriors kneeling around him in abject grief. Her anguish too great, she collapsed.

Her husband was dead.

Stancliff chuckled, looking out the window. His footsteps moved past her and he crossed the room to where a large table stood. Upon it sat a flask of wine and several goblets. Isabel heard the sounds of the liquid, splashing into a goblet. She heard his swallow, and his sigh of contentment.

From beneath her tousled curtain of hair, she watched him with all the hatred that burned within her. Just a short distance away, Rowena rolled to her side and moaned. Though Isabel wished to hasten to her sister's side, caution held her where she lay.

Through narrowed eyes, she watched as Ranulf grabbed up a cushion and tossed it to land near her sister. He laughed.

He took a vial from the leather pouch at his waist. He tapped the vessel at the edge of a flask of wine. He had just returned the empty ampule to his pouch when the door flew open.

Ranulf staggered inside. Blood stained his torso, drenched his braies. His eyes fixed upon Isabel, glassy and flat. "He is dead."

Isabel buried her face against her knees, wishing she could burn the memory of this moment from her mind.

"What hath happened to Rowena," Ranulf inquired.

"Delicate girl," chuckled Stancliff. "She watched from the window and fainted from the excitement of seeing you vanquish the Dane. I have placed a pillow beneath her head and expect her to revive shortly."

Rowena moaned.

"Ah, I see. And Isabel?"

"Sadly, I found it necessary to subdue her."

"Hmmmm," came her brother's simple answer.

"Let us drink to our victory." Stancliff lifted a goblet and poured it full of the tainted drink. He extended it toward Ranulf.

Isabel sobbed. She should let Ranulf die. He had murdered Kol. She would have him hear her judgment before he descended to Hell.

"Coward!" she shouted, pointing a finger at him. She trembled.

Ranulf trembled, too.

"Coward?" Suddenly, he lurched toward her. She screamed as he fell upon her, a forced embrace. He smelled of blood and sweat.

She struggled, hating him, until he whispered in her ear. "Trust me."

She stilled. What was he saying?

"Just this once. Trust." His lips pressed against her ear. He withdrew from her with a whisper. "Redemption."

Stancliff stood rigid and watchful, straining to hear any words spoken. The polished goblet glowed mellowly in his hand.

Ranulf moved toward him, using chairs and tables as a means of support. He groaned softly with the effort. Stancliff's teeth shone like pearls behind his wide-mouthed smile.

Isabel watched, knowing not what to do, as Ranulf took

the goblet from Stancliff's hands. Ranulf turned. His dark eyes gleamed with sure intent as he stared at Isabel.

Somehow he knew the wine was poisoned.

She shook her head *no.* He gave her a small smile, but lifted the cup to his lips and drank.

Stancliff leered. "You are the champion. Our true king."

Ranulf swayed, and dropped his sword. The clatter echoed off the walls of the room, an ugly sound. He sighed softly and lowered the goblet to the table.

Stancliff stared at him as if waiting. Curse him, she saw the smile twitch upon his lips.

"My lord?" His query rustled from his throat, as smooth as velvet. "Are you well?"

Ranulf coughed. "Aye. I am well." Below his boot, blood puddled in a dark footprint. "My sword. Would you give it to me, friend?"

"'Tis my honor," Stancliff gushed genially. He bent to grasp the sword by the hilt.

His lips pursed with the effort, Ranulf switched their goblets. Unaware of the exchange, Stancliff stood. He extended the sword to Ranulf.

"Place it in my hand, please. I feel so weak. Another sip of wine would fortify me."

Stancliff slid the cup closer to his lord. The metal made a low, grating sound against the trestle.

Fumbling now, his movements slow, Ranulf grasped his goblet. "To my most faithful comrade in arms. My dearest friend." With clear effort, Ranulf lifted the cup in a toast. Had Stancliff sensed the anger in Ranulf's voice?

Clearly not, for Stancliff smiled with all the confidence of a victor. His hand lowered, grasped the remaining goblet.

He lifted it to his lips and drank.

A look of satisfaction warmed Ranulf's face. He rasped, "And to my Isabel."

Stancliff's eyes, too, settled upon her, openly hungry.

She shivered in revulsion. Both lifted their goblets again. When they were finished, they set them on the table.

The two men stared at one another. A slow smile spread across Ranulf's face. Perspiration glistened upon his upper lip. "I think I must sit down. The battle has tired me. How my head aches."

"I will summon the medicus. Your wound requires attention."

From her place on the floor, Rowena moaned again.

Ranulf lifted a hand. "'Tis nothing. But perhaps Rowena—"

"Aye." Stancliff smiled, but almost instantly, the smile turned bitter. With a low gasp, he lifted a hand to his throat.

"Are you all right, friend?" Ranulf's eyes gleamed.

"Yes, of course," Stancliff answered, his voice hollow. He coughed.

Ranulf's expression grew hard as shale. "Are you ill? Odd, but I feel it, too, the burning in my throat."

His laughter sent chills down Isabel's back, for it was the laughter of a man who faced death.

"Mayhap when we broke our fast this morn the food was tainted?"

Stancliff stared, stricken, into Ranulf's eyes. "Mayhap."

"My innards feel"—Ranulf paused, and placed the flat of his palm over his stomach—"as if they boil, hot."

"Yes," whispered Stancliff. His brows creased and his lips parted as if he found it difficult to breathe.

Ranulf chuckled. "My mouth is dry, and I cannot seem to swallow."

Stancliff lifted his eyes to Ranulf's in sudden realization.

Ranulf leaned back in his chair, and closed his eyes. "Damn you to Hell, Stancliff."

Stancliff gaped at him, leaning heavily upon the table for support. Ranulf peered out from between slitted lids.

"My only regret is that I shall die a scant moment before you." His hands trembled, gripped the hilt of his sword, where he held it between his legs.

All at once his eyes widened. "Father." A faint smile curved his lips.

"Ranulf!" Isabel screamed, as his dying eyes turned to her.

He said, "I truly loved you, Isabel. In an honorable sort of way." He coughed, a watery, sick sound. To Stancliff, he muttered, "And you. I will await *you* in Hell."

Ranulf's head lolled back.

Isabel cried out in grief. She had despised him in the end, for having killed their father, and for his cruel punishment of Kol. But he was Ranulf. Despite his sins, she had loved him as a brother for so very long. A vision of him, as a blond little boy, surfaced in her mind, the boy who had been her protector since her birth. Aye, he had loved her, despite the demons that had tormented his later life.

Stancliff turned his eyes, full of realization, upon Isabel. "You told him. You betrayed me."

"Where is my son?" she begged. "You must tell me."

"I was the hero. I would have been king, and you my queen. I could have given you everything."

Isabel took several steps toward the door. He lunged, blocking her escape. From his belt he pulled a long dagger. "I won't go. Not without you."

His skin had gone pallid, but Isabel knew he had enough life remaining in him to kill her. He leapt up and charged toward her. She screamed.

Behind Stancliff the door crashed open, against the wall.

Above her, Stancliff raised the dagger—

He slumped, staring down at her with his terrible, jealous eyes. A low death-sound burbled from his throat. She watched as he foundered to his knees, then fell, facedown, to the floor. The hilt of another weapon protruded from his back.

Isabel looked up.

Kol knelt upon the ground behind Stancliff. "Damned traitor."

Their eyes met for just one moment, before a ragged sigh broke from his lips and he, too, collapsed to the ground.

Kol refused to die at Caervon. Dying elsewhere would thwart the intentions of his enemies; enemies who, even now lay wrapped in linen, awaiting their own burials.

Isabel walked alongside his litter. Though too weak to grasp her hand, she held his in between both of hers. As they made their way toward their encampment, he heard the voice of Rowena, and also Aiken, who had sworn his loyalty, along with many other Saxon warriors, to Kol. Every Saxon account concurred. There had been no attack upon the abbey. Godric remained unharmed.

Kol did not meet Isabel's eyes, nor did he look at the faces of his men. Despite her own injury, when they arrived at his tent she insisted on tending the wound on his thigh herself. Afterward, she spread furs over his body to keep him warm.

"Isabel, bring Father Janus."

"I will not." She lowered herself to kneel beside the bed, and laid her cheek against his chest. "My prayers will reach God. There has been too much death this day, and I will not allow Him to take you from me." Her tears spilled onto his linens, but her tears alone could not wash Ranulf's poison from his veins.

"Love, bring the priest."

Epilogue

Mmmmm. Very well done for a dead man."

"Are you certain? Aught we do it again to be sure?"

Kol lay beside Isabel. Both were naked, their limbs twisted into the bedclothes. Lovemaking had never brought him such bliss. With Isabel, he felt completed, on so many levels.

Isabel rolled onto her side, and planted a kiss on his mouth. Mischief sharpened her gaze. "Are you well enough?"

"Certainly I have proven myself."

"Beyond question," Isabel purred.

"I have only Ranulf to thank." His smile changed, grew more pensive. "He is the reason I live today. If he had not wiped most of the poison from his blade, I would have died upon the field."

"Then in doing so, he saved both our lives." Isabel clasped the bedclothes at her chest. "I suppose in some way, he achieved the redemption he sought. He held terrible secrets, but was not a wholly wicked man. I wish you could have known him as a boy."

Kol did not answer, but tucked a single, wild curl behind Isabel's ear.

After an extended silence, Isabel asked, "Would you think me wicked, for holding a secret of my own?"

Kol's heart stopped. He pushed her flat onto her back, and crouched above her, and glared down into her wide, violet eyes. "No secrets between us. I've had enough of that for a lifetime. Tell me what you meant by 'secret.'"

To his surprise, Isabel's eyes glowed with excitement. "Careful how you seek to pry the truth from my lips."

Kol's brow arched in question. "What dost thou mean?"

Isabel considered him from beneath lowered lashes. "What I mean is . . . you wouldn't want to hurt our child."

Kol froze above her. A thousand thoughts crashed through his mind, garbled and confused. "Our child?"

"Aye, beloved," Isabel whispered, her eyes agleam with sudden tears. "Your babe wilt be born before winter returns. Godric will have a brother or sister."

Kol's heart nearly fell from his chest.

"Isabel." He clasped her face in his hands, and kissed her lips, her cheeks, her eyelids. Even her nose. An energy he could not contain charged his limbs. He leapt from the bed.

Isabel clasped the linens to her breast and sat up, her hair spilling over her shoulders. "Husband?"

He shoved open the shutters. Outside, Calldarington slept beneath a blanket of stars. Not for long. All would share in these good tidings.

He bellowed, "I will be a *father. A father!*"

From the ramparts came the sound of cheers and the posts of spears thumped against the wooden walkways.

The last remnants of his mother's curses—whether real or imagined—fell away. The few demons who had lingered to taunt him that this bliss would never last, shriveled into dust.

He turned to Isabel. "How can I be worthy of a gift such as this?"

"Thou art worthy, Kol." She smiled, clearly content with her world. "Thou art worthy, and wanted, and never to be forgotten."

About the Author

Jolie Mathis lives in Texas with her husband, two small children, some spoiled animals, and a houseful of books. She loves history, flea markets, reading, and cooking.

Visit her website at www.joliemathis.com, or e-mail her at jolie@joliemathis.com.